KIDNAPPED

A CASEY CORT LEGAL THRILLER

AIME AUSTIN

AIME AUSTIN
www.AimeAustin.com

LOS ANGELES, CALIFORNIA

KIDNAPPED

A CASEY CORT LEGAL THRILLER

AIME AUSTIN

Kidnapped
Aime Austin

This edition published by
Moore Digital Media Inc.
1125 N Fairfax Avenue
Unit 46071
West Hollywood, CA 90046
www.*aimeaustin*.com

ISBN: 978-1-64414-058-1
eISBN: 978-1-64414-057-4

Scripture quotations are taken from the Holy Bible, New Living Translation, copyright ©1996, 2004, 2007, 2013, 2015 by Tyndale House Foundation. Used by permission of Tyndale House Publishers, Inc., Carol Stream, Illinois 60188. All rights reserved.

Cover Designer: Wicked Good Book Covers
Cover Images © Depositphotos, Shutterstock

Kidnapped/Aime Austin. — 2d ed.

"Adoption is, in its perfect form, suppose[d] to be about finding homes for children that need them, not about finding children for parents that want them."

— Claudia Corrigan D'Arcy

Pure and genuine religion in the sight of God the Father means caring for orphans and widows in their distress and refusing to let the world corrupt you.

— JAMES 1:27

1

Alile Useni Rubadiri
March 10, 2005

"I am Alile Useni. Born in Buram in Sudan. I am eighteen years old. My parents were killed in a siege on my village," I repeated aloud for the hundredth if not thousandth time.

My neighbor's "Shhhh" was as sharp as a knife. "You've been mumbling to yourself for hours."

Silenced, I turned my head. The Yoruba woman cramped next to me gave me an evil glare then her heavy lids came down over her large brown eyes. Her scarf, a tower of blue, green, and gold tilted to the side, bumping against my own head. I wanted to shove her and her silk back across the armrest. Doing that would draw the wrong kind of attention, though. I needed to be very careful in the next few hours. I was so close to reaching my first goal, I could taste it.

Ignoring her invasion of my narrow space, I did what she'd done, closed my eyes. One minute I was staring at the back of my lids. In the next second, I was seeing Kantayeni. Her beautiful chubby baby face floated before my eyes.

Then the ugly one of my Aunt Umi erased that of my daughter. Umi's last words to me rang in my head like a perpetual bell. "Get me three hundred thousand kwacha by your next birthday and I won't turn her over to Robert Chiwasa."

Chiwasa ran an orphanage in the next village. The orphanage used to be a place, especially in the beginning of AIDS, where a mother whose husband had died could drop off her child indefinitely while she got a job or got remarried or otherwise figured her life out. But since Chiwasa had gotten a second wife and a big brick house, the babies didn't stay too long. No one had the guts to ask where they'd gone.

I had no idea how she expected me to come up with that kind of money. No one I knew had anything like that. Ready to throw myself on my father's mercy for the final time, I'd left Yeni in Umi's house and run the thirteen kilometers to my father, asking him for the money or at least for him to do something about my aunt's threats.

The face of the man that had held me up to the night sky, and had told me a thousand stories was closed to me. He'd pushed me out telling me it was Umi's right to ask for that now that I'd made another mouth to feed. I should get the money, he spat, in the same way I'd gotten pregnant.

I'd told him months ago, when a bump formed in my dress, when he was holding the broomstick over my head, that his brother was the father. He'd called me a liar and beat me with it anyway.

When Yeni was born looking exactly like uncle Onani, I thought he'd finally believe me. But his face and that of his new wife were closed to me, now and forever it seemed. Now that I was no longer his pure little girl.

Defeated, my breasts rock hard with milk for Yeni, I dragged myself back to my aunt and uncle's, ready for a sleepless night caring for Yeni and finishing the housework I hadn't completed while in the capital. But the door was locked tight. Not a single sound came from inside. The metal bars shut me out of getting in the house. The white stucco I'd painted myself hard as a rock. For hours I stood there, pounding on the door and crying, milk running down the front of my cotton dress, until I lost my voice.

Despite the darkness, I started the long walk to the orphanage in Chitedze. Maybe Umi had already taken Yeni there. I may have nothing, but I could figure out how to scrape a living from the dirt like so many others. My father had always said the Europeans had come because we had hectares of rich and fertile land. I'm sure I could find a bit to farm. The big companies didn't watch every hectare. Lots of local people had taken a few rows of corn and peas for themselves.

Or maybe I could take Yeni to the city. Daddy couldn't turn me away with a baby in my arms. Or if his lock were as tight as Umi's, I could stand with some of the other people on the side of the road looking for day work. I could cook. I could clean. I could wash clothes. I'd been doing all that for two and a half years. Yeni was still small enough I could strap her to me with a cloth. I'd make sure she was good and quiet. At least until I collected enough kwacha to figure out my next step.

Halfway to Chitedze, the pain in my breasts became too much to handle. When I could no longer see anyone in either direction on the road, I huddled under newly planted stalks of maize. I squeezed out as much milk as I could, spilling it into the brown soil. I tried not to imagine the worst about the orphanage. That Umi had taken Yeni there and she was gone already.

The rumor was that they were sold to the highest bidder. I wasn't one hundred percent sure I believed any of that gossip, but my mama always said there was a bit of truth behind stories like that. Certainly, the last thing I wanted was to lose Yeni to the richest European who wanted to save an African baby.

I'd never get her back then. In the morning, I took myself to the front door. My milk came again when I heard the babies' cries through the window. No longer ashamed, I knocked anyway. After five minutes of talking with a matron and walking through, I was convinced that my baby wasn't there. I sighed with relief. Umi wasn't so heartless after all. I walked back home weak with hunger and exhaustion. Umi still refused to answer the door, though.

Completing the triangle one last time, I took the long road to Lilongwe. Instead of my father's house, I walked into the city. A man approached me. For three dollars, I did for him what I'd done for my uncle. For three more dollars I did it again. By the end of the week, I had enough money for a clean dress and a bus ticket to Nairobi. I didn't know where I'd go after that, but I dreamt of flying to London, to Paris, to somewhere I could get enough money to get Yeni and save her from a life like mine.

I opened my eyes, blinking back the tears that came when I thought of my daughter being without me. She'd have formula instead of mother's milk. Learn to roll over from Umi or worse from someone at the Chitedze orphanage. Maybe even take her first step without me. After that, though, I'd be there for every milestone, I silently promised her.

We'd be safe and free in this beautiful new place with its running water inside the house, and shops that had all the food you could ever want. Where you could summon the police if anything bad ever happened and not worry that the corrupt ones would blackmail you. I never wanted my baby to live like I had. Never wanted her hiding from men who treated her like she was an adult, even when she was a child.

"Ma'am, would you like breakfast?" That proper English voice came from a tall pale woman on the other side of me. I'd watched her walk up and down the aisles the whole flight. No matter how many pins she shoved in her nearly colorless flyaway hair, it wouldn't stay off her face. Right now, before she'd asked me the question about breakfast, she'd blown strands from in front of her eyes. It hadn't worked.

I must have been staring at her a long time. I didn't tell her the only white people I'd ever seen were foreign workers sent to help us find water, or plant their strange seeds. She did a slow blink, her eyelids covering then revealing light nearly colorless eyes.

"Breakfast? It's a proper English one today."

I nodded. Five seconds later, the woman in the dark blue uniform let down the tiny table built into the seat in front of me and a small gray tray appeared. There was a sausage, bacon, eggs, tomato and mushroom all cramped into the small plastic rectangle.

"Tea? Milk?" she asked, standing again each of her hands on a different kettle.

I nodded. Cloudy tea filled a small plastic cup. Juice covered in thick foil stood next to it. Yogurt was another foil-topped container. A small cake wrapped in paper crowded out any remaining space on the tray. With my hands, I picked up the sausage and bit into it. The taste was odd, salty, but I ate it anyway.

"Roll?"

The woman in blue was back, this time with a basket of bread.

"Can I have two?"

She nodded and put two different kinds of bread in front of me with a pair of tongs.

I'd seen more food on this flight than I'd ever seen in any one meal. What was worse was the amount of food the other passengers threw away. Earlier in our flight, the attendants had slid entire trays of uneaten remains into thick blue garbage bags.

I carefully wrapped the bread and cake and juice in a napkin and shoved them into the nylon pack I'd stuffed under the chair. There was enough food in there to feed my old village for a week and me for longer if I planned carefully.

Everything I didn't save, I ate. My stomach felt full to bursting, but I couldn't carelessly tip the food into the blue trash bag like many of the passengers around me. I just couldn't. I swallowed down bile. Maybe I shouldn't eat. What if Yeni didn't recognize me with fat cheeks or a big stomach.

Minutes later, the plane took a steep dip and the food I'd stuffed down nearly came back up a second time. I swallowed the spit in my mouth again and again.

The Nigerian woman turned toward me and slowly lifted her eyes.

"First time on a plane?" she asked in softly accented English.

I nodded afraid to open my mouth.

She patted her headscarf back into place then turned to look out of the tiny window. I wished I'd had that seat. If I could press my forehead against the cold glass, it might make me feel better. But after seeing the way people had rushed to their seats hours ago like squatters in a newly empty hut, it didn't seem like the kind of request that would be honored.

A screeching noise came over the loudspeaker drowning out whatever the woman next to me was saying.

"Ladies and gentlemen. We'll be landing at London Heathrow airport in thirty minutes' time. We don't have clearance for landing yet. We're waiting on air traffic control. We know you have many choices of airline. The folks up here on the flight deck and the One World Alliance thank you for choosing British Airways."

Choices.

I'd had precious few of those in my life. Choosing clothes, food, and airplane companies was so odd to consider. Maybe this is what life had in store for me. Maybe I'd be like these people flying from one continent to another looking like they didn't have a care in the world. Sure that they could go anywhere anytime they wanted.

The plane jerked again. It felt like falling. I closed my eyes. Opened them again. No one was screaming or in a panic, so this must be normal. Out of the corner of my eye, blue and green silk shimmered. Then a strong hand covered my own that had been gripping the armrest between us.

"I remember my first flight out of Africa. You'll be fine."

The warm hand reminded me much of my mother's. The Yoruba woman didn't say another word, but she didn't let go either. Not until the plane stopped moving.

***

Asylum.

The words crept diagonally up the airport wall. White letters against blue background. In more languages than I recognized. None of which was my mother tongue. But I knew better than to expect that here of all places. This was England, not Malawi where Yao had been the first words I'd heard spoken.

I shook my head as the queue of people pushed at me from both directions. Arabic, that was the language I was to declare as my own. If I wanted to stay in this adopted country, I had to repeat the story I'd been supplied in Arabic. And I'd learned it, the Arab's language with its swooping letters written backward. I wasn't nearly as stupid as my uncle had always said. In a matter of months, I'd learned enough Arabic to pretend I was from Muslim northern Africa.

While the group of travelers moved forward, I worried the small blue and white paper in my hands. I'd filled it out like I'd been told with a mix of lies and truth. I'd practiced my new truth for the nine hours it had taken us to fly from Nairobi to London.

I couldn't stop my lips from moving as I rehearsed my answers one last time. My name was now Alile Useni. My middle name was a popular Arabic last name that would not arouse suspicion.

I wrote my date of birth as 24 May 1986. I'd added four years to place myself firmly in adulthood. I didn't want anyone to herd me like the child I really was. A child in the eyes of the law if not in the eyes of men.

In my village, men had been the law.

I skipped the sections about my whereabouts in the UK. That would be anyplace where this government chose to house me. Occupation and passport number I left blank as well. I'd be more than willing to do any work that I could get although I hoped beyond hope that I could go to school first. I'd always wanted to be a girl who finished school.

There was only a single girls high school in my village. I'd always hoped that I could one day be one of those confident girls in a starched pink and white uniform walking about as if they owned the world.

My father had said that paying my fees would have been a waste of money. I was luckier than most as my mom taught me from my brothers' discarded school books when they were away. Even if I never made it to school in the UK, I was here to make sure that my daughter would.

Yeni.

A wave of longing so big came over me that it nearly drowned me. My hand shook as the line moved forward. The paper fluttered to the shiny floor. I bent to pick it up. The people behind me bumped and almost knocked me over as I was only two or three people away from the border protection officers. The other passengers were probably eager to get home or start their vacations. No one glanced twice at a girl like me.

I didn't see any guns or armed soldiers, but the very pale men and women looked less than friendly. Their whole job was keeping people like me from coming into their country. My whole job today was convincing them to let me stay. Then I could send for Yeni.

I looked to the paper which revealed my last lie. Place of birth: Buram, Sudan. A city nearly destroyed by war and lacking any kind of formal administration was now my claimed home.

"Ma'am, please step forward. Number two is free." A woman in a purple suit and white gloves waved me to the desk. I handed over my wrinkled paper to the official seated behind the desk.

"Where's your passport?" The man examined my paper, never once looking in my direction. Instead his pale hand extended beyond the counter…waiting.

I reached into the pocket of my rucksack, retrieved the booklet with the Sudanese national bird, a secretary bird, on its green cover. I handed him the documents I'd traded my soul for. I took a deep breath and said the words I'd practiced a million times in the last few months.

"I claim asylum."

2

"Stand up. They only get you if you're lying down," the woman with the emerald green hijab said to me. As quickly as I could, without attracting too much attention, I stashed the picture of Yeni in my shirt pocket. Yearning that had stolen my breath went as swiftly as it had come.

I turned to the woman who'd spoken. I listened to her further admonitions to shake out my shirt and brush off my skin in a soft-spoken voice and did as I was told. I scratched the bumps that had risen under the red blouse I'd been wearing for two or three days.

I only had four shirts in my pack. The white one was filthy, as was the yellow. I was saving the last blue one in case I had a meeting with someone who could make a decision about me staying. I didn't know when I'd be able to wash them or even where.

"Don't scratch! That will only make it worse," another woman whispered fiercely from her cot across the room. This was in heavily accented English. There were thirty-six of us in this big sterile room. I'd counted the bunk beds hundreds of times to help me to sleep, to keep me from losing my mind with worry about my flesh and blood thousands of kilometers from here.

"There are bugs. I didn't think there were bugs in England," I whispered. Though after I said it, I realized it was stupid and juvenile. Of course there were insects. There were more of them than there were of us on earth, one of the village girls who went to school had shared breathlessly after coming home from a science lesson, books weighing her pack down.

"There are bedbugs everywhere," the second woman said to me. She was black like me. For the first time in months, my curiosity overcame my self-protective nature.

I tried not to let the itch bother me as I sat down again on the mattress and leaned my body against the metal pole that held the bed up above.

"Where are you from?" I asked a skinny black woman in Arabic. It was the first time I'd talked to anyone—voluntarily. The smuggler's advice had been to keep my mouth shut and only talk to the government people in charge of my asylum claim.

Women who'd lied to get into the country, women like me, had had their claims denied when their roommates alerted the authorities. There were limits to the number of people the UK would let in. He'd said we were all in a fight to the death competition for the few spots in the quota.

She shook her head as if I'd spoken a language foreign to her. I asked the question again in English.

"Somalia," she answered.

I nodded. There wasn't a need to say much of anything after that. Conflicts dotted the African landscape like wildlife.

"I'm from Iran," the green-scarved woman said in Arabic. "You?"

It was the common language here in this place, after English.

Malawi nearly passed my lips. My spine went rigid. I was horrified by the momentary lapse, even if it had only been mental.

"Sudan," I said. "South Sudan," I corrected. I mentally reviewed the facts in my head. The war had started in 1983. It was calm for now, but tensions could flare up at any time. I'd had to leave because I was displaced. Because I was raped by a gang of men when I'd been trying to find firewood while my family was staying at the camps near Darfur. "There are to be two countries one day soon. That is the hope after the cease fire."

They both nodded, the weight of men's conflicts weighing heavily on all of us. Asylum wouldn't exist otherwise. The women glanced at each other, something passing between them. I didn't know what and immediately regretted saying anything.

Over the last five months it had taken me to travel from my home country to the UK, I'd been told time and again that it was best to say as little as possible about anything. Any kind of disclosure invited questions. Warm brown skin and compassionate eyes, like my mother's, had made me vulnerable. I'd be careful not to make that mistake again.

I decided the safest route was to change the subject. "Where can I wash my clothes?"

"The sink?" The Somali woman shrugged. Her own clothes were dusty and stained.

"They come by every two weeks. The next pickup will be in the Friday," the Iranian woman said in halting English.

I lifted my blouse from my pants and shook it again. Chill air stole up my chest as the huge institutional door swung open.

"Useni. Ahmadi. Dongxiang," a sturdy white woman in a tidy uniform bellowed.

Tentatively, I raised my right hand as did the Persian woman and a Chinese woman who had been next to me on the bus here from the airport.

"Great. You three. Pack your stuff. You're going to housing provided by the Home Office."

I turned my back to the center of the room and slipped Yeni's picture into a pocket I'd sewn on the interior of my backpack. My fingers lingered against the slick papers, feeling for the four photographs I'd smuggled this long way. There was little else to pack as I'd not changed my clothes since arriving to this place.

I hoisted the pack over my shoulders and stood at attention as I'd learned across the days and miles traveling from Malawi. The uniformed people who work for governments and NGOs rewarded obedience.

It took the Chinese woman a bit longer. She had draped all sorts of silk around her bed. My village could have eaten for a week on what those silks probably cost. I wondered, not for the first time, why she was here. Looked to me as if her life was just fine. She was heavy. A lone fat person in a room of skinny women. I'd only seen fat women in the cities I'd passed through. In the countryside, everyone was coaxing their next meal, their very survival from the land.

Ten minutes later, the three of us, joined quickly by a few more, walked in queue behind the white woman in uniform. When we stepped outside whipping wind and ice-cold rain greeted us. No one offered an umbrella or plastic coat.

Following the others' lead, I ran to a van, its back doors open. Though I'd lifted my pack over my head, I was dripping with water. I squeezed into a seat as new passengers pushed us along the bench. The matron slammed the door once we were all in and banged on the window with her fist.

On cue, the driver shifted into gear and pressed the gas.

"Where are we going?" one bold woman asked a different uniformed matron who occupied the passenger seat to the left of the driver. She was kind of smiling, and looked a lot friendlier than the woman who'd led us to the van. Maybe it was that smile that had made one of the women comfortable enough to ask a question.

"Hounslow," she said before turning to the driver and speaking rapid-fire English with such a heavy accent I couldn't catch every word.

"That's right next to the airport," a woman whispered from the last row in the van.

My heart sped up as fear crawled through my veins. They were moving us because we were going to be shipped out of the UK. I just knew it. All the talk of applications and hearings and required paperwork had been no more than a false promise.

I'd sold everything that I could to get the smuggler to ferry me here and I was going to be chucked out before I'd even had a chance to tell the story I'd bought and paid for with my body. That woman's comment had caused frantic chatter to start up and spread through the van like measles through a refugee camp.

"Ladies. Stop," the half-smiling officer in the passenger seat started, "no need to panic. We're moving you to better accommodation. Your applications will continue to be processed by the Home Office. Now please be quiet so the driver can concentrate."

Relieved silence quickly spread through the van. Though it took nearly an hour before the vehicle stopped and parked, I don't think we'd traveled more than a few kilometers. I'd never seen so many cars move so slowly. The official consulted a clipboard she lifted from the dashboard. "Useni."

"Yes." I snapped to attention.

"You're here on Saint Paul's Close. Get your bag."

She lifted a large black umbrella and stuck it out the door as she opened it. In a single move, she was out of the vehicle and opening one of the back doors. Four women got out before me so I could slide down the seat and out of the van. I stepped under the umbrella and followed her to the front door.

I took a quick glance around the neighborhood. Dozens of two-story homes flanked the quiet street. There wasn't a single person standing outside. It was startling to see no one in a city as big as this. In the last months I'd been through Lilongwe and Nairobi. Even on a bad weather day hundreds of women, men, children, and livestock filled the streets traveling from one place to another or peddling food and sundry goods on the streets.

"This here is your new home," the woman said as we walked up the short walkway. Almost all the houses had two or three cars in the drive. There were none here. A dirt path beaten between tall grass that tickled against my ankles led to the front door.

My eyes must have been wide in my astonishment at how grand the home for refugees was.

"It's one of our bigger residences. It's a semi-detached knocked together. You'll be sharing the place."

"Sharing?" I asked dumbly.

Her laugh was a hoarse crackle. "The Home Office weren't going to do up six bedrooms just for you." She knocked at the door, then pushed it open. I held my tongue about the fact that it wasn't locked.

"Who's here?" she called out.

A few women were sitting in chairs in the reception room. A small kid, maybe two or so, ran up to the woman, looking up at her with inquisitive brown eyes. He was a little darker than my daughter, his curls tighter, his cheeks more rounded.

I had no idea you could bring kids to this country. How had I not known that? A terrifying dread paralyzed my limbs. Maybe I didn't have to leave Yeni with Umi after all. Maybe I could have found a way to break in and steal the daughter they hadn't really wanted.

"This a new one?" a woman asked pulling me from my thoughts. She was heavy, wrapped in a paisley dress, her feet in sandals. Everything about her looked tired even though it was still morning.

"Yes. She's called Alile Useni. Where's there a free bed?"

The tired woman gestured toward carpeted stairs. "Up there, second door on the left. Girl left last week."

With a grunt of acknowledgement the officer took off toward the stairs. After a few seconds, I realized, I was to follow. Gripping the shoulder straps of my bag, I ran up the narrow stairs to catch up. She pushed open the door to the bedroom and I stepped in behind her. I wanted to laugh at my naïveté. Not my own house, nor my own bedroom. There were five beds crammed into the room barely leaving enough floor space to stand.

She pointed to a mattress stripped of any sheets. "That'll be yours. Bathroom's down the hall. Someone will be by to check in on you. I have to go, we have a bunch more stops, and between the rain and the traffic…"

I think she felt a bit guilty about dropping me here. I think her job probably required she show me around or get me settled, but I could sense her desperation to leave to take the rest of the women in the van to the places they would sleep tonight.

"It's okay," I heard myself say. "I'll be fine. I'm sure the other women here will help me out."

"Yes, of course they will. They're a nice group. Even some Africans like you, so you should feel right at home."

I gave a tiny smile. If Africans could get along so well, there wouldn't be a hundred conflicts in half as many countries. She handed me an envelope.

"It's twenty-nine pounds. You'll need to buy food and personal supplies with that. There are plenty of markets on the high street. It's about a half-mile walk that way." She pointed out one of the bedroom windows.

"Thank you," I said tucking the envelope into the front pocket of my pack. If I could save half, I'd be that much closer to paying Umi and getting Yeni. A little two- or three-year-old girl ran to the door of the room and peered at me shamelessly. All at once an idea struck me. Maybe I could get some allowance to get Yeni. I could split off some money for Umi and use the rest for a cheap plane ticket there and back.

"Good luck," she said and ran down the stairs. I peered out the window and she was in the van in an instant. Doors closed, it pulled away from the curb.

I turned to the bed, set down my pack, and slipped Yeni's photos from the pocket. Maybe I wouldn't have to wait until I had money after all. If that boy downstairs was here, there was no reason my daughter couldn't be. I'd search for sheets first, a place to wash and hang my clothes, second, and then tomorrow I'd find the office that would allow my daughter to come home to me.

3

Paul Cooke didn't meet my eyes.

"I don't think I can do this today," he mumbled.

Of course Paul would have some kind of artist's "emergency" that he needed to attend to on the day we came to the registrar's office. I firmly closed my ears to his words. Another few minutes and this would all be settled. The next chapter of my life mapped out only in need of quick execution. This chaotic time would be a distant memory when my belly was full of a brand-new life. A girl, I hoped.

When I didn't think anyone was watching, I touched my abdomen. The beginnings of cramps I felt there was like a kick in the gut—and not from the inside. My period was just around the corner.

I wanted the sore breasts and heavy feeling in my uterus to be a baby. But the ten or well, okay, twenty negative test

sticks I'd buried under wads of tissue told me different. Trying to get pregnant was starting to get more clinical than
pleasurable which was making Paul a bear to live with.
Maybe it would be better on our honeymoon without the
pressure of the hospital hanging over our heads.

Distractedly, I looked at my watch with its huge dial,
then I looked at Paul. We didn't have much time before my
shift at the hospital, but there was still enough if this government office proved to be one of the efficient ones. I figured there were fifty-fifty odds on that one.

The US, despite all the talk about it being the best country in the world, hadn't made any progress in the bureaucracy department in its two-hundred-twenty-nine-year
history after breaking away from England. Or alternatively
the Americans had made a lot of progress in adding layers
to the British bureaucratic nightmare.

There were cities, counties, states, then the federal government. It had taken me a half hour to figure out where to
get the license we needed to get married. I'd already notified the register office back home of our intent to marry
abroad. That had taken ten minutes. Cleveland, Ohio, had
already zapped an hour and a half from my life and I didn't
even have the license in my hand to show for all that time
wasted.

"It's half eleven," I said adding the same hopeful note to
my voice that I used with scared patients. "There aren't too
many people in line at the Cuyahoga County office. I'm sure
we'll get up to the window in ten, fifteen minutes' time. You
should be able to make it to the studio by one o'clock. I
think this buyer may be the one to catapult you," I added
hopefully. "I have a hip replacement scheduled at one as
well."

See, I wanted to say, we're a busy couple with a bright future. You'll be a top artist before you know it. I knew better than to say any of that, though. He'd just as soon call me a patronizing cow. I did not want to have that fight in this echoey hall.

I opened the messenger bag that I used as a stand-in for both a purse and briefcase and looked for my list. The wrinkled sheet would reacquaint me with what was next.

After we got the license, we'd be finding someone to solemnize our marriage. There's a word I'd had to look up. It basically meant a vicar. We'd need one or a local judge. I was hoping we could convince one of the judges on my list to marry us this weekend or next. I pulled my empty hand from my bag.

Damn, couldn't find it. I thought back to a few hours ago wondering if I'd left it on my desk at the hospital or even worse on my desk at home. I knew there were judges in this building or in one of the ones next door.

I'd hoped to cross two things off my list this morning so I wouldn't have to come back downtown. Damn, I'd have to find a way to get Paul to do it, or push a morning surgery and do it myself. Maybe I could keep morning surgery and make calls from my office. I snapped my fingers thrilled with my own problem-solving brilliance. Yes, that's what I'd do.

"No…I'm not worried about being late," Paul said.

My mind tried to make the trek from missing lists to my fiancé standing and talking in front of me. With laser precision I focused in on him, but Paul didn't meet my eyes. He looked from the barrel-vaulted ceiling to the Ionic columns to the marble staircase. Anywhere but at me.

"Fiona, I'm so sorry," he whispered, his voice barely audible in the grand entranceway.

I closed my eyes, making Paul disappear from my peripheral vision. I did not have time for this. There was no time for a row about money, or art, or us trying to get pregnant and him being a stay-at-home dad. All the things we'd agreed on a few months ago that he wanted to change out now.

We could do all that later. After we left this office, we'd have the rest of our lives to argue about all that. For now, we needed a license to get married to get to the married-couple fight that was obviously in our future.

Just. Not. Now.

When the wooden door opened wide, I propelled myself from the cold wall with my equally cold hand.

A smiling couple exited through the wooden door marked with the number 146 and Marriage License Department on a small metal plaque. A civil servant's hand beckoned us in.

"We're next. That was quicker than I thought." I sighed with relief then walked on through. Living with an artist was a tricky bit of business. Temperamental didn't cover it. Despite the ups and downs, I couldn't wait to start our life together as a married couple. If things were permanent, Paul would finally be able to settle into our relationship. I would no longer worry that he'd run away. That's what commitment did, kept people by your side.

Notwithstanding the fights, Paul Cooke was a great foil for me. He was playful where I was serious. He was laid-back where I was plagued by ambition. Those were all the good parts. He was also beset by a certain moodiness, though. I was still trying to convince him to give antidepressants a try and I think I was winning. He was a single prescription and one baby girl away from being the perfect husband and father.

I stood at the counter and looked at the clerk standing there shuffling papers.

"We're here to get a marriage license," I prompted. "Fiona Rose and Paul Cooke." Looking down into my bag, I found what I was looking for this time. Got my passport out and slapped it on the counter, then added the application we'd filled in together last night.

"Both of you need to be here," she replied barely sparing me or my documents a glance in between filing tasks.

"Paul's..." right behind me was what I was going to say. But when I glanced over my shoulder, I found out he wasn't behind me at all. Nor was he next to me, or anywhere in the small baby-boy-blue room, hot and close with steamy radiator heat.

"Paul," I leaned back, turned my head, and whisper-shouted through the door. Despite my attempt to seem quiet, my voice echoed through the marble and stone hallway. The building was quite grand. Reminded me that America did have some kind of past beyond day before yesterday.

In fact, we'd walked by a bride and groom snapping pics when we'd come through the three-story entranceway. Paul had agreed it was beautiful enough to have a wedding. I'd been doing some mental planning of a cute civil service ceremony instead of paying attention to what he'd been trying to say. Something in the pit of my stomach told me I was going to regret that—very soon.

"Pardon me," I said. "I'll go grab him. He must have wandered off to look at the art and architecture." In the decade or so we'd been together, it wouldn't be the first time he'd disappeared—wooed by the turn of a wooden furniture leg or curve of a woman's sculpted marble ear.

I walked into the hallway, looking right then left wondering which bit of stone had caught his eye this time.

"Paul?" I called again, not afraid to make my voice louder. I stalked down into the grand entrance. I looked up at the high vaulted ceilings. Maybe my partner had gone up the stone staircase hoping to see the Beaux-Arts styling up close. I'd never been in the courthouse before and had been caught a bit off guard with its beauty. Paul had been right when he told me it was one of the most handsome buildings in Cleveland. Certainly was a far cry from the set of boxy sterile rooms that were my home away from home at the Cleveland Clinic.

"Paul!" My panicked voice got me dirty looks from a few people in the lobby. Like all the people in the Tube who stared at you oddly if your finger so much as grazed your nose, I put them out of my mind like those busybodies on the train. I'd never see them again, so who cared if they thought me crazy.

The second floor had bigger doors to what looked like serious courtrooms, but no Paul. I was dripping sweat now. The eight-hundred-dollar parka which had been such a great idea a few days ago when arctic winds were coming across the lake from Canada was suffocating me now. Instead of a cold March morning, it was practically spring outside.

Damnit.

God damnit.

I ran back down the stairs at breakneck speed, nearly losing my footing. I grabbed at the stone banister. My sweaty hand couldn't gain purchase on the slick surface. I righted myself in the last second. No reason for an orthopedic surgeon to be the patient and not the doctor.

Pushing open the heavy wooden doors, I looked through the fog and drizzle that had replaced last week's snow. The shock of the moist air hit me and I unbuttoned my anorak as quickly as my fumbling fingers would allow.

"Paul!"

I saw him then. He was hunched over, hands thrust in the pockets of his not-warm-enough corduroy jacket. Soaked through with rain, he would freeze when the temperature inevitably dropped.

"It's our turn. I told you it wouldn't be that long. It's wet out here. Come back inside before she skips to the next person in the queue." I rubbed my hands against my scrubs trying to dry them.

"You're not listening to me, Fiona," Paul said finally meeting my eyes. "You never listen to me. I can't do this."

I could see my measured breaths in the air in front of me. Puffs of condensation disappearing every two seconds into the mist.

"Do what?" I tried not to sound like I was scolding a toddler. I probably failed.

"Marry you. Be with you. Be what you want."

His words mingled with the white puffs of warm air coming from his own mouth. I was sure I wasn't understanding what he was saying. I tugged at his jacket. "Let's talk. I'm sure there's a restaurant in there," I said pointing to the hotel cattycorner from the courthouse.

He didn't resist and a couple of minutes later, we were sitting in a nondescript beige and gray lobby. It wasn't as pretty as the courthouse across the street, but at least it was dry.

I didn't dare glance at my watch, but I couldn't help the jiggle in my leg. The plan had been to get registered, try to book a judge, then have Paul drive me back to the clinic and himself home to Cleveland Heights. Ten minutes was all I had to spare for this tantrum of sorts, I was sure, before I was MIA for surgery.

And while the US hospitals seemed to allow surgeons more latitude than the NHS, I was thinking being a no-show wasn't the best career move I could make after less than a year at my job. I was still on a kind of informal probation while they sussed me out.

"I've bought my tickets, Fiona," Paul said when a metal pitcher of hot water and tea cup with a bag arrived. No strong milky tea like my grandmum had made came from this place. Firmly, I tamped down any nostalgia that threatened to bubble up.

"Tickets? For what? Where?" I asked while I poured the water in the cup.

"I'm going home."

I dunked the teabag, once, twice, then a third time. I opened a sugar packet and added the contents. Poured in the gray-looking milk. Stirred. Held my breath. Let it out.

"To High Wycombe?" I asked in my nice wife voice. I'd worked on not being strident, not being loud, trying to care for his fragile male feelings while ignoring my own. It's what made women different from girls. What made marriages last. It was the exact opposite of what my mother had done through three different marriages.

His "Yes" came with no elaboration. No explanation.

"But you hate it there."

"I hate it here."

"Since when?" Though I knew it to be true. I'd studiously ignored the signs. Instead I'd hired a builder to turn what he'd called a "three-season porch" into a fully heated studio. I'd convinced myself that paint and carpet and insulation would make a difference. It hadn't except maybe to resale value.

"Since always. You decided to move here because you decided that money was more important than family and friends."

"What are you talking about? You helped me fill out the thousand pieces of paper I needed to get my license to practice in the States. You helped me fill out the immigration papers. We made this decision together."

He shook his head like I was hopeless, like we were hopeless. "I can't stay."

Of course he couldn't stay without some kind of visa. He wasn't a tourist. And after quitting school, he wasn't a student either. That left husband as his sole means of staying.

"But that's why we're getting married. After you dropped out of the Institute, you can't be here legally unless you're married." The "to me" part I kept to myself.

"That's part of it. I never wanted to be a teacher." Paul's art school stipend had come with strings—he had to act as a teaching assistant for a few classes.

"It was just a year-long stop gap measure while I got settled."

"That's just it, Fiona. I waited whilst you went to medical school. Waited whilst you did your specialist courses. Waited whilst you decided where you wanted to work. Pulled up stakes to come to the States, leaving me mam and me mates behind. I need something for me." He half stood, then when he realized he wasn't going to shake me off so easily, sat down again. This time it was his knee that was jiggling, his hand along with it. "I gotta go. I gotta pack. My flight leaves tomorrow."

"You rat bastard. Why did you come all the way down to the courthouse if you had no intention of marrying me?"

"I wasn't sure until I got down here. I thought maybe there'd be a sign. Something telling me this would all be a good idea."

I closed my lids so I didn't roll my eyes too hard. Even in Cleveland, which was more Birmingham than North Yorkshire, he'd started wearing beaded bracelets and talking about spiritual vibrations. All seemed harmless enough until these bloody vibrations now controlled his decisions.

"How long do you think you'll be home?" I gave it two weeks, tops. His mam drove him around the bend. She'd been pressuring him to work for the Royal Mail or Inland Revenue or something equally mind numbing for years. She'd be right back at it once the newness of his return had worn off. I kind of wanted to order a civil service costume to get him prepared for the straight jacket he was about to walk into.

"Don't know yet, going to New York City."

New York City?

That certainly wasn't home. He would have fun in New York. Maybe meet a low-maintenance girl in New York. I didn't like the idea at all. Time with his mam was practically a direct path back to me. Time with his mates, not so much.

"I thought you were going back to the UK?"

"Frankie and Ian are in New York on a street called Jane of all things." His smile was sad and wry at the same time. I could already feel a tug in my heart at the absence of that expressive face, his blue eyes framed by crinkly bits of skin that had come on in his thirties. "I'm going to stay with them for a couple of weeks then travel onward. I promised me mam that I'd be there for Easter dinner."

Mrs. Nice Lady left the building with his admission that he'd rather run through the pubs in New York City than be with me.

"And that's it," I said. My voice was shrill, but I couldn't control it. Wasn't trying to control it. "You're walking away after ten years? No real discussion. No real good-bye. Instead, you tell me this on the steps of the courthouse."

"It's more like we're in a pub." His eyes were earnest, but also steely with determination.

"The location doesn't matter. Why didn't you tell me this earlier, like this morning, or last week when I was filling out the paperwork and you were signing your name?"

"Fi, I love you. I do. I'm not ready for all this. The settling-down bit. The having-a-baby bit. Buying a house. It's all too much. I feel like we just got out of nappies ourselves."

My head was going to explode. Blood and brains right there in the gray and beige lobby.

"Last week would have been a good time to mention this, Paul. When you were buying tickets and texting your mates. I have to go. I have to get back to work. You know, work, that thing that pays for plane tickets and electricity and heat."

"You promised you wouldn't throw that in my face—being an artist."

"A starving artist," I threw in his face because what did any of the earlier promises matter. If he hadn't kept his, why should I keep mine.

"You're going to be late," he said stiffly, all traces of warmth gone.

"What if I'm pregnant, Paul? Have you thought that part through?"

"Are you?"

If he'd touched me out of something other than obligation over the last months, he'd probably know the answer to that. "No. I got my period," I said letting him off the hook. I wasn't like one of the girls from Eastenders who strung a bloke along based on a fake pregnancy.

"I know how much you want a baby, Fi. But I think you want it more than you want us. You and me, I think we're broken."

My pager sounded. It certainly wasn't broken. I looked down at the black gadget on my hip.

"I've got to go scrub in. I'm sure you can make your way home." I grabbed the keys to the single car we shared and left the not-quite-right tea and the man I thought was going to father my child in the crappy hotel—not quite pub.

4

"Alile Useni? Is that what you're called?"

"Yes." It was the first question that Justine Hawley asked. She'd introduced herself so hastily, that I hadn't quite caught it. Fortunately, her name was on the cluttered desk in the tiny office that she shared with someone called Nina. We were the only two in there now. I took my right hand and pushed it down on my left to keep both of them from shaking.

"Don't be nervous. We're not here to retraumatize you in this substantive interview. To evaluate your claim, I have to ask you a list of questions. They may make you feel uncomfortable, but it can't be avoided. Do you understand?" Her tone was matter-of-fact, but there was still kindness there.

"Yes."

"Do you speak English? I see that you're from Sudan, do you need an Arabic interpreter?"

I was supposed to speak Arabic as my native tongue. I'd practiced and practiced for the last few months, but I wasn't perfect, especially at reading. An interpreter would probably be a native and catch me in my imperfections. There were way more Muslims here than I'd heard about. Women, their faces covered, lots of children in tow, were on the high street all times of day and night. It was no stretch that one of them could work for the Home Office.

Of course English was the official language of Malawi so I knew it pretty well, not as well as the language my mother had spoken to me, but well enough. I had to take it on faith that this Justine wouldn't be able to distinguish between Malawian and Sudanese accents. For once British ignorance about Africa would be in my favor.

"English is one of our two official languages," I stated.

"Right, of course. Lots of African countries follow that model with English being the official language but everybody speaking a different tribal language at home. Lots of strife there, though, despite that, yeah."

I may not have gone to school much outside of my tutoring by Mama, but by my way of thinking it was the ancestors of this woman who'd caused the strife in the first place. When I didn't say anything, Justine picked up a stack of papers and straightened them at the corners.

"Date and place of birth?"

"Buram. In Sudan. Twenty-fourth of May...nineteen ninety."

"You're a minor?" She leaned forward in her chair so quickly it squeaked in protest.

I'd made the mistake of answering truthfully. Heat flushed my face. I was thankful like most whites, Justine wouldn't notice. "Eighty six. Sorry, I couldn't think of the right number in English." The last words were rushed. I'd never get through this interview if I stumbled on the easiest of questions. While Justine scratched the biro against the paper form on her desk, I took a few deep breaths.

"Look, Ms. Useni, I'm more than happy to get an interpreter to join us." She looked down at another stack of papers on her desk. "The earliest availability is in three weeks' time."

I couldn't see how delay would be good for me. I needed to get established as soon as possible and get one of those family visas that allowed a resident to bring her child here before Yeni forgot about me, before Yeni thought someone else became her mother.

"No, I'm fine. A bit nervous, but fine."

For the next hour, I answered all of her questions, this time without a single mistake or a moment's hesitation.

"In order to claim asylum, you have to show us that you have a fear of racial, religious, or other persecution because of your political opinions or tribal affiliation."

Having studied this time and again, I knew that better than anyone. I took another deep breath. I'd told a lot of stories to put a smile on my mother's face while she lay dying, and a lot of lies to keep my uncle from between my legs.

This one, this lie had to be the best one of my life. After a long moment in which I tried to mold my face into one Justine could have sympathy for, I began.

"I was born in Buram in the Sudan. I lived with my mother and father and two brothers and one sister." The first part was a lie, the second part the truth. The man who coached me had told me that sticking close to the truth was best. The fewest mistakes were made that way. I continued, "I'm a black African, Masalit, one of the disfavored ethnic groups.

"About a year ago, maybe a bit more, the Janjaweed came to my town. They killed my father and brothers. Then...then...they took my mother behind the house. She screamed for them to stop, but they didn't. Not until...she was dead when I found her later. Then they came back for me and my sister. Six different soldiers—"

Justine's hand flew up, first to cover her mouth, then to swat at me like I was a fly buzzing too close. I stuttered to a stop.

"No detail is necessary. We're sensitive to sexual assault and don't want to cause you further trauma, so let's move on. What would happen if you return?"

"I think the Janjaweed might kill me. I have no parents or brother to protect me. My younger mother didn't...survive. My older sister can't...hasn't...mentally, she can't cope with life. I am alone and at the mercy of the government which is killing all the non-Arabs. I'm a Christian and a minority there."

"Do you have any children?"

"I got pregnant and had a baby in October two thousand four. I was alone." All of a sudden, I could not speak. It was as if a large rock had clogged my throat. I turned away silently swallowing back tears.

"Where's your baby now?" Justine's question was a whisper.

"I don't know. She was taken from me because she was mixed. She was probably given to a Muslim family. At least

I hope that's true and they don't know about me. That they love her like a daughter. I can't think of or consider anything other than that happening."

"I'm so sorry that you've gone through this. It's such a tragedy what goes on in Africa these days."

Justine Hawley closed the folder and stacked her pen a top of it. After waiting for a year, the interview felt somehow unfinished. There had to be more to the decision that could change my life and that of my daughter.

"How long before you decide if I can stay?" I asked.

"I myself won't make the decision. I'll give over your papers and someone else will be in charge of that. Eliminates bias, I think."

"When should I hear from you or the other person?" I knew I shouldn't pressure her, but uncertainty was killing me. I never thought it would take a year just to get an interview and who knew how long to get a decision to stay—right to remain she'd called it earlier.

"Let me check on something. Can you stay here a bit longer?"

"Yes. Of course, yes."

I'd worried the hem out of the side of my skirt by the time Justine Hawley had returned some twenty-five minutes later. All the sympathy had been drained from her face. It was a pinched mask of disbelief when she came back into the room. I tried to smile to relieve the tension. It didn't work.

"I have to warn you." She sat heavily in her chair, but seemed to loom over me nevertheless.

"What?" I tried to keep the question short to hide the panic closing my throat.

"You can be convicted for using false documents or false passports to enter the country." She tossed the small green booklet with its gold-emblazoned secretary bird at me. It fell to the floor before I could catch it. I retrieved the forged document from the floor as if it were the most precious thing in the world.

"These were issued in Sudan..." I tried to explain. To fix whatever had been broken when she'd left the room.

"Your application can also be damaged if you have given false evidence or don't have a legitimate basis for claiming asylum."

There was no question there. I didn't know how she wanted me to refute the claims she was making. I relied on the excuse my smuggler had told me to use, after pushing me out of his bed in the middle of the night—my body having been all I'd had left to barter—promising me he had government ties that got false information printed on official government paper.

"The war in the Sudan has made the government unstable. I don't have a way for you to verify my information. That's the exact reason I'm here. I got the documents from official government channels. But there's so much corruption..." I left her to fill in the blanks on that part of my story. She looked a bit unconvinced, though. I bowed my head in silent entreaty.

"We will take that into consideration." This time her voice was a bit less harsh, though.

"Is that it?" I stood. There wasn't anything I could do to make this better. I wanted to get out before she thought to bring in that interpreter or some fancy machine that would show my papers as false.

"Yeah. You will be notified of our decision."

5

Casey Cort
April 16, 2006

"So why didn't you bring that guy Miles to dinner, lieb, I made plenty."

If the smell wafting through the kitchen was any indication, there was enough food in my parents' West Boulevard home to feed half the members of the local parish. Too bad not a single one of them was here to take the heat off me. All of a sudden I was sad that I'd discouraged them from inviting Father Boyle.

"He's in Philly with his own mom and dad," I said hoping beyond hope that would be the last of the impromptu interrogation. My mom stirred, and poked and looked for a long moment like she'd gone back to food and was going to leave the topic alone, when she turned, towel in hand, and looked at me with a squint. Lines deepened around her eyes.

"Oh, with Linda and Emmanuel Siegel, that was his dad's last name, but not his mom's, right? Linda wasn't Siegel."

The dig was subtle, but it was there as she pointed out all that was nontraditional, meaning non-Catholic, about Miles' upbringing.

"She kept her maiden name. It's Miles' middle name." I needed some Imodium to stop the flow of the diarrhea of the mouth. I was talking fast because I didn't want to talk about how quickly Miles had been to abandon this dinner. Or discuss how serious we weren't.

I'd promised myself that we wouldn't be more than friends with benefits this time around, but I was afraid I was falling for him…again. I certainly wouldn't lay out my feelings like a buffet he could pick and choose from like I'd done the last time. Night after night in his bed or mine, I promised myself I'd be smart and savvy and sophisticated and not get hurt.

"But you said…" my mother probed none too gently.

"Mom…" There was a warning tone in my voice. I had invited him to Easter dinner. He'd said yes before he'd been summarily called to the City of Brotherly Love. And when the people who supplemented his income and expensive clothes habit summoned, Miles went running.

I'd been too embarrassed to tell my parents that their invitation had been rebuffed at the dead last minute. So I'd showed up alone knowing there were going to be questions I couldn't adequately answer.

"He's still living at his place, and you at yours?"

My mother's eyes didn't quite meet mine. I just knew that she wasn't asking me about sleeping arrangements. She had to know that I wasn't a virgin and hadn't been for years. It wasn't the forties or fifties. Far from it.

Once a sitting president had talked about his sex life on television, and oral sex in the Oval Office had become water cooler chat, all bets were off as far as I was concerned. But I gave her what she wanted—a reasonably chaste daughter—because I wanted to enjoy this dinner and all others in relative peace.

"He still lives in Coventry, Mom, and I haven't moved since law school. How did you make the lamb?" I asked quickly trying to smooth over my blunder. Because of course I had moved out of my Shaker Heights apartment for a brief moment. Back when I thought I was going to move in with and marry Tom Brody. For that rich scion of Ohio's most powerful political family, these Catholics had been willing to make an exception. Miles, half Jewish, didn't get the same pass.

"Will he be back tonight?" my mother asked, her back to me. She bent, the oven opened, and the yeasty smell of brotchen filled my nostrils. Feasting was way better than talking.

I didn't want to talk about Miles. I kind of didn't want to think about Miles. Not on Easter Sunday, the most important holiday of the year. Miles and I had been on, really on, then off, and now on again. In the latest go 'round I'd said yes to the sex and work pillow talk, but I was keeping my heart out of it this time. Broken hearts were hell to heal, and I wasn't ready to double down.

"Are you talking about your Miles?" my father asked right on cue. I swear after a gazillion years together my parents knew how to make a coordinated attack. The CIA should have recruited these two instead of letting them languish in retirement.

My mom nodded toward my dad as she eased a beautifully browned rack of lamb out of the oven. My mom poured out the meat juices into another pan where she'd already browned flour. Her ridiculously good gravy would be up next on the table. My stomach growled in anticipation.

"I didn't think they were the kind of people who celebrated with his mom being so...outspoken and all and with his dad being Jewish," she said, her hand never stopping. She'd perfected talking and whisking years ago. "Or are they doing something for Passover. That's always the same time of year, right?"

We weren't from the same universe, Miles and I. He was half black, half Jewish, Ivy League, and one hundred percent from a well-off family. I'd call them rich. He'd disagree. He'd say we were more similar than different. With my working-class Catholic roots and state school pedigree, I certainly felt very different. But I didn't want to broadcast that to my parents. I didn't want them to have any more reason, than they already did, to dislike Miles. I wasn't at all sure what our future held, but whatever my decision, I'd need their backing. I always had.

I gave my father a look that he understood without words.

His nod was nearly imperceptible to anyone but me. I loved my dad more than anyone in the world. We'd had a lifetime of communicating wordlessly.

"How's work?" he asked changing the subject just as I'd needed him to.

"Good," I said putting on my winningest smile. "Pretty good. Lulu's been a real help."

"How so?" my dad asked, his accented English full of sincerity. Somehow Lulu's rich Jewish family didn't rub them the wrong way like Miles' rich Jewish family did. My mind skittered away from the other reason they might see Miles as different. I turned toward my dad's open, welcoming face.

"She's provided a steady flow of adoption referrals." Slowly but surely I was transforming my practice. The juvenile cases that had been my bread and butter for nearly a decade were all gone. Closed and archived in storage and on backup tapes courtesy of my secretary, Leticia.

Criminal was nearly done as well. I was finishing up a couple of appeals, but taking no new work. Divorce…and custody weren't so neatly wrapped up. But I was thinking I'd keep those cases and call my practice a full-service family law firm. For the first time I could see both the forest and trees and a future of my own making, not one that had been imposed on me. It was a great feeling being in control of my destiny.

"What was wrong with criminal work?" my father asked. He more than anyone else had always supported my criminal practice. He got it.

"It was morally dubious," I said undercutting the arguments I'd made over the years about everyone's right to a good defense. Marc Baldwin and Jarrod Carter had made me question all the things about criminal law that a great defense lawyer has to learn to ignore. I wasn't that good.

"And adoption isn't?" my father asked. His gray eyes pierced mine with an intensity I'd never seen before. Our usual ease with each other vanished in an instant. Something I couldn't put my finger on was troubling him about the focus of my new practice.

Saddled with the choice between two uncomfortable topics, I glanced toward my mother who was adding copious amounts of butter to the mashed potatoes that I may as well have smeared on my hips, skipping their trip through my digestive system.

She hadn't batted an eye at my father's tone. I was one of the few only children I knew, and not for the first time I wished for brothers and sisters. Someone to take the heat off. Someone to help me parse the subtext of family language, navigate the waters of family strife. But I didn't have any. My devout Catholic parents had deviated there, and no amount of probing had ever yielded a proper answer as to why.

"What are you talking about, Dad? Couples who can't have kids of their own find unwanted kids to make a family. I go to court and make sure the family can be together forever. What's morally dubious about that?"

My mother bustled and set a platter on the kitchen counter. I helped myself to a couple of chops, green beans, and the potatoes I should resist, but couldn't.

"I've read stories in the paper about mothers who were coerced into giving up their babies," he said.

My parents quoted the Plain Dealer like it was the gospel according to Newhouse.

Standing from the counter-height stools, I lifted the platter of meat and another of potatoes and carried them to the dining room. My father followed, his hands carrying the plate I'd started to prepare for myself on a stack of clean ones. My mother brought up the rear through the swinging door with gravy and the brotchen on a hand-carved wooden board she'd brought from the old country.

"That may have been true in the nineteen fifties. Particularly with some Catholic charities," I said unable to help myself from the dig that did make my mom wince as intended. "But things are much different now. A lot of adoptions are open. Or the kids come from orphanages or group homes where they've been effectively abandoned.

If juvenile law taught me anything, it's that institutions can't raise kids. I'd go to bat for a parent, any day, who wanted to pull a kid from that system."

My father carved quietly, laying lamb chops on two plates. He helped himself to a bit of the rest and chewed thoughtfully while my mother flitted around the kitchen turning off knobs, piling pots in the sink, capping this and corking that. Most nights I didn't say anything, but I wanted her to enjoy the feast she'd made for us.

"Sit down, Mom. Please," I called to her. "You should enjoy the food you've cooked for all of us."

Reluctantly, she came into the dining room, untied the apron dotted with unnaturally bright red cherries and electric-yellow flowers, hung it over the back of one chair and sat on another across from me. I stood and took her plate, filling it with a little of everything and placing it before her.

"There was a story on one of those news shows a few months ago." My father had laid his knife and fork against the china.

I took a crusty roll, buttered it, and sat back ready for a lecture about how the world worked by way of 20/20, 60 Minutes, or Dateline. Those shows were ratings grabbers and my parents tuned into each and every one of them.

"About adoption?"

My father took up his utensils again, carefully cutting his lamb, not switching his knife and fork hands like most Americans. My German Polish parents had all but assimilated into this country except for a few little things. The knife-in-the-other-hand thing being one of them.

"There was a woman on there who runs a...how did she call it, Birgit?"

"A blog, Peter. It's called a blog."

"Right. She has this website where she writes about her life and people can comment on it. Anyway..."

"Anyway, Dad." As much as I didn't want to talk about Miles, I wanted to hurry this discussion along as well. They took these sensationalist news shows a little too seriously in my opinion.

"They did about forty minutes on how adoptions are not really ethical. That people are essentially paying for babies. You might be interested in this." He hunched his shoulders, leaning forward. "The average adopting family pays something like forty thousand dollars for a white baby, but less than half for a black child."

"Dad, I'm not getting in the business of brokering babies. I'm helping people who need to finalize adoptions, solidify the relationship, get some certainty."

I put down my own knife and told them the story of Jackie Lopez, now Mitchell. It had been the first adoption case I'd closed, a pro bono referral from Lulu's white shoe firm.

"The girl, Jackie, had been in the guardianship of Steve and Bonnie Mitchell, distant family friends who'd taken her in when she was two. When Jackie had turned eight, the Mitchells had decided to make the arrangement permanent."

"That sounds good."

"It is, Dad. You remember when I was in juvenile court? How there were kids lingering there with the state trying to take them away, but really having nowhere to put them except into one foster care placement after another? I still think that's shit.

"But for those kids with a grandmother or aunt or someone, I want that relationship to be permanent, so that neither the county nor the parents can come back and upset a good thing. That's all. I'm not going to be in the world of people paying for babies. I don't know anyone who is, and even if I did, I'm not going there."

My father held up his hands, knife and fork still backward, in surrender. "Sounds like you know what you're doing."

"Thanks for trusting my judgment." I shifted in my chair remembering I was now an adult, not the child who'd been lectured in this same room time and again.

We ate in silence for a few minutes. But it didn't last long. My mother didn't sit so well with quiet.

"So when do we get to see Miles again?"

I sliced a bit of the lamb. Loaded my fork with some creamy potato and a green bean. I chewed and swallowed while I considered the best way to answer her. I loved my mother's desserts, but was thinking of coming up with an excuse so I could take my serving of blütennusskranz to go.

I came up with a lie instead. "I know that you don't like the idea of me moving in with Miles, Mama. Before he left, he hinted that he was going to talk to Linda and Emmanuel about something important. I think he might pop the question."

"Doesn't seem like you've been together long."

"I'm thirty-four. Been around the block a bit. It's been almost eighteen months if you add it all up. Long enough to know my own heart."

"Would you have children?" she asked. It hadn't been on their priority list to be fruitful and multiply. But it didn't mean they didn't want it for everyone else. My mother was always sending congratulatory cards for births and christenings in the parish.

"Of course, Mama. I'm not that lapsed as a Catholic. I've always wanted to have a family. Two or three kids, probably."

All that was true. I'd wanted kids for as long as I could remember. The father in my fantasy had changed from my high school sweetheart, to my college boyfriend, to Tom Brody. It was just as easy to slip Miles into the mold.

The image it conjured up of little curly-haired children running through a big house in Shaker or Cleveland Heights suddenly warmed me more than the thought of hazelnut and walnut cake.

"Have you thought about what it would be like for the kids?"

"I suspect we'll cross that bridge when we come to it. I think my job is flexible enough that I can stay home with the little ones when they're still small."

"I don't mean your job, honey."

A chill stole down my bones. I put down my utensils and pushed away the delicate china plate in front of me. "What exactly do you mean?"

"This country, lieb, it's not always a nice place for people like Miles."

"People like Miles? Lawyers from Philadelphia?" I prompted though I knew I was being deliberately obtuse.

"That boy Troy Duncan was killed for being in the wrong place. What if your children are in the wrong place?"

"Mama, that won't happen," I said only half believing it. "This isn't Nazi Germany or World War Two Europe."

"Your father and I love our new country. It has been good to us and mostly good to you. But we don't want you to make it especially hard on your children if you were to marry this Miles."

I rubbernecked between my parents who suddenly looked like strangers. "You did not raise me like this. Why are you talking about Miles this way. He's a great guy from a great family." I stood up and shoved my chair back from the dining room table. "One day he'll be your son-in-law and the father of your grandchildren. You're going to regret this day."

Full of righteous indignation, I left my parents' house, without the dessert.

6

"Are you late for something else?" my sixty-two-year-old fractured humerus asked me.

I'd tried to make my glance at the clock to my right subtle, but I'd failed. I'd moved right on after Paul had left. It was 2006 and women—especially thirty-six-year-old women—did not need a man to make a baby, or make their family complete.

While Paul had probably been drinking and shagging his way through New York City, I'd signed on at Ardendale Cryogenics, had been put through a battery of tests, and had bought one of those fertility monitors.

After peeing on test sticks for the last month, I'd finally gotten the little smiley face letting me know my luteinizing hormone had surged and my eggs were ready to meet a sperm.

Two days ago I'd let the clinic know that I was at my most fertile, and they'd urged me to come in right away. Surgeries had piled up back to back, though, and tonight was the end of the narrow window when I could become pregnant, otherwise I'd have to wait for a whole new cycle. I needed to get to the clinic at least an hour before closing time.

Ignoring the patient's observant question, I said, "I'll prescribe pain killer. Two weeks' worth. You'll have to—"

"Paging Dr. Rose. Fiona Rose."

Bollocks. I could not handle one more surgery. Someone else would have to take this one for the team.

"Isn't that you, Dr. Rose?" my patient, still prone on the examination table, asked. I didn't ignore her this time. Talking about anything other than her care, though, was going to push me off schedule. And now I had to add this damned page to my to-do list.

"Yes, you're my priority, though," I said in my best customer service speak like we'd been taught during orientation. "Now back to physiotherapy. I know three times a week can sound like a lot, but you'll want to do it to get your range of movement back as soon as possible."

I was filling out the little referral sheet to tear off for the fractured humerus, when the hospital pager at my waist buzzed against my skin.

"Do you think you should get that?"

"Let me just hand you this. Call us if you've any questions." I tore off the last pink sheet and handed the sheaf of directions and information to the woman. It was only when I was in the antiseptic-laced hall that I realized it was going to be hard for the patient to manage a stack of paper with her non-dominant arm. I didn't turn back, though. A nurse would handle it, I reassured myself.

I was moving toward the nurses' station to answer the damned page when Dr. Bloom intercepted me. "Done with your post-ops yet?"

The US was known for its fast-talking, quick-moving life-style, but somehow all of that had been slowed down in northeast Ohio. Everyone wanted to chat about the intermi-nably gray winters, or the Indians, Browns, or Cavaliers. It made all the chatter about Manchester United seem quaint in a way.

"Two to go, but I need to answer this page." I tried not to let my impatience show through. Normally, I liked the folksy friendliness of these American Midwesterners, but for once I wished they were more like the people from home, tight upper lip and all that.

They needed to leave me alone if I was going to make it. It was half past three, thirty minutes after the end of my shift. The fertility clinic closed at six. I was counting back-ward to see just how much more time I could be at the hos-pital when Dr. Bloom asked another question I didn't quite catch.

"Come again?" I prodded.

"What was the page?"

I pulled down my eyebrows and pushed out my lips. "Just my name, then my first name."

Without asking, she pulled the remaining folders from my arms. "That's a personal emergency. I'll take over. Your past shift anyway. Go home."

"Are you sure?" I tried not to look too joyful with her offer. I was supposed to be a serious doctor concerned with her patients, not someone happy to skive off.

"Anything complicated?"

"Osteotomy and hip pin."

She waved her hand at me. "Go home."

I took a deep breath, swallowing down the unexpected tears that nearly bubbled up. If I got over to the clinic before six, I could be pregnant in the time it took for sperm to meet egg.

"Paul not back?" Debra Bloom probed.

"Don't know if he's coming back. I thought it was a tantrum and he'd be home after a week of drinking with his mates, but…"

"But the clock's ticking." Dr. Bloom awkwardly shifted my files under her arm. "I don't want to overstep, but I've been thinking about giving you something." From the other doctor's pocket a card the color of Easter eggs appeared. "You mentioned that you were thinking about IUI or IVF, but I think you should maybe consider another way of completing your family. All God's children deserve a forever home."

"Ah, okay, thanks," I stuttered awkwardly. "The page." I pointed toward the ceiling intercom and pivoted on my clogs. I continued my walk toward the nurses' station. She'd never seemed like the bible-thumping, proselytizing type. But with Americans you never knew.

For all the talk of escaping religious persecution, it seemed like a super Christian country. I dismissed that thought and shoved the card deep into my lab coat pocket. I didn't have time to work out this particular American paradox. The mental hoops I was jumping through to keep up with Paul's month-long absence were enough.

Before I could ask the duty nurse what the page was about, she spoke. "Dr. Rose. You got a call from a Dolores Watson. She says it's an emergency."

I tried not to roll my eyes too far back into my head. Everything was an emergency for my new next-door neighbor. She'd met the removals lorry before we did on the day we moved house.

From what she'd told me—one of the few times she'd accosted me in my driveway—she was the nearly full-time care giver for her grandchild newly out of foster care and that girl's little brother.

The granddaughter/mum was still down at the pubs, though, to Mrs. Watson's continued horror. And mine too, I had to admit. I'd never leave my babies for a moment, not to run out for a pint or a date.

That was a paradox of another kind, women who had babies and didn't want them and those of us who wanted them, but didn't have them. My mother was the former to the tune of six of us by three different fathers. I was, of course, in the latter category.

I picked up the heavy beige phone receiver and dialed the number the nurse had written on the yellow message slip. "Mrs. Watson. Doctor Rose returning your call." I kept my voice brisk, not wanting to invite more than a just-the-facts rundown of the so-called emergency.

"Fiona Rose, your front door is open." No preamble, like she'd been waiting by the phone for my call.

I looked around the room, but there weren't any windows here. It hadn't been raining when I'd left the house, in fact it had been another one of those warm days that hint at spring. None of those Lake Erie winds that would chill you to the bone could have blown it open. I shivered with worry about a break-in. I didn't have much for anyone to steal, but I treasured what little sense of security I had left without Paul.

"Did you close it?" I asked, hoping a visual barrier would keep all but the most persistent thief away.

"It wasn't quite open," she hedged, "but it looks un-locked. Without Paul around anymore, I didn't want anyone to come in. Since I didn't have a key," she hinted broadly, "I wasn't able to lock it up tight for you."

That sounded like she'd been in my yard poking around, probably seeing if Paul were still working in his studio. At least the door was closed, though. That brought me a mo-ment of reprieve from worry.

I think he'd said something about giving her a cup of tea and a Cornish pasty a few months back. I tried to look at the positive side of that. I didn't know any of my other neighbors. At least Mrs. Watson cared enough—or too much.

If she didn't knock, did that mean Paul might be home? Had he left the door ajar while dragging in his oversized rucksack?

Hope bubbled up. Maybe I could skip the clinic and try getting pregnant the old-fashion way. Relieved, I nearly sighed into the phone. I knew it wouldn't take too long for that man to come to his senses. He'd probably left not five minutes after Easter dinner this Sunday past. His mam was crazy enough to have caused all four of her sons to have emigrated far from England.

"I'll be home in about ten minutes' time."

"My eyes will be peeled."

When I pulled up in the drive, the curtain of the Watson house twitched not once, but twice. I lifted a hand in reassurance before I walked the three brick steps to my door.

I had to push open the front door with a bit of effort, but it was unlocked like she'd said.

"Paul?" I yelled. My voice echoed off the walls of the too empty rooms. Despite the cold and darkness, I sprinted from reception to lounge to kitchen to dining room.

No Paul.

Half the time when he was home, the kitchen was lit and yummy smells of roasting meat came from the oven. The other half, he'd be in his studio, long having lost track of time. I pushed through to the conservatory. It was empty and even with the smell of warm radiator in the air—so, so cold. Paul wasn't coming back. If weeks of drink with his mates and dinners with his mam hadn't sent him back to me, I couldn't think of what would.

I wandered back to the front door and inspected the lock and jamb. Nothing was amiss. I'd probably run out the door, late, forgetting to lock anything. Having to make my own coffee and get my own toast and marmite had thrown off my already abbreviated morning routine.

I chucked my useless keys on the tiny table I'd installed by the entrance. After I tripped over a flyer for a new pizza place in University Heights, I looked to see what else had obstructed the door. Three days' mail lay in a discarded heap inside the vestibule.

I think every woman over eighty in Cleveland had broken their hip this week. I'd reamed more pelvises and cemented more metal in bone than I'd ever imagined I'd do when I chose my specialty. I bent my aching back down to pick up the mail.

Paul's name graced most of the envelopes. One from the gas company, one from electric, another from the water and sewer authority. It was all Paul. Of course he'd set up everything.

I'd been knee deep in paperwork for the clinic and getting acquainted with my colleagues and duties. I added name change to the list of things I'd have to get to in the next couple of days I was off. The last piece of mail was something from the Art Institute—a bill it looked like. That, I'd leave in Paul's name.

Technically I wasn't at all on the hook for it.

My earlier enthusiasm gone, I dragged myself up the narrow stairs, dropping my scrubs, the minute I reached my bedroom door. The crisply made bed reminded me one more time that I was alone. No husband. No partner. And without either one of those, no baby. I'd had a schedule, a timetable, a plan, and Paul in one moment had blown all that to smithereens.

In my underwear, I wandered to the room that was to be for the baby. A recliner in the corner was the only place to sit in the room. I stepped into the room, feeling goose bumps rise up my nearly naked body.

Memories flooded my head. I ran my hand along the smooth finish of the brown wood heirloom dresser and matching changing table we'd found at an antique store in Chagrin Falls. The wood floors Paul had refinished gleamed in the weak setting sunlight. The walls were a gender-neutral teal.

My favorite childhood animated characters from Chorlton and the Wheelies jumped and played just under the crown molding. A bear laughed. I'd spent hours imagining sharing my childhood favorites with a son or daughter of my own. They'd have had my dark hair, but maybe Paul's fair skin. I'd rolled the imaginary dice in the genetic lottery hundreds of times queuing up lists of possible results in my imagination.

Deliberately I closed my eyes, then opened them again. No Paul. No baby appeared. I clapped my hand on my abdomen, empty, barren like this room, like this house. I shut off the light and slammed the door closed.

After a quick shower that chased away the exhaustion and brought back the elation of what was to come, I pulled on sweats and ran out the door, making sure to lock up this time.

Ten minutes later I was in the lobby of Ardendale Cryogenics which was as generic looking as its name. For the first time, I noticed the walls were nearly the identical color of my very empty nursery. Taking it as a positive sign, I took a confident stride to the expansive reception desk.

"Afternoon, I'm on deck for insemination."

"Fiona Rose?"

At my affirmative nod, she clicked at the keyboard in front of her. "I love that accent. Irish, Australian?"

"English," I answered for the thousandth time. It was the question patients asked more often than what their surgical outcome would be. The accent made them trust me more than all the data I could throw at them on rehabilitation and survival rates.

The receptionist smiled like I'd gone permanently into her good books.

Ten minutes later a suited woman I'd never met, opened the door to the clinic's inner sanctum. The hairs rose on the back of my neck. She had that officious look of someone from an insurance company. The kind of woman whose job it is to say "no" all day.

"Do I need to change into a gown?" I asked while we walked down a winding corridor.

"Not quite yet. We'd like you to talk to Doctor Ivanova."

I followed her to a bright and spacious office I hadn't visited before. I'd only met and spoken with Dr. Ivanova in the exam room while she and her team had performed various tests.

Candid baby photos decorated the walls in a careful pattern. Pink frames alternated with blue. The woman left me alone. I hated all the insurance paperwork in America. The care was great, if you could afford it. I probably needed to remind them that I was paying out of pocket, so we could skip all this and get to the procedure.

I wouldn't be surprised if a big smile was making its way all over my face. I was about ten minutes from being pregnant. I mean, I knew that there was only a twenty percent chance from this first time, but it ratcheted up to eighty in just three or four months. I would probably have a winter baby.

I could see Charlotte now. I'd already chosen her name in honor of my grandmother. Her cheeks would be ruddy with cold like the donor's picture standing alongside some New England lighthouse. I'd bundle her up in one of those new prams that looked old-fashioned and take her for long walks through the neighborhood.

I'd show her off to Mrs. Watson, maybe join one of the local new mum groups, so I could swap stories about spit-up and sleep.

"Doctor Rose?" a voice asked breaking into my thoughts.

"Yes." I stood awkwardly while Dr. Ivanova strode through the door and took a seat behind the expansive desk. When she didn't offer to shake my hand, I sat.

"Sorry to keep you waiting—"

"Fertility must be a lot like obstetrics. Babies have their own schedule." I tried for camaraderie.

Katya Ivanova barely cracked a smile. I looked her up and down then, her perfect white wool suit was as flawless as her ash-blond hair. Maybe clinical practice was different from a hospital. My lab coats and scrubs were required dress and closely monitored.

"These are for you," Ivanova said. She'd pulled two manila folders from a stack on her desk and passed one across to me.

"What's this?"

"Normally I don't share raw test results with patients. I know you'd likely ask for them, so—"

"I'm confused. We're scheduled today, right. My fertility monitor indicates the window closes tomorrow."

"We have called you and left messages asking you to come in, but...We won't be performing IUI today. There'd be no chance of success."

Whatever smile I'd had earlier had long disappeared. I had ignored their calls about test results because I didn't want to waste my time. I felt sorry for patients who drove across town, knocked their budget out of whack on parking fees, only to hear one tiny bit of information. So yes, I'd ignored their calls.

I wanted to ask about a thousand questions, but couldn't think of a single one. Instead I opened the folder, pressed my finger hard to the paper, watching the blood disappear from its tip. I traced all the black words swimming until I got to the one labeled diagnosis.

"Hydrosalpinges?" I racked my brain trying to remember what in the hell that was. It was jumbled up in my head with thousands of other long, complicated, Latin-sounding words I'd had to memorize to pass one exam or another.

"Blocked fallopian tubes."

I sighed in relief, my whooshing breath ruffling the paper under my index finger. Blockages in the human body could be fixed especially in this time in medical history when lasers were as common as scalpels. Fallopian tubes weren't nearly as complicated as stopping a human heart to fix diseased arteries.

"Laparoscopic, followed by IUI or will I have to step up to IVF?" I asked proposing a quick and easy surgical solution to my condition.

"How long did you and your former partner try to get pregnant?" Dr. Ivanova posed instead of answering my question. These doctors in the softer fields like to chat, so I'd indulged her. Since there wouldn't be a procedure this month, I had the time.

"Don't know. We were never really great with condoms, so I got an IUD. Took it out about six months before I moved here. About eighteen months then?"

"The hysterosalpingogram films show the dye not getting through."

"Jesus, Mary, and Joseph." I knew I sounded like my hypocritically devout mother, but I didn't care for once about trying to sound more English than Irish. "Which surgery would be better?" I knew that a scalpel and now precisely focused lasers could solve more problems than they could cause.

"Dr. Rose, there really isn't a surgical solution for this. The blockage goes beyond the tubes, discharge from an untreated infection has led to a hostile uterine environment."

"Infection?" Ivanova had made my body sound like a room full of Tories.

"To be frank, this is usually the result of some form of STD. There's a script for azithromycin in the folder to clear it up once and for all. I wanted to be discreet."

Untreated infection. Christ. Paul had given me Chlamydia early on. But we'd both been treated and had been faithful after that. At least I had. Now all those late nights he'd spent in his studio started to take on a different meaning. It was starting to look like he'd taken my dream for a baby from me in more ways than one.

Like I'd mastered in medical training, I pushed all the feelings down for processing later. Turning to the analytical, I met Dr. Ivanova's eyes. "Bottom line it for me."

"You'd be best served, given your advancing maternal age, to consider other methods for completing your family." A lot of words to say, the factory was closed down and forever out of service. It was like Margaret Thatcher had been through my body and treated it like an old manufacturing town.

Wordlessly, I flipped through the printouts in the folder. Even without any training in radiology beyond the basics, I could see that my tubes were blocked. I'd have to research the rest, but I had no reason to believe Dr. Ivanova was lying to me.

Gathering the folder, I stood.

"Thank you for your honesty."

"I'd be happy to refer you to a counselor if you like. This news can be very hard for some women to take."

"That won't be necessary. If you don't mind, I have an early surgery." I turned on my very unpregnant heel and showed myself the door.

7

"Can you watch him?"

Before she could push little Eligu toward me, I pulled the little boy onto my lap. He curled into me like I was his second mother, which I'd kind of been since I'd moved into this refugee house in a place the woman from the Home Office had called The Midlands. All I knew is that it had been a long drive from London many months ago.

"Where are you going?" I asked in English. It was the most universal language among the asylum seekers, not to mention that it was the language of the country we all wanted to stay in. I didn't understand the women who chattered to each other in their native tongues. Though having English knowledge didn't seem to count toward much when it came to decisions about staying.

"To work." Dinha said that with a wink and a nod. I looked at her boy, lighter than me and his mother with his wavy hair already long at eight months old.

"How long will you be gone?"

It was already past six o'clock. I'd eaten dinner with Dinha and Eligu. With that injera she always made and stewed vegetables, she was able to make the twenty nine-pound-a-week stipend last longer than I was ever able to. I didn't understand her need to do what she did for money. Not when we had a roof over our heads and food in our mouths.

"Till I can make two hundred. The doctors said Eligu needs that more expensive formula, and I've got to put something aside for the future. When I get asylum, I want to start school for nursing. The help they say you get here isn't really enough."

I nodded though I didn't really believe her story. I'd done what I had to do or when I'd had no choice, no other currency. Secretly I wondered if she somehow enjoyed the attentions of random men. Instead of saying anything to her, I cuddled Eligu all the closer. My Yeni was older than this now, but holding Dinha's little one reminded me of the weight of having my own baby on my lap, lying against my breast in those first weeks before Umi locked me out. I pushed away the thoughts of those desperate days and focused on Eligu whose hands were roaming across my chest.

"He should still be on the breast," I said, my voice low. It wasn't my business, but I don't know how Dinha had given it up so easily, that soul-deep connection to her little one. I'd suffered for days as I walked from Lilongwe with my breasts hard as rocks, milk leaking into my dress until a kind woman had given me some leaves to make it stop.

"The punters, they were just...too freaky...that's the word they use here about it. My milk was for my baby. If he couldn't have it, no one else could either."

Punters was one word for it. I could think of a few others that I'd use to describe the depravity of men who liked things like that. I didn't share those experiences with Dinha, though. I wanted to push them down so deep, I'd never remember them again. Taking care of her baby was one way to do that. I made motions toward the door.

"You go. I'll make sure he gets a bath and gets to sleep."

Dinha didn't look once back before her skinny blue-sequined body disappeared through the front door.

I didn't bother to stay downstairs for too long. This house I'd been moved to a couple of weeks ago was in a town they called Wolverhampton. Its name made it out to be much more than it was. While it was bigger than the place I'd stayed in London for a week, the brick building was packed to the ceiling with black and brown women and children. There were ten of each. The kids mostly weren't in school yet and none of the women had legal jobs. That was a lot of people crowded into a small space. We all irritated each other. To avoid the fighting, I took long walks during the day. At night I took solace in Eligu. I was happy to hold him, and unlike the other women here, I didn't charge Dinha a single quid.

Every day I was here, I alternated between regret on not finding a way to get Yeni on the journey across Africa with me and relief that she didn't have to be in a place like this with its roaches, and rats, and people with no soul left in their eyes.

Refocusing on the present, I peeled Eligu from his clothes while the bath filled with warm water. Keeping all my attention on him was the only way I could push away the soul-crushing regret of giving up, of leaving Yeni behind.

I stripped his soggy diaper and lifted the baby under his chubby arms. I held him so his fat baby toes skimmed the bath water, bubbles tickling his ankles.

"How's that water, Eligu?"

If his "ayeeee" was any indication, he loved the bath. Gently, I lowered him in, keeping my arm around him the whole time. This tub was way too big for babies, but there wasn't anywhere else I could think to wash him. The kitchen sink was always full of dirty dishes, and even if it wasn't, I'd seen too many roaches around there.

I kept this bathroom scrubbed every morning, even if that stuff they gave us to clean cracked my hands, but I could see Eligu catching some disease in here for sure if I didn't keep it spotless.

I made noises pretending the soap was a boat that nibbled at his toes, then an airplane that dropped suds in to his hair. One-handed, I rubbed in between all his little rolls of skin and made sure to get all the soap out of his hair and away from his eyes.

"You're good with him," a woman said. Her clipped tone wasn't from one of the women who lived here. I nearly dropped Eligu when I jerked around.

I thought if I'd learned nothing over these past months, I'd learned to be aware of my surroundings. Somehow this baby boy had lulled me. I looked the woman in the eye. From the sympathetic smile, I could tell this woman was from one charity or another.

I did my best to smile back. Sometimes they dropped off money or soap or clothes and they liked us to be grateful. Over the last year, I'd mastered grateful.

"I'd shake your hand, but yours are full. I'm from Raha. I'm called Emma Graham."

"Raha, from the Arabic, like comfort or relief."

"You speak Arabic? Where are you from?"

I lifted Eligu from the water and wrapped him in the thin towel I'd pulled from the line earlier. I could tell he was tired as his squealing had stopped, and his eyelids were barely able to stay open.

"Sudan." Short, to-the-point answers. I looked down, fiddled with Eligu's towel some more.

"I'm so sorry for what's going on in your country. It's always about oil in the end, yeah?"

"Men will always fight to gain power." It was my usual non-political, non-committal answer to these types of people. She nodded like they all did as if I'd said the most profound thing ever.

"How long have you been here?"

"In the UK? About a year. Another few weeks before I get an answer from your Home Office, I expect."

"I wish it were that way, quick and fair. Some people have to stay in temporary housing for years though. Huge backlog we're seeing." They all said that. If she had free stuff, I wanted to get to that so I could put Eligu down before he got cranky.

"What is Raha?"

"We're not just handing out soap or giving free dental checkups," she answered as if reading my mind. "Not that there's anything wrong with those. Soap and good teeth are important. Raha is kind of like a social worker. We try to fill in the gaps to give you guys what you need."

"Do you really think it will be much longer?" Maybe this woman, this Emma, had some way to get my "right to remain" papers. I cuddled Eligu closer and walked from the bathroom to the hallway. Emma followed along without asking if I wanted privacy. They never did, these workers, assume you were entitled to any kind of private space or time.

"There's talk about there being a new fast-track scheme coming, but for now, the average wait is about eighteen months."

That burning feeling I sometimes got started in my chest again. That feeling that Yeni was thousands of miles away and no matter what I did, get asylum, get enough money, get help, that I'd never see her again.

"I can't wait that long." Desperation made my voice breathy.

"It's better to be here than there, yeah?"

"Yes, but I...worry for the safety of the rest of my family...I hoped to bring them here once I was settled." It was the closest thing I'd said to the truth in weeks. Something about this Emma made me want to share my secrets.

"You do a really good job with your son there. He's got to be a comfort for you during this hard time."

"He's not mine. I'm watching him for one of the other women here. She's...at the high street...buying formula."

"I don't work for Home Office. We know that you can't really live on the welfare payments. I don't care if some of you are working on the side."

My relief was probably visible.

"I have to..." I stood fully and walked to the room Dinha and I shared with four others. I pulled out some clean sleep clothes for the baby. Laying him on the bed, I tickled his belly while I taped the plastic and paper diapers into place. I put on some sweet-smelling lotion that one of Dinha's punters had given her. Then I gently slipped one foot, then another into the pajamas that made him look like a fuzzy rabbit when zipped.

I scooted backward onto Dinha's bed and wrapped him in my arms. Slipped a dummy into his mouth and rocked him slowly. He was asleep in less than a minute. My Yeni would have taken the breast and a whole lot more rocking than this before she finally settled. I wondered if she'd grown out of that already.

Dinha complained, but Eligu was an easy baby. I was thinking he took after his father, whoever that was. I'm not sure Dinha really wanted a baby or looked at little Eligu as her way to remain in the UK. He was her half-English anchor to the land here.

"What kind of job do you want if you get your refugee status? What kind of job did you have back in Africa?"

"I was only a girl, so I had to help my mother and aunt cook and clean and care for the ones younger than me. I never got to go to school past a few years. I was hoping to do that, get some kind of an education. If I got that indefinite leave to remain, then maybe…"

I honestly couldn't answer this Emma Graham. I'd never given much thought to what happened to me. I was planning to send for Yeni and put her in school. She would be able to grow up and be anything, even prime minister of this great country. Myself, I'd sacrifice whatever I had, do whatever job was needed to give her that future.

"I'm asking because you're really great with that baby. And you just said you cared for younger kids. Raha has a partner that places women like you in au pair programs. You can go to school, have free room and board, and all you have to do in return is care for the children of the house."

My heart sped up a little. I could go to school. Maybe earn a certificate or something. If I could have room and board, I could do what Dinha was doing, put aside a little something for the future.

"I'd be very interested in that, I think."

"Here's my card," Emma said. I took the thick square of paper and tucked it into the pocket of the jeans I'd gotten from a different worker last week. "Come in tomorrow around eleven. I'll help you fill out the application and get you on your way. I think you'll like it better than being here. Did I forget to mention you'd have your own room and bathroom as well?"

No more sharing. No more scouring. I could save money, send for Yeni or maybe even figure out a way to get her myself. Regret over all the past decisions left my heart. I didn't like it when one of the NGO people said something like "things happen for a reason." Maybe, though, maybe she was right. Maybe my uncle, and the men who I'd had to use my body to pay along the way, were the price for this clean and bright future for me and Yeni.

I swaddled Eligu a bit tighter, then lay next to him unable to sleep a wink. I counted the minutes until the sunrise.

8

"Sunday night?" Miles asked for the third time after the host seated us in a tall leather booth at the back of the bistro. "Does Lulu honestly think that Sunday was a good time?"

"It's weird, I agree, but Lulu would like me—us—to meet her new guy." I wanted to meet the person who'd captured her heart more than I wanted a good night's sleep.

"I have to go before Judge Boyko in the morning," Miles said as if I hadn't heard him the first three times. "You know how new judges can be..."

New judges were like new lawyers, nervous, eager to show they knew what's what. In a judge, though, that could have some unpleasant moments.

"He was in Common Pleas from the time I graduated, though, so it shouldn't be too bad," I soothed. It was times like these that I had to remember Miles wasn't from here. That he didn't realize Cleveland moved at its own pace, with

AIME AUSTIN

its own cast, kind of like the old Hollywood studio system where the same actors took on different rolls in one film after another but the complexion didn't much change. Rather than explain any of that, like I was some kind of Midwest cultural interpreter, I laid my hand atop his to stop its insistent tapping on the table.

Miles shook his head, then slipped his hand away. He shook the wrinkles from his napkin and placed it on his lap then he picked up the overlarge laminated menu.

Shaking off the quick flash of unease his movements caused, I too turned to food, flipping my plastic menu from back to front not trying to ignore the tempting pictures of the decadent treats.

Every women's magazine article on maintaining a healthy weight skipped one super important fact. Eating your feelings tasted good. Inadequacy tasted like potato chips. Anxiety was honey-almond flavored. Loneliness was double-stuffed chocolate cookies. I wanted all the carbs from the menu, the bread and potatoes and butter. But knew if I wanted to keep Miles, keep fitting into my new clothes, I'd better not indulge.

I'd decided before we even got in the car, that I was having whatever fish they had with whatever vegetables they could cook up. I liked my newfound figure and was unwilling to risk it on deep-fried anything.

I didn't even have to glance down at the menu to know deep fat fried in batter was this place's specialty. Its proximity to Jacob's Field and the smell of fry oil in the air was all I needed to know I needed to stay away from most stuff on the menu.

Mentally I batted away all the uncomfortable feelings that he didn't love me enough, that these two hours with my best friend could somehow ruin his future because he didn't prep enough, that I was settling...again. Instead, I pasted a huge smile on my face and kissed him on his stubbly jaw.

"So what's up with Lulu that we couldn't all have met near where we live on the east side?" For a half a second, I regretted bringing Miles. It had seemed easier to have a buffer. I'd wanted him by my side in solidarity—especially if the new guy was a jerk. I was starting to notice Miles made things hard if they weren't going exactly as he'd planned them. For things to work, I was going to have to be the accommodating one.

Immediately, I chastised myself. Maybe I was being unfair. I didn't have court in the morning. During most of the years I'd been practicing law, the kinds of cases I'd worked could have been handled in my sleep. Miles was working at a much higher level. The stakes were greater in federal court. I was patient as I explained for a fifth time why we were five miles from the Heights.

"She's got a new guy. Maybe he's not from the Heights. Who knows? I'm sure she doesn't want to be here any longer than you in case we hate him."

"And you don't know who it is?" he asked for the ten thousandth time.

"Someone from the firm. They all kind of run together," I said. I'd been on pins and needles with curiosity for days if not months, but wanted to play it cool for everyone involved. So I said, "I probably met him in passing and didn't give it a second thought. Lulu's been playing it pretty close to the vest. I'm so glad that she's found someone that I kind of don't care if he has two heads as long as he's nice to her. She used to have a thing about being with guys who weren't always nice." That was something my best friend and I had in common. I was hoping that we'd aged out of that.

Miles covered my hand with his under the table and gave it a squeeze as he cut his eyes my way, squinting a little while he did it. I wanted to tell him the hint wasn't so subtle. I'd allowed my ex Tom Brody to treat me like crap, not once but twice.

At least I'd wised up and broken up with him the second time around which was why I was sitting here with Miles and not in Lakewood at the obligatory Brody weekly family dinner watching them plot the ruin of one person or another.

Speaking of family dinners, I broached the topic I'd studiously ignored. "My parents really missed you at Easter. My mom really did it up with her homemade bread and lamb." I'd tried not to say anything about how much I'd missed him over the holiday. How much I'd wanted to show my parents that I was healed and whole and on to bigger and better things.

"I've had her strudel, I don't think your mom does low-key."

He was right about that. He and I had first really clicked on the night when he'd dished up my mother's famous strudel to my friends during my portion of the New Year's progressive party. I changed the subject because guilt wasn't sexy.

"How was Philadelphia?"

It was the first time I'd worked up the courage to ask. Couldn't bring myself to pose the real question of what his parents had wanted that would make him cancel plans with me. I wanted to think I was more important than a new watch or a bigger stipend.

"Philly was the same," he said evenly.

"My parents were a little weird about me doing adoptions. They made it sound like I was brokering in newborns stolen from their mother's arms. As if it was the nineteen fifties or something and I was some evil house mother plucking infants from the arms of 'girls in trouble.'" I did air quotes around those last two words.

"Sounds odd. Adoption in the US is mostly on the up-and-up. Not something that comes across my desk ever, and we see nearly every human depravity there is."

"I know. Weird, right?"

"Maybe it's some European thing. Is adoption big over there, do you know?" He'd traveled the world before his fifth birthday and knew all sorts of odd things about different cultures. It was odd for him to ask me a question like that. He continued, distractedly answering what had obviously been rhetorical. "The US is the country of the orphan train. Probably not an old-world tradition."

"You're probably right about it being a cultural difference. They asked about us, you know. Birgit and Peter," I said rounding back to us.

Miles' eyebrows lifted slightly. "What did they want to know?"

"If we were serious this time." If you were going to break my heart again, I wanted to say.

"I love you, Casey," he said. Those three words smoothed over all the ruffled feelings. "Who couldn't love your pluckiness," he continued. "But we're young, right. Who knows how the future will go?" And with that last question, I was ruffled once again. Pinning down a future with Miles was like trying to hit a piñata while blindfolded.

I changed the subject away from needy girlfriend. "Are your parents going to Greece and Turkey or doing that northern Africa tour your mom talked about?"

"Can I get you anything to start?" the server interrupted. "Maybe some of our specialty beer-battered onion rings, fried cheese wedges, or fried pickle chips to share?"

"Water, please," I gulped.

"Can I have mine sparkling, with lime. We'll hold off while we wait for the rest of our party," Miles added smoothly.

The waitress darted away as quick as she had come. I saw Miles glance at his watch when he didn't think I was looking. I slipped my hand to his knee, found it jiggling, patted him until it stopped.

"My parents are getting divorced," he said matter-of-factly. I nearly fell off my chair. The devastation of that kind of news hit me in the solar plexus and it wasn't even my parents.

"Oh, gosh, I'm so sorry. I don't know what to say."

Miles swallowed a couple of times. I really wished the water were already at the table. Didn't seem like a good time to wave over a busser, though.

He swallowed hard, then spoke. "They've been together thirty years."

"Wow. So have mine," I responded. My parents were a unit in my mind. I couldn't imagine them in different houses, with different lives. My head jumped right from the fact of it to the why of it.

Why two people who'd been together longer than they had would end it. It had to be an affair. His mom, probably more than his dad.

"Did they say why?" I tried, and failed, to clear my mind of judgment over ending such a long-term marriage. That was one thing I appreciated about being Catholic. We were in it for life.

"My mom is going to Greece, Turkey, and Morocco without him."

"So your dad doesn't want the divorce?"

"He's devastated. He's never lived on his own. I don't think he's ever gone to sleep or woken up without my mom. She says she wants to live life, stretch her wings, be who she really was meant to be before she dies."

Sounded like his mom had rehearsed that speech a time or three.

"At least you're not a kid in that situation. I've done those cases as guardian ad Litem, and the kids can't really make heads nor tails of it. Sometimes they do well long term, sometimes they don't," I said trying to offer what sympathy I could, make the best of a bad situation. Miles had moved out, though. Moved on. His life wouldn't change too much. He had a great job, didn't need them as backup. Not in the way I needed my own parents.

He swallowed again. "I think Mom wants to sell the house."

"The one you grew up in?" I hadn't seen it. But the way Miles described it, the house sounded like something from one of those perfect family dramas. Two stories, big sunny rooms, expensive but cozy, lived-in furniture, a kitchen full of laughter. If his parents were divorcing, though, maybe I'd made it out to be more than it really had been.

"It's home."

Those two words felt like another kick in the gut. On the one hand, I wanted Cleveland to feel like his home.

Our home.

Yearning for a family of my own, that I'd thought had gone a long time ago, was returning with a swiftness. On the other hand, when I took my own needs out of the discussion, I understood Miles deeply.

Even though I'd called Shaker Square home for most of the last decade, I couldn't imagine not being able to go home to West Avenue. I always knew where I could go for commiseration, for a home-cooked meal, for a night of sleep, or long term if I needed it.

"You can always come to West Boulevard," I said. I bumped my shoulder up against his. He didn't budge. I felt like a rat running through a maze, not at all sure which tunnel to select to get the reward of his smile, his attention, his love. I tried another. "Why does she want to sell?" His family was the kind where the mortgage was probably paid off. Where there was no financial reason to get rid of it.

"It's an old house. A bear to take care of. Fixing leaks, tuck pointing brick, managing renovations. All of it. My mom says she's exhausted. Wants a maintenance-free condo where she can come and go as she pleases."

"And your dad can't just keep the house? Take care of it himself, at least the small stuff?"

I knew my father would be up on a ladder pulling leaves out of the gutters as soon as it was warm enough to work outside for a stretch. If I weren't still really mad at them for their closed-minded comments, I'd probably have been in the kitchen eating my mom's butterkuchen and drinking tea with them after he was done working outside. I'd ignored their overtures over the last week, though, until I cooled down enough to speak with them rationally.

"My dad likes to think of himself as handy. I'm not sure anyone else in the world sees him that way. Let's just say, managing details isn't in his wheelhouse."

"Even if they don't sell the house, he might have to figure it out. They don't expect you to move home and take care of things, do they?"

I'd met those kids in college and even law school. Mostly the kids of immigrants who took care of everything, whose families were bereft without them and their language skills.

My parents were by no means perfect, but they did have strong boundaries. All of us in the Cort family knew where our responsibilities began and ended. And the taking care went one way. That might change in the next twenty years, but for now it was as it had always been.

"Let's not talk about this." The water finally came and Miles took a long drink, cleared his throat. "I've been calling both of them trying to get them to reconcile. They've never fought. They aren't fighting now. If they go to counseling, I'm sure they can fix it."

That sounded unrealistic and immature. I'd met his mother. From keeping her own name to speaking her mind, she was as thoughtful and direct as they came. But I let him keep his illusions, for now. I sipped at my own water and zipped my lip.

"So Lulu…" I changed the subject back to what I'd wanted to avoid in the first place. After skidding along the third rail of divorce, being a little inconvenienced by leaving the east side seemed like a little thing.

"Has had some bad relationships," I started. "She went through a bad-boy phase. If this new one works at the firm, at least he has an upstanding job. Probably doesn't deal drugs, or ride motorcycles, or have another woman on the side."

"Still hurts, huh?"

"Not really." I took a deep breath, exhausted with all the times I had to answer for Tom's behavior like he wasn't a grown man responsible for his own mess.

It had killed me the first time, I'd admit that. The second time we'd broken up had been a relief more than anything.

"Some men visit hookers. I guess they can't integrate the whole Madonna whore thing. I don't know. Not my problem any longer or ever again. We don't have any problems in the bedroom." I slipped my hand up from his knee. He caught it and moved it back down to a safe zone. The tension of broken relationships shifted and I leaned in to give him another kiss. This time he angled his head toward mind and returned it. He let go of my hand and I craned my neck over the top of the booth. On cue, the restaurant's front door opened.

This time I was the one squinting because it was Lulu, but wasn't. Normally, I could spot her from a thousand paces because some part of her was always sparkling, glasses, jewelry, an errant rhinestone hair comb she must have dug out of her nineteen eighties nostalgia box.

But today, I could barely make her out in the dim light. Even what I called her Joseph and the Technicolor Dream Coat was missing in action, replaced by something from a display ad for spring jackets from the Burlington Coat Factory. It was so gray, I could only imagine it on one other person, my own mother, for whom color and style were foreign.

"Lulu's here," I threw at Miles over my shoulder. I stood ready to wave her over, when my own arm stopped, paralyzed in midair. Lulu's eyes widened a bit when I saw whom she'd been hiding for the last many months. Betrayal slammed into my chest. Now I knew why she hadn't introduced me to her boyfriend.

9

"Dr. Rose?" At the sound of my name, I stood from the square cloth and metal armchair in reception and took the cool outstretched hand. "Welcome to the Hudson Agency. I'm Paola Castro Hudson."

The woman who had come to collect me was tall, thin, and amazingly turned out. I'd have been scared to wear pastel suede outside of a hermetically sealed room. First Ivanova, then Hudson. Maybe the Cleveland fertility scene was more fashion conscious than I'd imagined.

I looked down at my own scrubs and immediately regretted my choice of clothes. Or lack of choice. Hadn't thought twice about it before coming over. For once I was okay having "doctor" in front of my name smooth over my sartorial faux pas.

"Are you the founder?" I asked turning the focus on her. Whenever I didn't know what to say to a patient, I asked them a question. People loved to talk about themselves.

"Twenty years ago, yes. Come to my office. Let's talk." I followed her through the plush carpeted halls, quiet save for the occasional whoosh of a printer or ping of email. The sound of raindrops didn't even permeate.

It was a big room, her office. Lucite desk, more pastel colors that remarkably didn't clash with her lilac suede. Nothing about the agency screamed, or more accurately whispered, that babies happened here.

"Those two," Paola said, then pointed to two large framed posters of what looked like models behind her. A young woman in one, a young man in the other. Dark hair narrowing to a widow's peak in both, hers shoulder-length, his cut like he was at Eaton. Both had green eyes, appealing freckles. Looked like an advert for NHS sexual health—the good, condom-inducing kind, not the disease-testing kind.

"Those two are my children. Adopted them from Guatemala when they were one and three."

"Beautiful," I blurted, though I was sure she'd heard that lots of times.

"Aren't they, though? But that's just the proud mother in me talking. They're literally the poster children for Hudson Agency. After I experienced the joy of completing my family through adoption, my husband thought I should share the knowledge and expertise I gained from the grueling process with other women and families, so here I am."

I ticked one box in my head: personal experience with infertility, and moved on to another. "How many adoptions have you completed?"

"We're not a volume agency. Very selective in fact. We work very nearly only by referral. Maybe we do twenty per year. We've completed about five hundred by my count, mostly families here in northeast Ohio, some Pennsylvania and Kentucky for those willing to travel for our services. Tell me, what brings you here? Are you...partnered?"

"I'm here because I'd like to bring a child into my life. My partner of ten years and I were working to get pregnant, but he left to...go home to England. He was homesick, I guess. I was ready to go the IUI or IVF route, but testing showed that I'm very likely infertile. Even with surgical intervention, there's little chance I'd be able to conceive on my own." I hoped my speech didn't sound as rehearsed as it was. Paola didn't blink an eye. She'd probably seen it all. If the agency did psychological testing, I prayed I was far down on the crazy chart.

"I'm sorry to hear that. I'm sure that you've heard all the platitudes. That children don't make a family complete. That we're whole just the way we are. I want to say, though, that my children are the joy of my life. I wouldn't be sitting here with you if they hadn't inspired me."

Impatient to get my questions answered, I interjected, "Do you have babies?" before she'd finished her "completing a family" speech properly. "Available for adoption, I mean."

She was unfazed by my rudeness. I liked that about her. "The easy answer is absolutely yes," she said pivoting effortlessly.

"Easy?" Adoption seemed like the hardest solution out there.

"If you've spent more than a few minutes on the internet, I'm sure you've read the dire tales of how few babies there are to adopt. The politically inclined will tell you either that birth control has been a success or there are too many abortions. Either way, their basic facts aren't true. There are babies available both here in the US and abroad. The caveat is that you must be open to taking a baby who is a different color than you. African American, African, Chinese, or from another part of the world that's not western Europe or North America. Is that something you can see your way to doing?"

My Irish mother might not like it, but I'd come of age in an entirely different era. One with a capital city full of immigrants of every stripe. I'd always envisioned a baby that looked like me and Paul, but that had been a biological fantasy. Instantly, I expanded my notion of what it was to be a mother. Excitement coursed through me. "Of course," I hastened to answer. "Color doesn't matter one bit."

"Good to know. Have you considered international adoption?"

I hesitated. Of course, I didn't want to seem picky, nor insult the woman in front of me whose own children had come from outside the States. At the same time, I didn't want to wait for the rest of my life either. Who hadn't seen the chat shows where bereft families had practically moved next door to some Chinese orphanage while waiting six months or more to get their baby out of there. "I have no issues with adopting a baby from another culture. My job, though," I plucked at my scrubs. "I'm a surgeon at the clinic. It doesn't allow for extensive travel."

"Those stories about wait times are for families doing it on their own. I don't want to sound mercenary, but there are some things money can buy. Cutting through red tape is one of them."

My sigh of relief was probably audible, but I didn't care. I'd already moved to a country where money could buy you medical care while others had none. Who was I to judge if money greased the wheels in other ways. I wasn't going to turn into a flaming Tory over this bit of business. Adopting had to keep me right in the Labour column.

"I appreciate that. Some of us have more money than time, I expect."

"It was great meeting with you, Doctor Rose. I'm going to turn you over to my assistant. You'll complete some forms and she'll go over the process with you, so you can make a fully informed decision."

I have no idea if I'd passed the test. Paola must have pressed some kind of invisible button, because the moment she stood, another impeccably dressed woman appeared at the door, knocking softly, then entering without waiting for a reply.

"Merrill Barrera." She extended her hand. I could do nothing else other than stand and extend my own. We shook. "Doctor Rose, let me take you to my office so we can start this process."

"I haven't...I didn't—" I was surprised to hear my own voice utter any hesitation. My heart was all, go, go, go, but my brain, my over analytical brain thought this was all going too fast.

"Yes, of course." Merrill patted me on the shoulder like I'd suddenly wandered from the geriatric floor. "I understand. This can be a lot for anyone to process. The application just gets things started. You decide where to go from there."

I let myself be led from Hudson's office to another that had Barrera's name calligraphied on the door. I didn't expect the room to be larger, but it was. In addition to the regular desk and two chairs, a six-person conference table took up half the space. She directed me to a seat that had a slim laptop on the table where a placemat would be. Obediently, I sat.

Barrera perched on the edge of the seat next to me and swiveled in my direction. "Here at Hudson we've streamlined the adoption process. What takes other agencies months, or years, takes us only weeks. The first step, of course, is an application, all of which can be completed online. The initial fee is seven hundred fifty dollars to submit this. Of course, once you fill this in, I'll be able to give you more information and answer any questions."

She lifted the top, entered her password, and a utilitarian fill-in form popped onto the screen.

"I'll give you five minutes."

Dutifully, I filled in my name, address, phone, all the vitals I'd put on a thousand employment and immigration forms. I ticked the box saying I owned my house in University Heights, and let them know that I had no illness that could shorten my life expectancy, that I had no known mental illness, nor did I have a criminal background. I stuttered when I got to the information about parent number two. Fortunately, the computer let me pass those sections without filling them in, no blaring red box jumped out highlighting the fact that I was single. Added my employer, my income, and that was it.

Like she'd been standing behind me, Merrill walked in at the moment I'd typed the last keystroke.

"Great. You're all done. Didn't think it would take you long at all. I'm happy to submit this for you. If you don't have a checkbook with you, we do accept credit cards as well."

I extracted my wallet and handed over my newly minted American Express card without any chip and pin like my Barclay's which had confounded the machines here.

"Be right back." In a minute she was handing me the card and a small duplicate paper to sign. She slipped the yellow copy over to me and I put both in my wallet.

"Thanks," I said, not sure what I was thanking her for exactly.

"Let me tell you a bit about the process, okay. In order to adopt any child here, in the US, or abroad, you'll need to complete what we call a home study."

"Is that invasive?" I asked. I'd read a tiny bit online about the process in between patient rounds. I wondered if someone did a white glove test or found moldy lettuce in the crisper would I instantly be deemed unworthy of a baby.

"Not at all. Rather than farm them out, here at Hudson we do them. I'm a licensed and certified social worker duly registered with the state of Ohio. So if you chose to work with us, I'd be doing the home study. You have to fill out a few more forms, nothing challenging for you, I'd imagine. Then I come visit your home, make sure you're set up for a baby. I'd talk to your references, clear you through state-required background checks, then that would be it."

"How many months?"

"Not months, weeks, Fiona. You set the schedule. At Hudson we do nearly everything in-house to expedite the process. No calling and following up with people. I would advocate for you and work on your behalf to make sure you're matched with a child."

"Wow. I thought I'd be in for a year or more wait."

"If you do it on your own or go through the state, sure, I guess. We're here for busy people who don't have that kind of time. Our fees are commensurate with that, however."

"How much will I need?"

"From a brief glance at this, you're in the mid six figures. So it will be no problem for you. Our fee is fifteen thousand.

Seventy five hundred would be due up front. Additionally, our home study fee is fifteen hundred, which would be paid initially as well. Including legal fees and whatever expenses the birth mother incurs, the total is twenty-five to thirty thousand dollars."

I sighed, relieved that I had been scrupulous in saving my pounds in an account I didn't share with Paul. With the exchange rate of one pound to two dollars, I could cover this without much effort.

"What's your placement rate?"

"Ninety-seven percent of families that pass the background check are matched with a child." Her ever-present smile was quickly replaced with a frown. "The three percent are mostly families with strict limitations that we could not meet."

"Limitations?"

"Often families want a child that looks just like the parents despite what they put on the application. I must stress, we're not an auto manufacturer nor do we make burgers 'your way.' Each child is a unique gift and we support families who honor that."

Looks weren't everything. Looks weren't any part of an equation in bringing a child into the world. My brothers and sisters looked like my mum and our dads, but they hadn't loved us any more for that. We'd still gotten the back hand or the strap when any one of us had gone astray. I would never be one of those people. My future son or daughter was too important to me for that.

"How would I get started?" Whatever hesitation I'd had earlier this morning was long gone. These people appeared to provide a sure path to parenthood and I was more than ready.

Barrera stood and glided to a white enameled file cabinet in the corner. The drawer slipped open silently at her touch, and she extracted a folder that looked like it had been hand-painted with watercolors. At her offer, I took it in hand, smoothing my hand over the slightly roughened surface. Bold pinks, purples, and greens evoked a brightly hued childhood I hadn't lived, but wanted my child to have.

"All the information and forms you would need are in there. If you leave us with a check for nine thousand, we can set up an appointment for your home visit. The forms would have to be completed by then. In the meantime I'll run the criminal checks if you sign a couple of authorization forms before you leave and that's it. We'd get the ball rolling. You could have your son or daughter in your home by summer."

Summer.

That was only a bit more than a month away. Reflexively my hand went to my stomach. Nothing slipped by Barrera's gaze.

"It's not as much time as a birth mother gets to prepare, but your motherhood journey can start soon. As I'm sure Paola shared with you, it's one of the most worthwhile."

"I can't wait to get started. Where do I sign?"

10

"I feel like you're avoiding me." Lulu's accusation came at me before her secretary was even outside of hearing range.

"I'm not—" My protest came fast to my lips.

"Oh my God." She threw up her hands with a drama and flair that had been missing for months. "That's the biggest damn lie you've ever told."

"What did you want me to say?" I threw back. I'd thought I'd worked through my resentment over the last three and a half weeks, but the angry heat creeping up my neck gave truth to that lie.

"You haven't even made an effort to get to know him." Lulu's own voice was on the rise. "Miles' pager beeped and you were both out of there before the appetizers could even come."

"He ordered a martini," I said with condemnation.

"That's your problem with my boyfriend, that he doesn't swill girly drinks?"

I very much resisted the urge to put my hands around my best friend's neck and throttle her for her lapse in judgment. I wasn't the least bit sure our friendship could survive—him. It made me so sad that she'd allowed a man, and a crappy one at that, to come between us.

In between my chest heaves, I spit out, "My problem with your boyfriend is that..." I trailed off, anger making me mute. There were so many issues I shouldn't have had to spell a single one of them out. But I did. "Let's see..." I lifted my fingers close to her face so she wouldn't have any problems counting. "One, he's married. Very, very married. I asked you point blank last year if being married is what made him off-limits, but you lied. That's not one, but two transgressions right there. Two...no...three...he totally dropped the ball, let me down when I needed him the most."

Not rising from her desk, Lulu batted my hand away. "He's separated."

"While you all have been up here in the ivory tower, I've been down in the trenches. Legal separation isn't really a thing in Ohio. He's separated from his wife like I'm separated from my apartment. North Moreland and I will be together tonight, though."

Lulu ignored the area of law that wasn't in her favor and plowed on.

"Is it that he has a wife or is it that he was your faculty representative in all that stuff that went down with law review."

I turned away and started flipping through the papers on my side of Lulu's desk. Like my cat Simba my attention was caught when the reflection of diamonds or rhinestones flickered across the wall. My heart lifted at the thought that

Richard Sinclair hadn't stamped out all Lulu's bling, when I realized it had come from the other side of the office. In our heated discussion, we'd missed the door opening and closing. The sparkle was from someone's very expensive watch.

"Casey," I said sticking out my hand. "Have we met before?" Something about the guy's light brown eyes were eerily familiar.

"Ron Pinheiro. I'm the pro bono chair here."

"Right, I think I remember your name from the NDA." I tried to arrange my face and make my voice sound as normal and professional as I can. There was no erasing the fight he'd come in on us having.

"We have a referral that Lulu said you could handle."

I sat up straighter and put on my serious lawyer face, somber, but caring. I'd cribbed that from television news anchors. The possibility of paid work was the one reason I was here. A potential client was always worth my time. Otherwise I'd have been happy to give Lulu the cold shoulder for quite a while longer. "Tell me about the case," I said in my most adult voice, trying and failing to push my best friend's betrayal out of my mind.

"It's a client actually, not a one-off. We represent Paola Castro Hudson. She runs her own adoption agency here in Cleveland."

"I've heard of them," I said. I'd put together a list of agencies, infertility clinics and the like. It was on my never-ending to-do list, to write cold call letters, send emails, or go on in-person visits to solicit work. My current caseload was heavy, though, and I hadn't yet executed the plan I'd put in place when I was making New Year's resolutions five whole months earlier. Maybe I could shortcut that today.

"With the interest in international adoptions higher than ever," Ron continued, "they need someone they can refer parents to, to help get the adoptions finalized quickly and put these parents at ease."

"Pro bono?" Free was a great way to get experience, but I was about at the end of the free tether. And if not today, definitely by my thirty-fifth birthday later this year. It was time I earned money for my expertise.

"Gosh no. This is a legit pay-by-the-hour referral. There are conflict issues representing the parents, while the agency is a client—obviously. Also, they're small cases and we need to save our resources for matters that have a much higher upside."

Gotta love big firms. My upside was in the tens of thousands of dollars. Dalton Lacey's was no doubt in the millions. I was happy to pick up their crumbs.

I sat forward in my chair, my body virtually humming with anticipation. My caseload could wait. I was ready to meet with the Hudson Agency today, assure them I was the best lawyer they could hire. I was getting better at the never-ending practice of selling myself. "Who do I need to talk to?"

Ron slipped a card from the folder in his hand and pushed it across the desk. His watch sparkled more than Miles' Tag Heuer. I was almost sure I'd seen a glimpse of a Rolex crown. Rich guys were as popular in law firm hallways as stray cats were in mine.

"Dr. Fiona Rose? Cleveland Clinic?" I read the embossed text. "Not Hudson?"

"We're still representing the agency side, but need to farm out the parent side. Their last counsel left them in the lurch and we were picking up the slack for a bit. There are no conflict issues so far, but in this business that could happen. I'm sure you've seen the cases of the parents who want to return their kids. Not saying this has ever happened at

Hudson, but our malpractice carrier doesn't like the potential breach of ethics even with a wall."

"I thoroughly understand," I said. Dalton Lacey's loss was my gain. I motioned for Ron to continue.

"This soon-to-be mom, she's got a girl from Africa coming to live with her from an orphanage there. May be one of the poorest areas in the world. She needs help from start to finish. I'll email Hudson that you'll give this Doctor Rose a call tomorrow. That work?"

My head was nodding so fast I'm sure it looked like a Cleveland Indians bobble head.

"Good." He shook my hand and gave me his best smile. A little zing of something reverberated through my body. "Nice meeting you again. Hope to see you around," he finished. A second winning smile flashed my way, dimples showing, before he took himself away to bill more hours.

"He's the cutest thing ever," I gushed. "Why aren't you dating him? If I weren't with Miles, I'd ask him out in a heartbeat." That last wasn't exactly true. I'd never been that bold, but if he asked I'd say yes. Definitely wouldn't kick him out of bed for eating crackers.

"Are you saying that 'cause he's rich. You have a thing for guys with money?" Lulu asked, eyebrow firmly up near her hairline. I shook my head vigorously. That comment hit a little too close to home. I'd surely date someone without money. None of them had asked me out though.

"It's as easy to fall in love with a rich guy as a poor one," I said embarrassed I'd let that cliché leave my lips. "I don't have a thing for rich guys." I could hear the defensiveness in my tone, but couldn't seem to do a thing about it. "Tom was in the same class and you thought Miles was a good match. You brought him to my apartment—practically set us up."

"Fine. Guilty as charged. Ron isn't my type." The fact that her answer was a relief gnawed at my gut. Miles was the guy for me. I was ninety percent certain, which was nearly one hundred percent if I rounded up. I'm pretty sure from reading women's magazines no one was ever one hundred percent certain.

"Too many morals or too single?" I asked. If she wanted to deflect, two could play that game.

"If you got to know Rich, you'd like him."

"Rich? Dick seems more like. I did get to know him. He said he'd help me. Then did nothing when that pack of raging hyenas, also known as our fellow students, hunted me down and threw me off law review."

"That's way in the past. We're talking ten years ago—"

"Ten exactly."

"Fine. An even decade. But almost a lifetime ago." I hated when she did this. If anything came out of her mouth akin to "stuff happens for a reason" I swore to myself I was going to chuck her out of her pretty window.

"For you maybe sitting pretty on the thirty-eighth floor of the Huntington Building." I pointed to the view we both knew well of Public Square and the war memorial.

"It's called two hundred Public Square," she corrected.

"Whatever. Do you remember going to breakfast just a few years ago when I didn't have enough money in my pocket for eggs and toast? Do you remember me, here in this exact office, hat in hand taking your offer to do pro bono adoption hoping it would lead to a more lucrative practice?" Richard Sinclair hadn't been the cause of my problems, but he'd had his hand in my demise as surely as others had.

"You're not poor," she poo-pooed. "You can afford breakfast nowadays."

It was true. My star had risen enough in the world that I could afford a twenty-dollar breakfast out. But it hadn't been too long since yours truly had been a budget buster.

"You're not listening, Lulu. That, all of that, I can trace back to one single failure on the part of your boyfriend." Like every innocent defendant out there, I'd put my faith in my representative, in the system. And like so many of my clients, I'd been sorely disappointed.

"What about you? On your high horse worried about plagiarism from some guy who'd already graduated. Everyone warned you to leave well enough alone, but you couldn't do it."

My mouth opened, closed. I couldn't believe she was doing what everyone else had done, making this my fault. As if the student who'd done the down and dirty wasn't the true culprit.

"So now we have no ethics. No morals. Only follow the rules when it pleases us? My only failing was calling out the truth? Good to know principles are on a sliding scale."

"I guess that means no double dates." The small smile from Lulu was a peace offering, but I wasn't quite ready to break bread.

"He's old enough to be our father. Okay, not quite. But seriously. He has a forty-something-year-old butt. He has a wife. He has a kid. How can you be in a relationship with a guy who can only dedicate half or a quarter of himself to you. I bet he wouldn't be so forgiving if you had a stray husband and couple of kids hiding in your apartment in Cleveland Heights."

"She's constantly in the hospital. She would be without health insurance if he divorced her. His daughter is in college in Tennessee. He's here now, spearheading our pro bono appellate practice. Death penalty and all that, Casey.

After all your speeches on the Constitutional right to a good defense, you have to appreciate that."

"I only gave those speeches because I had to take those jobs to pay my rent." That wasn't quite true, but I didn't want to have anything in common with Professor Richard Sinclair of the sliding scale morality.

"So he could never be redeemed in your eyes." She looked so sad, I kind of wanted to run around her desk and hug her.

Instead, I said, "It's not only that. You've changed."

"How have I changed?" She asked so earnestly that I started worrying anew that not only was Sinclair some kind of master manipulator, but she wasn't even aware of the ways in which he was altering her.

"You're dressing differently. You're talking differently."

"You mean the bling and the faux Ebonics?" she asked. I winced inwardly. All the Tommy Hilfiger and sparkling rings on both hands had been a bit much for me. Even last year's rhinestone granny glasses and multihued outfits weren't subtle. I'd grown used to all of it in time because she wasn't what she wore. I didn't want to be the kind of friend who judged someone based on the superficial. Even if Lulu hadn't been what she wore exactly, she'd always had a definite sense of style—a way she'd wanted to appear in the world.

"Well, it was the you I met," I said. "I've always loved that girl."

"And you think I, reform Jewish girl from Cleveland Heights, was being true to myself?"

Ah, Jesus. I hadn't had enough coffee for this conversation. What in the hell did I know? I'd never had a sense of style. For the last few years I'd vacillated between the adult version of Garanimals from Lane Bryant and now I wore the same from the mannequin matching outfits from Ann Taylor's downscale cousin Dress Barn.

"So this." I waved my hand up and down. "This Sinclair subdued you is the real you?"

"It's more real than I have been. I'm in love. For the first time, I think. Real love. Not puppy love, not high school, not college hookups. Soul-deep love with a guy who peeled back the layers and found the real me. And loves that person he discovered."

And there wasn't a damned thing I could say to that. I wanted that more than anything. I'd rounded Tom up to that. Maybe was rounding Miles up to that.

"Does that mean Ron's up for grabs then?" It was my agree-to-disagree moment. My second very adult moment of the day.

"He's all yours."

11

"Congratulations on your journey to becoming a parent!" Casey Cort crowed with great enthusiasm. Way over the top, if you asked me, which no one had. I was adopting a baby, not picking up my national lottery winnings. She was a pleasant-looking woman, but the big smile didn't suit her. I tried to work my face to pleasant to at least get halfway to where she was.

"I'm looking forward to what the future brings," I replied. Arranging my hands on my lap, I patiently waited for what was next. My quiet unsettled her a bit, I think. It often did that to people. I had never gotten a lot from useless banter and small talk, though, so I hadn't mastered it. There were plenty enough blowhards in the world to go around.

"Well, then. Let's get started," Casey said. She cleared her throat and opened a folder on her desk. Extracting several forms, she clicked her biro into place. "Adoption of children where the parent or parents have consented is pretty straightforward. What I'll need from you today is a host of standard personal information and for you to execute a retainer agreement."

I nodded. Merrill Barrera had outlined what to expect, but I couldn't help myself when I asked, "How do things work in America if you can't write a check?"

What I took to be the lawyer's true face came out then. It was both pained and empathetic. She took her work more seriously than most. She'd never had made it as a surgeon, maybe even would burn out as a lawyer, if she didn't detach. Someone who cared, though, would probably be a good thing for me and my new little one. "Not easily. I've represented those parents without so much as a bank account. You don't want to be them."

After that sobering little revelation, she took me through a series of questions. The same I'd answered for Paola and Merrill when she'd done the home visit.

"Mrs. Barrera indicated that you may be receiving a child from abroad, is that right?"

"Yes, I told her I was very open to adoption from one of the countries affected by one-child-birth policies or war or famine. Somewhere children have been left without parents."

When she'd let me know that there were far more of these children available than those to be born in the US, I knew it was the right choice. Had to be better than posting my lonely single person photo on line with my proverbial hand up screaming "choose me!" I knew my pale narrow face would be no competition for the cherubic Americans with their perfect teeth and open smiles.

"That's very noble of you. There are very many children who need solid, permanent homes. I'm sure Hudson has made you aware of possible attachment issues and that you may need special support, right?"

I'd heard the whole spiel on how children aren't something you can return. I myself had seen those horrific stories of children who had to be returned because they couldn't form an attachment. The internet and Paul-induced insomnia had given me those. I knew that wouldn't happen to me, though. I was grateful to have the education and resources to solve any child-related problem. I'd scoped out the clinic and there wasn't anything wrong with the human body, outside of stage-four pancreatic cancer, that couldn't be fixed.

"You're a US Citizen, then?" Casey asked bringing me back to the present.

"No?" I could feel my face pulling together in a frown. Most people assumed the accent said otherwise. "I'm from the UK."

"Right. To be clear, I'm asking specifically about citizenship and immigration status as it pertains to your ability to adopt a child."

"I'm here on an H1B visa."

"So you're not a legal permanent resident? Green card holder?"

My mind scrabbled for purchase. Had I skipped over something really important? Something that would stop me from having a family? Paul and I had mused over the fact that if I had a baby here, they'd be a dual citizen. Might even have a weird American drawl when they spoke, but this, this I hadn't considered. Unlike a bunch of my colleagues, I was already a citizen of a first world country, I wasn't interested in adding citizenship to a second, especially one without universal health coverage.

"No. From what I understand, I can stay here as long as I'm working at the clinic."

"I'm not an expert in immigration, so I'll take your word on that. I'm asking because non-residents aren't generally permitted to adopt children."

"No one at the agency mentioned this. Are you sure of your facts?"

Casey hesitated for a long moment. "I only did some preliminary research," she admitted, "as I assumed that you were a citizen or green card holder. She mentioned you were British, but what your accent maybe has nothing to do with what your status may be."

While my mind was reeling as to what the solicitor was saying and how it would affect my chances at adoption, my pager buzzed against my waist. I couldn't gather my thoughts in time to press the button to read the tiny LED characters before my phone came to life, beeping a tune in the bag that I'd slung over the other chair in the room.

"May be a patient issue." I gestured to the dark-colored heavy phone on her desk. "Can I use it?"

She rolled away from the desk in her high-backed leather chair. "No need to press anything." Casey stood and walked around to my side of the huge desk. "You can dial normally. I'll step out. Give you privacy."

After the door clicked shut softly, I pressed in the unfamiliar number from the pager. "Doctor Fiona Rose."

"Merrill Barrera here. I have good news."

"Merrill, as a matter of fact I'm at Casey Cort's office. The solicitor, um, lawyer you recommended. She's saying that—"

"Fiona, listen to me," the voice said on the phone, its stern tone enough to make me stop my rambling and take notice. "Your baby is here."

"My what?" I was normally very in control of my world. A surgeon had to be that way. There wasn't much that I didn't understand, or that could throw me for a loop, but I'd been surprised twice in ten minutes and my brain couldn't keep up.

"Your baby is coming to Cleveland Hopkins." Merrill spoke slowly and clearly. There was no mistaking what she'd said the second time.

"How—"

"We're an adoption agency. We specialize in babies. There's a little girl landing in two hours. Can you be there to pick her up?"

"Of course." I borrowed the yellow pad the solicitor had been using and scribbled down the pertinent information about flight times and terminals. I put down the phone and tore off the sheet.

I stepped out into the reception area where Casey was chatting with another woman.

"There's a baby."

"What?" the women cried in unison.

"I know. It's fast. I have to be at," I looked at the paper, "Terminal C."

"I'll drive you," the lawyer announced, then suddenly looked as if she'd thought better of it. "It would be nice to be there, but I don't want to impose..."

Suddenly, I didn't want to face this alone. This yawning chasm of instant parenthood, something I'd all along planned to face with Paul by my side after nine long months of preparation, loomed large.

"Please do come. I'll drive, though, as I have a car seat."

"You bought one? Already?"

"It goes from baby to toddler. Merrill said it was better that you be prepared. I guess she was right. Why don't we drive there, then maybe you can help me to install it."

"Perfect," the lawyer said hugging herself a little. "I'm excited for you."

"And the citizenship stuff?"

"We can figure all that out later. Let's go get your baby."

Months or years later I hoped I'd remember more about this day, because by the time we arrived at Cleveland Hopkins, not only couldn't I remember driving there—scary because it was all on the wrong side of the road—but anything leading up to the trip either. As I pulled into the car park, my heart sped up more rapidly than it had been the twenty minutes prior. Any faster and I'd be a patient in my own hospital.

"Let's install the seat," I declared when I'd finally gotten my hands to stop shaking long enough to turn the car's engine off and jiggle the key from the ignition.

With that prompt, Casey was out of the car and standing by my boot. I popped it open and I could hear the sound of tape ripping from cardboard.

Two graduate degrees and miles of school between us and it took us an hour to get the car seat situated in the back.

"Thanks," I said slamming the back door with finality.

"When it's my turn, I'll definitely call one of those services that does this for you. I even think I'd heard they'll do it at the Shaker fire department."

"Totally agree with you." I laughed with relief. Relief at getting the seat in. Relief that my daughter was here, waiting for me to meet her. Relief that I wouldn't have to spend months or years waiting. Relief that my real life could begin now.

Casey surveyed the electronic board in the small and quiet airport. "Flight twenty-four thirty-five lands in twenty minutes. You ready?"

"According to my mum, no woman is ever ready." Whether that said something about my mum or if it was indeed true, I was about to find out.

The solicitor sat while I paced the passenger waiting area. After US nine eleven attacks, no one was allowed back at the gate like when I was a kid. I was forced to stand in a pre-screened area thick with waiting family members and hire car drivers dangling black names printed on stark white paper.

What seemed like hours later, but was probably all of fifteen minutes, a small stream of passengers appeared. Men in suits came through first, probably from the first-class section. Tired rumpled people came next. It was probably the last leg of a series of long flights for many. The flights I'd taken for the interview and when I finally arrived with Paul weren't so far in the past that I'd forgotten how long it took to get to a small city like Cleveland.

Families with children straggled through next.

Though it probably annoyed the hell out of the parents, I gave a long glance at every baby who came through. The way their mother's clutched them close, I knew none of these was mine.

Last, but not least an exhausted woman shuffled through the door. Asleep on her shoulder was a small girl, probably a year old at most. Her curly hair was barely contained under a white cotton knit cap. A feeling of rightness squeezed at my heart.

This was her.

This was my daughter.

"Fiona Rose?" The woman approached me.

"Yes. That's me." I reached out my arms and she put my baby into them. Like all the mothers I'd seen moments before, I clutched her close. She smelled like sugar, and honey, some kind of cream, and baby.

"This is my daughter," I said. I knew those four words were the truest I'd ever spoken.

"What's her name?" Casey asked. It was the most perfect question. I had the most perfect answer.

"Charlotte. Charlotte Rose."

12

"Took nine years."

"Nine years? What took that long?" I turned my back to Justin McPhee, flagging down one of the waiters. Most seemed as ancient as the old steakhouse that filled half the bottom of my building.

Every time I was here, and that was rare, it brought back the mobster movies that had been popular when I was in college. I'd have bet my meager savings that at least one hit had been ordered in this place.

"For you to buy me a drink."

My heart went into overdrive and the possibility that I'd slighted Justin. He'd offered me the keys to juvenile Court, which I'd grabbed up with two desperate hands, and all I'd sent back was a thank you card. I didn't have a chance to blurt out an excuse or apologize before the waiter I'd summoned lumbered over.

"What's your fancy?" the black-vested man asked me when he approached our table.

Beer didn't seem appropriate or adult. "A Sidecar," I answered.

Lulu and I had decided many moons ago that we needed drinks that wouldn't make us look unsophisticated when were out with other lawyers. We'd pulled her dad's college bartender guide from the bookcase in his den and tried out a bunch of mixers from his supply. I'd landed on a cognac drink and Lulu on a vodka-laced Cosmo. I pretty much thought I'd won in the sophistication department.

A lot of sugar mollified the alcohol that tended to burn through my stomach lining like it was on fire.

"And you, sir?"

"I'll have the stout on tap."

Beer. He'd had the balls to get beer and I hadn't. But I was a Sidecar girl, right? To have a signature drink meant that you had to actually order it and drink it. I openly stared at Justin while he chatted with the waiter about happy hour specials.

Lately I was comparing every man to Miles. Justin wasn't spared. He was okay looking, maybe even a little cute in that Cleveland west side sort of way. I knew, like me, he'd probably gone to Catholic school and potatoes had been a substantial part of his diet growing up.

His red wool vest did little to hide his growing middle. Miles would have ordered a craft beer, then sipped at it. He also played basketball and biked regularly, helping keep my boyfriend slim and trim. I hoped that the longer I spent with him, the more likely I'd be to take up biking and sports. With effort I was sure I could be one of those sporty girls the Ivy League seemed to spit out by the dozens. The kind of girl made for a man like Miles.

"You're working for Paola Hudson now?" McPhee posed when the waiter left to put in our order.

"It's why I wanted to have this drink," I said. "I'm happy to have the Hudson agency on board. I want to make the transition as smooth as possible, though." I'd been more than a little bit curious when I'd seen Justin's name on some open files. Why someone still eking out a living in juvenile court was pushing this cash cow off his plate made me wonder.

"Transition?" he said turning his full attention toward me. Little dimples I'd never noticed before hollowed out his cheeks when he talked. I had kind of a soft spot for dimples. Refocusing on the business between us, I pushed his face and any cuteness there from my mind.

"The transition from you as the attorney they refer parents to—to me," I painstakingly explained.

"Right." His monosyllabic answer did not give me a lot of clues. This was not the loquacious guy I'd met at a bar association luncheon who had single-handedly changed my career trajectory. I pressed a bit more.

"You did do work for Paola for the last six years, right? When the referral came in, I asked who they used before and they mentioned you. I was surprised that I knew you." Awkwardly, I patted his hand. I was trying for chummy this time. He pulled his arm back like I had the plague.

"It's a small pool of attorneys in Cleveland." Sounded like something I'd have said to mollify Miles. It seemed patronizing coming from someone else's mouth.

Drinks appeared on the table with a clatter. I took a sip of the sweet and bitter liquid. While wiping the circle of beaded water from the surface with my bare fingers, I searched my head. There was something going on here, but I couldn't put my finger on it. I wanted information though, so I pressed ahead.

"I'm handling my first adoption for a mom. She just got her new baby yesterday." I could hear the unusual spark of joy in my voice, but those five minutes had been the most amazing thing I'd ever witnessed. I could kind of tell Charlotte and Fiona were meant for each other. It was like watching two people fall in love at hyper speed.

"Super fast?"

"Totally. I'd assumed people waited years to adopt. Up until now, I've been doing the ones where the families have had kids in long-term custody but wanted permanence."

"These from cases in Juvie? Did you step up to help some of those guardians become permanent?"

"Yes and no. They're from juvenile court, but not my cases, exactly. I had been doing some pro bono at Dalton Lacey." I'm not sure where that twinge of guilt came from, but it wasn't warranted. Pro bono was pro bono.

"Fancy."

"Just a friend from law school. I'm sure you have some at Dalton."

"Ronaldo Pinheiro and I were in the same class at Case. There are a few more, but we were in the same section together first year so we got tight."

"It is a small world. He's coordinating the adoption pro bono program. He referred me for paying cases."

"Nice of him."

"Totally, right."

"What's up with the Valley girl speak, you're from the west side right?"

"Grew up on West Boulevard."

"I graduated from Saint Ignatius."

Of course he had. It's where smart Catholic boys went to school.

"St. Joseph for me." It was the female equivalent.

"Even more fancy." His tone said that fancy wasn't good.

"I was on scholarship. My very devoted Catholic parents thought this kind of education was super important. I'm grateful they were so focused." Admitting I was a scholarship kid was new for me. I used to be mortified, but was learning to accept that I wasn't anything like Miles and that was okay.

"Wait. Did you go to the Valentine's Day Dance…it was my senior year. Graduated in eighty-seven. I think I remember you there."

"The one in Rocky River where Joe Meniconi let a gaggle of geese in. I was a sophomore."

"I love that you knew when to use the word gaggle," Justin said, his tone softening.

"Flock of seagulls. Cauldron of bats. Murder of crows. Cackle of hyenas. Thunder of hippos. That's Saint Joe's for you. I'm pretty sure there was a quiz on that one."

Justin's laugh was full and throaty. "I love it. Are you first generation? My dad's Irish. My mom's Polish."

I didn't tell him the map of Poland was all over his face. Instead, I said, "My dad's Polish by way of Germany. He picked up my mom there and they both came here to Cleveland."

"Sounds like my dad. He picked up my mom in a dance hall. They'd deny it to the parish priest, but there was much drinking, dancing, and probably premarital sex back in the seventies."

"They all deny it." Not that I'd ever asked my parents or anything. God knew I'd never broach that subject to my dying day. But I'd run into some letters from my dad when I was spying in my mom's closet that mentioned a pregnancy scare, long before they were married or I was born.

Justin threw up his hands. "Hey, my sisters were virgins until their wedding day."

"I'm one too."

He dissolved into laughter. I held back the urge to join him. Catholic guilt and all that.

"Did you have nuns or lay teachers," he asked. On familiar ground, I relaxed.

"Mostly lay after elementary. I think they ran out of nuns. Women not taking the vows and all that. You?"

"Lots of Jesuit priests. I think there may have been stealth nuns in the place, though."

"Stealth?"

"Can I ask you a question. You met a lot of nuns, right?" I nodded bracing myself for the unexpected. "There was this one teacher who subbed in and out. She was like the permanent sub. I have some thoughts about her. Questions."

"Thoughts? Questions?" My mind ping-ponged between depravity and the Catholic church. It was not a good place for a mind to be. So much lay in that space.

"Most nuns gave up the habit and the wimple, right?"

Clarity dawned like the sun after a thunderstorm. I turned the tables.

"Wait, wait, let me ask you a few questions?"

"Direct examination, counselor?"

I nodded semi-seriously, trying to keep a smile at bay. "Did substitute teacher wear colors? You know other than gray, slate blue or black."

"No," he answered like a good witness should. No embellishments. No exposition.

"Was her hair always pinned back? Like ten bobby pins more than normal?"

Justin briefly closed his eyes in memory. "Maybe."

"Did she wear a big cross, not gold, but wood. Maybe with a crucified Jesus to boot?"

"Check."

"Beads on her wrist."

"People wear those for meditation."

"Your Honor, direct the witness to answer the question," I said to some imaginary arbiter. We both smiled then. Breaking from my role, I said, "Meditation beads? C'mon. This is Cleveland, not L.A."

"Oh my God. She was a stealth nun." Justin reared back. I could see a whole new understanding dawning for him. I'd had plenty of these women in my schools. Working in the office, in the school library, puttering around in service of God.

"I don't think she was under cover. You didn't read the signs."

He threw back his head in laughter and this time I joined him. It was crazy the Catholic thing. So many rules. So much that went unspoken. Miles didn't get it. He was a died-in-the-wool atheist and didn't understand how or why my parents were the way they were in light of the world turning away from the church.

"A pandemonium of parrots," I interjected. His laughter was so lighthearted and joyous, I wanted more of it.

We laughed so hard the rest of the patrons turned around. These were older men, some of them criminal defense attorneys I recognized, who probably hadn't looked up from their bourbons in twenty years.

It took me a full minute, but I managed to get my giggling under control.

"So you're really in the adoption game now." Justin observed.

Silently, I reassured myself I wasn't a sellout. That I had the right to make a living.

"I'm looking forward to working with Hudson," I said brightly. "I made a promise to myself after a few cases that went sideways that I'd change my practice. This is really a shift in a new direction."

"Does that mean you're leaving Juvy? Come to think of it, I haven't seen you around in a long time."

"I already left," I admitted. "Judge…" I stopped myself cold. I'd been about to give credit to the Brody family for getting me out of court, which was true. A thousand percent true. No matter how much I'd wanted it years ago, I never again wanted to be associated with my ex-fiancé's family. "It had to go, that part of my practice," I continued. "Two hundred fifty dollars maximum per case is no way to assure great legal representation for those parents and children."

"They need people like us, though, don't they? We're not the lawyers who catch as many cases as possible and churn the files for the fees without really helping the families. You were one of the ones who cared."

I found that I couldn't dine or righteousness or Catholic guilt.

"To be frank, it was going to bankrupt me, Justin. Maybe you have a different situation than me. Half the people I went to school with had families who were supporting them. Not mine. I have loans. A lot of loans. And obviously I like to eat," I said pointing to my newer thinner body which still, in a lot of ways, felt like my older fatter body. "Since I don't want to move back in with my parents, I need to do what I can to pay the bills. And Juvy wasn't cutting it."

"Not when you have cases like Grant." The way he said Grant suggested that maybe he thought I had something do with the judge's disappearance. I almost defended myself. Almost. But I was tired of that. Defending Grant. Defending my criminal practice. I'd never committed a crime. I'd done nothing, was doing nothing unethical. I pressed on.

"I want more cases like Grant. Which is why I'm excited about Hudson. It seems pretty straightforward. I walk the parents through the paperwork and probate court. Everyone comes out happy. Plus I get paid. Why did you stop doing it?" This was the thing I was most interested in. Communing over nuns and Polish parents was fine, but I could do that with countless people. I really wanted to know who gave up a cash cow for peanuts from Cuyahoga County. I half wondered if he'd found something even more lucrative in the family arena. I was more than willing to supplement what Hudson was going to bring in.

Justin drained his beer, signaled the waiter for another.

"You want a refill?" he asked.

"I'm good." I said waiting for what was to come. I clasped my hands on the smooth wood the same way I'd done through my first eight years in Catholic school. After a moment of quiet, Justin's wide hand landed on top of mine. It wasn't…unpleasant. It was actually kind of nice, this moment of communion. It was nice to spend time with someone who got me. Who'd lived a life so much like mine.

"You driving? I take the Rapid."

"So do I, but I'm good."

"Suit yourself." Justin was quiet for a long moment. He took his hand back, rubbed it through his hair. "To answer your questions, I think Paola and Merrill and I didn't see eye to eye."

"What's there to disagree about?" I was pretty sure that nearly everyone loved babies. It's what had kept our fighting, warring species alive.

"You'll find out they have a very streamlined process. You'll have to be on board with that."

"After the never-ending cases on Twenty-second Street, I think I'll really appreciate streamlined. People get their babies, we finalize who's the legal parent, I get paid. I can't see the downside." And I really couldn't. This had to be what was in the best interests of orphaned children.

Justin mumbled something under his breath.

"What?" I leaned forward. "I didn't catch that?"

"Nothing. I wanted more time with the cases. Maybe I'm too set in my ways. I think cases shouldn't be rushed."

"Between the Adoption and Safe Families Act which only gives parents of kids in foster care six months to get their shit together and Ohio adoptions which are generally finalized in six months, doesn't seem like there's a lot of time anymore. I used to hate it, that rush. Maybe it's not right in Juvy. Probably not. But for adoption. Seems more than right."

Justin looked as if he wanted to say more. Instead he downed his beer.

His shrug was nonchalant. "Maybe, maybe not. Are you still doing felonies? GAL stuff in Domestic Relations?"

"I'm not trolling for criminal anymore, so any assignments I get are the only cases I take. It's ninety percent pleas anyway. You know those post-decree custody cases can linger forever in Domestic. I might keep doing them. When they're not your bread and butter, they're not as stressful."

"You seeing anyone?" he asked in a one-hundred-eighty degree turn.

"You mean a guy?"

He nodded.

A little zing of awareness snuck through my veins. Was he thinking of asking me out? Mentally, I shook off the feeling. What in the hell was up with me these days? I kind of felt a pull toward every guy I was sitting down with. Reminded me of my hormonal teenage years when every male within a three-mile radius inspired sinful fantasies I used to own up to back when I went to confession. This time I charged it up to my alcohol-lowered inhibitions. I had no idea how to answer, though. I was either soon-to-be engaged—again—or still at friends with benefits. I opted to round up in my answer.

"Miles Siegel? He's an AUSA."

"Wow, you're dating the enemy. Wasn't that a movie?"

"I think Julia Roberts was Sleeping with the Enemy, but I'm pretty sure her husband wasn't a prosecutor, just your run-of-the-mill psychopath. You know we're all on the same side, Justin. We all want justice and judges who follow the rules. He's a good guy, Miles."

"A good prosecutor?" He snorted like that was the biggest oxymoron of all time. "There's not a soul in this bar who would agree with you."

This was the opposite of a cop and prosecutor bar. They drank way on the other side of town where the patrons were more sympathetic to their brand of justice. But Miles was not the same as all those others. Suddenly it was imperative for me to let Justin know that about my boyfriend. That even if I was a sellout on the legal front, I certainly hadn't sold out in my private life.

"He was a cop before that, so he knows how prosecutors operate."

"A cop turned prosecutor. Oh, this gets better and better." If I hadn't been dating Miles, I'd have agreed with him—one hundred percent. The cops and prosecutors I'd met while defending my clients hadn't endeared me. And definitely not my last cop client either. Miles was different.

"He's black, though, so he knows how it can go." I kind of wanted to cringe at the way that came out, but I soldiered on making my case for Miles. "He was there for me during the Troy Duncan case."

"You represented a cop there too. Which side are you playing?"

"The side of truth, justice, and the American way, Justin."

Suddenly exhausted, I lifted my purse from the chair next to me and slipped out my wallet. Justin waved my money away.

"Thanks for taking the time for a drink," I said. "I've gotta get going. Have to pull together that paperwork for that first adoption they referred." I was a little tipsy and a lot tired of being on the defensive. My guess was that Justin hadn't left Hudson, maybe Hudson had left him. Probably too self-righteous for the clients' taste. I scooted from the bench and stood.

"Those parents got the baby how quickly again?" he asked after tugging on the sleeve of my spring coat.

I slung my purse and bag over my shoulder. "A few weeks. She's a single mom. I realize now that if you're open to all ethnicities and backgrounds, it's much easier. Less of a wait. It's both amazing and sad at the same time."

"Amazing and sad. How you put that is perfect." His eyes went soft and sentimental. I chalked it up to the twenty-four ounces of beer running through his veins. "It was amazing and sad talking to you today, Casey. Have an amazing and sad day and life."

"You too, Justin. Maybe that should be your last beer."

He nodded gravely. "Stout is amazing in taste and sad in how it makes you feel."

"Okay, thanks for the drink. Have a good night." I left out anything about it being either amazing or sad.

13

"Uh oh."

My heart started pounding the second the words left Dinha's mouth. The blood rushing past my ears was so loud I didn't hear the rest of the words she was speaking.

"What is it?" I looked around frantically for Eligu. But he wasn't lost or hurt. He was on the floor looking for something disgusting to put in his mouth. He was as safe as he could be in a rat-infested house.

"A woman from the Home Office is here," Dinha announced.

"That's normal," I said more to myself than her. It was normal. Someone from the government was always stopping by to make sure we weren't working or had done something unauthorized.

Freedom came with a lot of rules.

Dinha didn't let me linger in my delusion longer than a few seconds. She shook her head emphatically. "No, it's not. This one, she's wearing nice clothes and she's carrying envelopes in her hand."

"What does that mean?" Dinha had been in this country longer than me. She knew the system, how things worked. I'd relied on her to tell me all the unwritten rules of which there were so many.

"They've decided someone's status. She's here to tell one of us in person." It was all women with us. No men in this house as cramped as my uncle's at home.

The breakfast porridge I'd eaten threatened to come right back up. On any given day I bounced between being sure I wouldn't be thrown out—forced to the Sudan—or being sure they'd put me in one of the jails here at Her Majesty's expense. I had no desire to go back to that detention center with its bedbugs and without laundry facilities. This place was no palace, but over the last months, especially with Dinha and Eligu, it had become home.

"How do you know?" I didn't test her often, but I did now. The fear of that truth she was speaking was shaking me to my core.

"Hasn't happened since you been here, but you see and hear things, you know?"

Dinha, a few of the other women milling around, and I watched the white woman, another one with colorless hair and eyes, as she poked at the doorbell. No one made an attempt to tell her the bell had never worked, not while any of us had been here at least. Finally, irritation causing her to blow at her flyaway hair, she knocked at the thick wood door.

Eligu picked up, dusted off, and tight at her waist, Dinha turned the locks and pulled the door open. Now that the weather had been more dry than wet for a bit, it didn't swell or stick like it had over the winter months. Despite the protesting squeak of the hinges, it opened easily.

"Hello," she said. Her tone was clipped and official. I feared Dinha had spoken the truth. When Dinha didn't say anything, the woman spoke again.

"Right. Hello. I'm here to speak to Dinha Be...Bekele. That right?"

"I'm Dinha," my friend said.

"Great. That's grand. Can you wait here? I'm also after Alile Useni."

I raised my left hand tentatively.

"Great. You're both here. Let me talk to you first, Dinha," she said. The two of them went outside on the steps while the woman talked and handed Dinha a sheaf of papers.

When she came back in Dinha's smile let me know that she was staying. I took a few gulps of air and waited for my own good news.

The woman poked her head back in. She pointed something at me, a pen probably, and gestured through the door. "You next. Do you speak English?"

"Yes."

"Come on out, then. I need to speak with you."

I stepped out the door and stood on the top step so I could look the woman in the eye.

"I'm Alile Useni," I said.

"Right. Yes. Well, I have bad news for you. Unfortunately the Home Office has decided that you're not eligible for indefinite leave to remain."

"What...why?" I swallowed once, then again, trying not to cry. This was my only plan. To stay, to make enough money to bring Yeni here. I'd planned to get a job because pounds here were worth millions of kwacha. I could have paid for someone to bring Yeni to me and paid my aunt twice what she was asking.

"Your documents can't be authenticated," she was saying while I watched my plans crumble to dust.

"There's a war," I supplied.

"I understand the complications."

"Complications? People are being slaughtered. It's practically a genocide," I insisted. That last word was foreign in my mouth, but I'd heard it on the telly here a dozen times. It usually made the guests on a chat show squirm in their seats and claim that the English had to do something for Africa.

"Again, we understand. There are refugee facilities in Uganda. Some have gone to Egypt."

I didn't want to go to any of those places. They weren't any better, and were probably worse than where I'd left. I'd figure something out. Even if it meant disappearing into some kind of shadow existence. But I didn't want to put this woman on notice. Instead I kept up the pretending, as I'd done for the last year. I hung my head and said, "When do I have to go?"

"Someone from the Home Office will be in contact to make arrangements."

"Thank you."

"Here's your official notice. Have a nice afternoon." The woman shoved a few papers in my direction. I took them and walked back through the door.

"Bad news?"

It took everything in me not to cry. Not to scream to the heavens that my life had been nothing but bad luck. There was an old adage about white men coming to Africa with the bible and taking all the land. I'd come to Europe with hopes and would leave with much less. There wasn't much out there for Africans. Europe had everything and they were keeping it for themselves.

I only nodded.

Dinha smiled. "I can stay. Section fifty-five or something like it. I can stay on account of my kid." She pinched his little tan cheeks. "Eligu. I love you."

"I have to go."

"Where? Are you going to run away. Try to find a place to stay in the UK? There are some that do it. I'd even say you could move in with me, but there's a man who says—"

I cut her off. "No. I can't live like that. It won't work for Yeni," I said all the while spinning out plans in my head to do just that.

"Yeni? Who's Yeni?"

"My daughter." There was no reason to lie or conceal the truth any longer.

"You have a baby? Where is she?" Dinha looked around the front room as if my little girl were going to appear.

"Africa." I heard the defeat in my voice, with the realization that I'd be lucky if I could ever get my girl out of there with no country to bring her to and no money. It was more than a year later and I was not any further than I'd been in Malawi.

"Why didn't you bring her?" I was grateful not to hear accusation in her voice.

"It was a long trip. I left her in a safe place. I have a little bit of time to go back and get her."

"How much time?"

I fell onto a broken down chair in the entranceway. My hands came up to cover my face as my head pulsed and my nose clogged. Tears were next. I felt the swish of air as the other women came to gape at me. Dinha must have done something because as quickly as their feet shuffled in, they shuffled out the way they'd come.

"A week, a year. I have no idea. My aunt threatened to take her to a local orphanage if I didn't pay. I tried to...gather...the money, but I couldn't earn enough, so I decided to come here. The life I could give her wasn't any kind of life. If I lived here, I could bring her, and she could grow up to be someone, anyone, not a servant, not a prostitute." I dropped my hands, realizing what I'd just said. "I'm sorry. I'm not saying you're bad. It's just..."

"Don't be sorry. Why do you think I do it? I don't want little Eligu here to do what I do for money."

"There are boys?"

"There are men who look for boys like they look for girls, if they look hard enough. That's the past, right? I can work now, for real, or go to school, and send him as well. Punters can go to hell. Do you think your aunt gave her away?"

"I don't know. I hope not. Letters to her and my father haven't been answered. I haven't gotten any mail here. I've been sending a few pounds every week. I've almost paid how much she asked."

"So you just have to figure out a way to stay here or go back and bring her here. Maybe try again with immigration or something?"

I could see that Dinha was happy, that she wanted to think there was some magic wand that could be waved to fix my problems like one had just fixed hers.

"Where? Where did you come from. I wondered about your claim to be Sudanese. You look like no one I've ever met from Sudan."

"Malawi." It was the first time I'd said it out loud in many, many months.

"What about all that talk about Sudan?" she asked in a whisper.

"I need to stay here. I need to get Yeni out of Malawi."

"What about your parents?"

"My mom is dead. My dad went to…he went to the city to look for work, then he stayed with a new wife and her kids. I stayed with my aunt and uncle."

"Where's the father? He a punter?"

"No, no. I wouldn't…sorry, I'm not—" I did, I had, but I wanted to forget all about those last months before I'd arrived in England.

"Don't be sorry. If we were allowed to work, don't you think I'd work in a shop or scrape gum off bus seats?"

"Of course. Sure."

"The dad?" Dinha asked again.

"My uncle."

"Oh—"

"He said it was my job to—"

"They always say that. Every girl I know has an uncle like that. The smart ones figure out how to outwit them."

I was unable to stop my face from falling in on itself once again. There were so many nights I'd found ways to avoid him until I couldn't. Maybe my father and brothers were right that I didn't deserve school. "I wasn't smart, I guess."

"No. I'm not saying this the right way. I mean the lucky ones get away. Not all of us are so lucky."

I tried to accept her apology, but she was saying exactly what I'd always known, what my uncle had said, it was my fault for smiling and not always keeping my clothes together after I washed. He couldn't keep himself from my temptation. I shook my head. I couldn't do anything to fix that part of my past. I could only do what was necessary to save Yeni's future.

"What time is it?" I asked Dinha.

"Three. Can you watch—"

· "No, I have to go. I have to figure out something." I turned from Dinha and little Eligu and ran upstairs. I'd pretended too long that they were like my family. It was time to figure out how to save my own.

One hour and twenty minutes and one very long walk later, I turned up at Raha.

"Is Emma Graham here?" I asked the woman at the front desk.

"She's got someone in. We're about to close."

"I have to speak with her." I leaned against the little reception counter hoping this woman could see how important it was. "I need to see her today."

"She'll finish up in about ten minutes or so."

I stood at the desk fiddling with the pamphlets until the woman cleared her throat and looked pointedly at the tattered chairs behind me. I took the hint and sat tucking my skirt modestly under my legs.

"Alile, right?" Emma said coming out, her hand extended. I hesitated a moment, then took it in mine.

"Yes. I wanted to talk to you about the babysitter thing."

"Perfect timing. I was just meeting with our partner at the au pair program. There are always families looking and not enough girls available. Those that speak English anyway. Right now there's a huge demand."

"I want to apply. I want to go." My voice had been too loud. She stepped back at my insistence. Normally I tried to be quiet and small for the English, but it was important that I get her attention.

"Wow. Okay. Come in to my office."

I sat in a small room. The grimy window looked out on a car park. For a country so wealthy, I hadn't seen much of it. Maybe the king and queen kept it all to themselves.

"Let me tell you about the process."

For twenty minutes she talked about applications and references and interviews over the computer. My hopes sank deeper than the deepest part of Lake Malawi. I didn't have references. I didn't even have a valid passport. I didn't know where I'd be next week. In war-torn Sudan or worse thrown into some other nation rife with tribal conflict. Of course I'd need papers. I'd just spent a year trying to get them. How did I think the rest of Europe would be any different.

Emma stopped speaking. I'm not sure if it was because she knew I wasn't listening or because she had come to the end of her speech. She pushed a thick stack of papers in my direction. I pushed them back toward her.

"I'm sorry. I made a mistake coming here. My asylum claim was not granted. I thought that perhaps I could find a place in another country, but I cannot complete any of this." I tapped the thick stack of paper. "I have no references, except other refugees without status. I can not apply. I...I..."

Emma stood so quickly, her chair rolled toward the wall and hit the window sill with a thud. "Come with me."

"What?" I asked. I was confused. Was she showing me the door this very moment. I lifted my bag from the floor and stood nearly as quickly as she had.

"I don't normally do this. Just come with me before I get in trouble," she pleaded.

Desperation made me follow her like a well-fed dog. We left through Raha's entrance and walked down a street filled with wood and stone buildings. Old ladies going about their day looked, but didn't look at the odd pairing we made. At a small door, wood framing glass, without any kind of sign, Emma knocked, then jiggled the knob. I walked behind her through what looked like a book and map store to a small area in the corner. An older woman stood at a large flat wood counter, a large map rolled to the very tip.

"Rita, this is Alile. She's interested in au pair work abroad."

The woman lifted glasses from her hair and put them on her nose. The glasses made her light eyes overlarge. "But you don't have all the necessary papers, yeah?" Rita got right to the point. I could tell there would be little beating around the bush with her.

"Unfortunately…" I started ready to launch into a list of suitable excuses.

"No need for explanation. I've already heard enough for a lifetime. I got one question: you ever care for kids?" Rita's face was no-nonsense. She didn't look like the type to be swayed by lies and half-truths, so I didn't bother.

"My daughter, Yeni, as well as my nieces and nephews." I didn't mention the care was involuntary or how old any of them had been. I'd practically been a child caring for children. It wasn't the kind of thing they understood here what with day care, schools for two- and-three-year-olds, nannies and au pairs.

"You have experience then. There's an agency we work with in Paris. Often there are parents who adopt African babies who are looking for help from a native that doesn't cost what a local would. Let me make a few calls. Would you be willing to go to France or Switzerland or Sweden? That's where the demand is nowadays."

I nodded vigorously. I'd had my heart set on brining up Yeni in the UK, but she was young, she could learn French or Swedish or whatever they spoke in Switzerland.

Apparently, there were blacks there as well. The world was so much bigger than my uncle's house and my mother's village.

"Yes," I said loud and clear.

"Come back tomorrow. About this time. I'll make some calls. Young pretty girl like you should have no problem getting placed informally."

She picked up a small camera from the desk, pointed it at me, and snapped photos. After that I followed Emma out the door. She went back to Raha and I started the long walk to the house that wouldn't be home for much longer.

June 29, 2006

I'd probably counted every minute in the twenty-four hours before I was back at the bookstore. Rita was sitting exactly where I'd left her among stacks of dusty books. If she weren't wearing a yellow shirt instead of white, I'd have thought she'd never gone home.

"Well, you're punctual," she said by way of greeting. "That'll be an asset in your placement."

"You found something? Where?" I took a deep breath to slow the speeding of my heart. Then I did all I could to hold back a sneeze from the dust I'd taken in. "I was thinking about Sweden last night," I said. "I hear its cold all year round. So different from Africa." When everyone had gone to sleep I watched a show about Scandinavia on the telly. Even though I'd had to prop my eyes open, I saw it through to the end assuming fate was on my side.

"Right. Sweden. I mentioned that, did I? Well, Europe isn't available right now. But there's a family in America that needs help."

"America. That's far." My heart sped up again. How many thousands of kilometers would that put between me and Yeni? If I couldn't afford to bring her to Europe, how would I afford America?

"It is far, but they have a greater need for girls. They don't have any kind of leave for mums there."

"Where in America? California? New York?" They were the only two places I'd really heard of.

She lifted a small white card from her dark wood table. "Ohio. Cleveland. It's a city in the middle of the country. Kind of like we are here in Wolverhampton. It's like Birmingham, I think."

"When would I go?"

"Saturday. You'd take a train to London. Fly to Detroit. It's where they make the cars and music. Then onward to Cleveland."

"Saturday?"

"Can you be ready by then?"

"How many children?"

"It's perfect for you actually. It's a little baby girl from Africa. The mum's a doctor. I think she's single, so probably not sleeping much just by herself. You'd work about forty hours.

"How much will it pay?"

"Oh, pay. Did Emma tell you? It's the same no matter the job. In America it's about two hundred dollars."

"A month?"

"No...no. A week.

"Also, you would have access to school and it's a city with public transport, so that should work. Is it a go? I have to give an answer to put the tickets in your name, or we'll have to call up another girl."

Two hundred...a week. I could save up enough to get to Yeni in a few weeks, and enough to bring her to the US in a month, maybe two. I was sure I could find someone in the village to fly to bring her to me. Not Daddy or Umi, but someone from the school. A teacher probably. They had the smarts to figure out how to bring my baby to me. I could pay them enough to give money to the right officials to get her the right papers. What had seemed so bleak just yesterday was now very bright. I'd all but stopped believing in God, but he was great. He had come through for me. My silent prayers had been answered.

"It's a yes. Definitely a yes." It was two days from today. I didn't exactly have much to pack. The clothes I'd brought, a few I'd bought, soap, and one new pair of shoes.

"Alrighty then. Be here at five Saturday morning for the early train."

The streets were supposed to be paved with gold in America. Surely I could figure out how to bring Yeni there before time ran out.

14

"She's sleeping," I said as I opened the door to let Merrill Barrera in. I glanced at the doorbell meaningfully trying to send my displeasure via telepathy. Once Merrill was gone, I'd tape a note over it threatening the next person who pressed it with certain death, except maybe the UPS lorry driver who made bulk deliveries of diapers.

I made a mental note to talk to him separately about leaving boxes at the back door. The doorbell back there hadn't worked since we'd moved in, so he could press that one to his heart's content without disturbing Charlotte, then leave the packages on the back step.

"How's it going? You've been a mother for one whole week!" Merrill nearly clapped with glee. Americans needed to dial it back a bit. Someone needed to tell them life wasn't a quiz show.

"Fine. Hold on." Without excusing myself I stalked to the kitchen and took the pad I used for shopping lists from the drawer. The top page was half filled with things I still needed but couldn't remember or didn't have the time to pick up. I tore it off, laid it to one side then made a note about the doorbell and UPS guy. Those I didn't want to forget. Even though Charlotte wasn't an infant, sleep for her seemed to be in short supply.

"Mommy brain?" Merrill was leaning against the doorframe, her face pulled into sympathy.

"What's that?" My brain felt fine, a little foggy, but fine, operational at least. I'd worked for hours on little or no rest off and on for years since I'd graduated medical school.

"It's what happens after sleep deprivation or maybe it's from having no one to talk to over the age of two. Whatever the cause, most women can't seem remember their names, much less full grocery lists."

"I'll get to the shopping later today," I promised. I did not want to in any way appear incompetent. There could be no reason for Merrill or anyone to think my daughter couldn't stay with me. "Charlotte hasn't much liked the car," I offered in explanation. "I'm not sure if the seat is uncomfortable or if it was the sun beaming in through the back window when we drove to Heinen's the other day." I could feel my face crumple as I nearly gave in to an overwhelming urge to cry. "How can I be so bad at this?" I wailed. "I'm a doctor. I've sewn people back together after hours on my feet. The care of one small human being shouldn't be this hard."

Merrill put a firm arm around my shoulders and guided me to one of the two charity shop iron stools that stood on either side of the glass-topped table where Paul and I had shared morning tea dozens of times. The memory of Paul and the realization that I was alone came crashing down upon me all at once. I laid my head on the table and cried. I wanted to be strong, stiff upper lip and all that, but caring for Charlotte all alone had brought home the fact that I wasn't superwoman.

"Fiona," she said, her voice at once both gentle and sharp. It was the kind of voice I'd always expected from my mother. I'd only gotten the sharp.

"I don't know if I can do this." I whispered the truth I'd bottled up over the last couple of nights.

"Of course you can," she pronounced. "Charlotte's sleeping now?"

I glanced at the clock on the wall. "Another forty-five minutes probably."

"Great." Her voice was all brisk efficiency now. She laid her palms on the table. "First, you need help."

"Paul was supposed to—"

"By all accounts Paul is long gone. It happens, Fiona. Men leave during pregnancy. They leave on day one. They leave on day one thousand and one. Women handle it. You're not the first single mother in the world. It's a little harder for you because you're in an unfamiliar city without lots of family and friends around, but that will change in time. Right now, we need to find a solution to the immediate problem. Can we agree on that?"

"Yes." My sniffle was loud. "Okay."

"You're going to hire a nanny."

"A nanny. I don't want Charlotte to be one of those posh wankers who isn't raised by her parents."

"I didn't say hand the child over and run away to the Caymans. I'm talking help. Another pair of hands to throw baby clothes in the laundry. To change a diaper. To sing her a song while you cook yourself dinner."

"Maybe a babysitter would work. I can book someone a couple of days a week if I put an advert—"

"Part-time help is not really a thing, Fiona. A mother's helper is not for you. Once you go back to work, you're going to need someone full time anyway. How about an au pair?"

"One of those young girls from Europe?" I flipped through my memories of British colleagues talking about hiring girls from Germany or central Europe to help out.

"Yes. You'd have to give her a room in your house and she'd have to enroll in school, but the cost is far cheaper than floating a kid through a traditional four-year school, and since they're usually young, they don't tend to step into the mother role."

I looked at the clock. Forty-five minutes had turned to thirty-five while we were talking. "How would I go about finding someone? It's hard to get anything going when she's awake."

"Hudson will handle it. We have some connections with agencies here and abroad. Let me take that one off your hands."

I'd not let many people take much off my hands. And with Paul I'd had to be in charge of paperwork if I wanted assurance that things were done right and on time. But Merrill hadn't disappointed me yet. She was a full-fledged adult who got things done. There had to be a special place in heaven for women like her.

I nodded willing to accept help I so desperately needed. "If that's not too much trouble."

"No trouble at all. My official title is social worker. It's in our job description to provide you the resources to make your life easier. Period. I'm not one hundred percent sure of the current numbers, but au pairs are paid about eight hundred fifty dollars a month plus expenses. Is that something you can handle?"

"Of course. That's legal, that low pay? What are the other expenses?"

"The upfront cost is about ten thousand. That's the agency cost, airfare, and administration which means you don't have to do any visa or immigration applications. You're to provide room and board which should really cost you nothing extra. You have the huge attic room and bathroom already furnished."

I'd bought a bed and laid out towels with the hope that my mother would visit, but like she'd always been, she was too busy managing the life of all of her siblings to help me with mine. Except for a visit from one of Paul's friends, the room had remained empty.

"Use of a car or a transit pass," she was saying. "I think that's about thirty a month for RTA and the last expense would be for any educational programs. We usually recommend you help them enroll in community college. There are a couple of Tri-C campuses on the east side which don't cost much. That's about it. You're free to pay more, of course. But you should see if you like her first before committing to that."

"How long would it take to find someone." I was warming to the idea of a full night's sleep or a nap or a bath or even the chance to buy groceries without a ticking time bomb of baby need hovering.

"Like adopting babies, it's unpredictable, but I'd let you know in a few days what the status—"

Merrill's last words were interrupted by babbling that was quickly ratcheting up to alarm coming through the baby monitor I'd clipped to my waistband.

"I've got to—"

"I'll be in the living room."

I ran upstairs only noticing when I got to the top that I had to pee like a bloke after too many down at the pub. But so did Charlotte probably. Slowing down to keep my bladder from explosion, I walked into the baby's room.

There she was, my little one. She was standing in the crib. As soon as she saw me, she raised her arms high. Everything else in the world gave way to this one little moment where my daughter wanted only me. I studied her thin cheeks, inquisitive brown eyes, the little curls that covered her entire head. She bounced on her pudgy little feet not the least bit patient with my parental scrutiny.

I gave in and gathered her up in one quick move and went over to the changing table. From how swollen it looked, I knew her diaper was full. I ripped open the tape and tossed the princess-covered plastic into the designated bin.

I plucked a few wipes from the warmer and cleaned her up. Then I got a new nappy from below and taped it closed. I marveled at my own efficiency. Just a few days before, this whole process had taken nearly twenty minutes and Charlotte and I were both nearly in tears toward the end.

I picked a short-sleeved onesie and matching pull-on pants from the drawer. Even with the infernal snaps, I was able to get it on in a few minutes.

As she promised, Merrill was down in the lounge casually flipping through a folder that had my name in big block letters on the front.

"Is this Charlotte?" she cooed, her voice pitched higher than a kite. I handed over my daughter as Merrill's hands were outstretched like she were going to take off in flight and I didn't think she'd take no for an answer. "You're so darling," she said turning the full force of her attention on the baby. "I love this sparkly pink dinosaur on your shirt. Do you love dinosaurs?"

Of course Charlotte didn't answer. She just stared her big-eyed stare at the woman.

"Can you hold her while I get a bottle ready?" I asked unnecessarily.

"Absolutely. I'll keep you company, right, Charlotte. We can talk all about your big airplane trip and your new and improved life in America."

I left Charlotte in her hands. After I disappeared into the WC to relieve myself, I went on through to the kitchen. Carefully I measured out formula and added it to a plastic shaker. I poured in distilled water from a jug on the counter. I shook it, then poured the mixture into a sippy cup, careful to screw the top down tight. I'd already made the mistake of not checking that. Had to wash two blankets and the chubby couch pillow in super hot water to get out the awful smell of soured milk.

"Here you go," I said coming back into the lounge. Charlotte let go of Merrill's black pearl necklace and held out her hands for the cup I handed to her. She turned it up and drank like a starving person. I tried to block the images that rushed to my mind of those distressed Romanian orphans who were on every channel when I was a kid as one NGO or another asked for money to ease their plight. It broke my heart to think that Charlotte could have been lonely, abandoned, rattling the side of a metal cot like jail bars.

"Do you have any more information on her birth date?" I asked Merrill as Charlotte sucked and swallowed.

"I did put in an inquiry to the orphanage. But it's not like calling down the street to contact people in these countries in Africa."

"She's thin, but the pediatrician puts her age at closer to a year and a half and not the year on the paperwork. She's the height of an eighteen month old, but the weight of a twelve month old."

"What about the other milestones?" Merrill's face screwed up in concern.

"She's behind on some. Her walking is still wobbly, but she's improving quickly. The doctor says taking her to some 'mommy and me' groups would help as kids copy each other."

"That's true. I'll ask about the age like I told you, but I don't know if you'll ever have a precise answer. A few months won't make a huge difference in school. In America the policy favors holding kids back from school anyway."

"And she's from Zimbabwe, right? Do you know her first language by any chance?" I asked. I only spoke English, but wish I could speak a few words of her native tribal language. At least for milk and food and sleep and nappy. Those things that I spoke of daily that seemed to dumfound her.

"That's our best guess. Information from these orphanages isn't perfect. Sometimes the babies are from neighboring countries. Famine, war, and migration make it hard to pinpoint. The AIDS crisis doesn't help either. So many babies are orphaned." She shook her head then bowed it in mournful prayer.

"Her initial HIV tests came back clear," I offered, my focus on the good news I'd had from her last doctor visit. "We'll have to check in three months and in six months, though."

"You being a doctor will make this transition so much easier."

"I hope so. I really do."

Unlike Paul, I wasn't one who didn't face the hard things. The meeting with Casey Cort had been as much the source of sleepless nights as Charlotte's cries. I hadn't had a moment to do any research on my own, but the idea that there was a chance this could all fall through, that Charlotte could be ripped from me was making what should have been a joyous time a bit hellish.

"Can I ask you about the citizenship adoption issue? That solicitor, Casey Cort, mentioned that this could be a huge problem. I had no idea that noncitizens couldn't adopt in this country. I don't want to lose her. I guess I could take her back to the UK if that's what's necessary, but I don't have a job, or anywhere to live in London right now."

"Casey's new to working with our agency, so you'll have to excuse her. Hudson has contacts in the state department to smooth over these kinds of…procedural…bumps. There are exceptions for everything in the US. Don't worry. Charlotte is yours. Such a beautiful name, by the way."

Just hearing her say those words was a huge relief. I'd tried not to panic, but Casey's words had set me on edge. I hadn't exactly had time to dwell on it what with Charlotte arriving a couple of weeks ago and my mad dash to get everything I needed, clothes, toys, a bath insert, and so on. Next on my agenda was to get a pram and maybe one of those cloth carriers that other mums used to tote their babies.

"Thank you. It was my grandmother's name. I loved her dearly. She passed recently in Belfast." She'd been my rock when my mother couldn't be.

"I'm so sorry to hear that." Merrill's face was sympathy again. I wondered if she'd taken one of those empathetic-listener classes as she always had the right face at the right time. I closed my eyes for a moment to rid it of the uncharitable thoughts. Mommy brain had made me a bit judgmental at a time when I was hardly in a position to judge.

"I'd have loved for her to have met my Charlotte," I said, my thoughts ping-ponging between legal matters and Merrill's faces and my grandmother's love. This confusion in my head was nothing a good night's sleep wouldn't cure.

"She will be your new family," Merrill soothed grasping my cold hand in her warm one.

"And it didn't even take nine months…" I whispered more grateful than ever that Charlotte had come into my life before I could talk myself out of motherhood without Paul.

"Waiting to become a parent is not all it's cracked up to be."

15

"Can I float something by you?" I asked as Miles took the dishes from my dining room to the kitchen. I stood from the table ready to carry the water glasses. The goblets would have to wait. I was saving the wine for later when I would really need it.

Towel thrown over his shoulder, he came back in empty-handed ready to get the rest. "Isn't that how we ended up back together? You coming to me for legal advice." Miles came around the table and hugged me from behind. Below my waist, I could feel that his mind wasn't on the intricacies of federal law.

"I'm one hundred percent serious," I said feeling uncomfortable in his grasp. We'd spent most of dinner talking about his job. Whenever I brought up mine, he'd changed the subject back to his boss, Chas Fitzgerald, or his least favorite colleague Rebecca Shaefer. But I really needed a sounding board and unfortunately after that last awkward and sad meeting, Justin McPhee was out as was Lulu.

"So am I." He did a little wiggle with his hips which emphasized his new agenda.

I took a deep enough breath that he released me from his arms.

"I'm serious and Lulu is coming over in a few." So we can't just disappear to the bedroom was the unspoken part of that sentence.

He stepped back shaking out his limbs like he'd just run five miles. "What's up?"

"It's an adoption case," I said hedging around the issue of confidentiality. "Hypothetically." If we were married it would be easier to talk about things like this. Spousal privilege had to trump attorney-client privilege any day.

"How many federal issues could there be in your garden-variety adoption?" I thought I heard condescension in his question, but shook it off as me being too sensitive. I soldiered on.

"With the popularity of international adoptions, you'd be surprised. The babies have to get visas before they can come in the country." A fact that had both shocked me and didn't at the same time.

"Seems simple enough," he said like babies and bureaucracy were a natural fit.

"I wish it were that easy. Here's my dilemma. I have a mom here on an H1B visa, so she's obviously a highly trained professional. She wants to adopt a baby from abroad, but there's no provision in the law I can find for it."

"Really, no provision? Did you look at all the relevant statutes? I thought everybody wanted to save babies?

'Family first' and 'family values' and 'middle-class families' have to be the three most used phrases by politicians."

"I did the research," I defended. Just because I wasn't Ivy League or big firm didn't mean I couldn't read a statute. "What I found was that noncitizens can adopt babies from the US. And US citizens can adopt babies from abroad. But not that third option of noncitizen visa holders and noncitizen babies."

He shrugged and went back to clearing the table of regular-size forks and the salad forks he'd insisted I buy. "So tell your clients, they can't have what they want."

"It's a single mom and she already has the baby," I said. Saying "no" would have been much easier months ago. Now that she'd fallen in love with little Charlotte, how could any of us go back?

"How did she get a baby without a visa. Did she smuggle her through customs in a carry-on?" He was paying attention now. Miles had a kind of spidey sense about people breaking federal laws. A shiver of regret passed through me and launched a worry that he'd seize upon this as the next wrong he had to right. The next case he and his FBI sidekick, that buzz-cut guy Valdespino, could use as a career maker.

"The little girl wasn't in anybody's luggage." I shrugged hoping he'd forget about what I'd just revealed. "The agency handled it. A nurse or something brought her here. We all met at the airport."

His brown-eyed laser focus didn't let up. That next question came to me like he was at the podium and I were on the stand in federal court. "What was the entry point?"

"Chicago, I'm pretty sure."

He nodded like he was flipping through a mental rolodex of customs and clearance procedures. I didn't point out that I'd never been outside the country. Tom and I had planned that bar trip that never came to fruition and after that I hadn't had the time nor money to do a bunch of international travel. Miles, on the other hand, had been to probably two dozen countries.

"So what's your plan to finalize the adoption? You'll take your chances going to court? Will the judge toss the case? Take the baby? Deport the baby? The mom?" He'd listed all the nightmarish scenarios that I'd mulled over instead of sleeping for the past couple of nights.

I couldn't see much of a way that the whole thing didn't end up another legal disaster with my name attached. It's why I was grasping at straws with him. I hoped he'd wade in with some obscure technicality I hadn't thought of. Wasn't looking like he was coming through, though.

"They'll probably make them both leave," I said. Fiona would lose her high-power surgeon job. Maybe England would take the baby if she went back home. Maybe there was some third-EU country where it could all work. All that was well beyond my research abilities and the scope of the matter I'd been hired to work on.

"Are they going to send her to central America or something?"

"No, Europe."

"So the worst-case scenario is that your client has to go back to Europe? If she's not some kind of political pariah, seems like she's made her choice by keeping the baby."

"She hasn't made any choices yet except adopt a baby. She filled out an application, did some home visits, and a baby from Africa was placed with her. Until I said something, she was none the wiser. The mom says the agency can get some special kind of dispensation."

"Loophole?"

"I guess. What I wanted to ask you was whether there was some kind of obscure law I might have missed?"

He shrugged again as if I was worried about nothing. "So they probably have some in with a congressman who inserted some kind of line of text in a bill giving them rights no one else has. Wouldn't be the first time that's happened."

"How would I go about finding that?"

"Ask the agency?"

"They're not my client," I said. The truth was that I didn't want to look completely incompetent. It was the same reason I hadn't called anyone at Dalton Lacey with the question. People were hesitant to give you more work when you were stumped by what they'd already given you. And turning down paying work wasn't something I wanted to do. I'd already spent the Charlotte Rose money a dozen times in my mind. New car, new clothes, or more new furniture were choices I'd cycled through a dozen times.

"Didn't you get the referral from them?"

"I think it would be a big conflict of interest to go to them."

"Maybe they'd appreciate a brush-up on the law."

"Dalton Lacey's their corporate counsel. They do not need any pointers from me."

"And Lulu is your best friend."

"So I need a fix for all of this."

"Maybe you can't fix it."

"That's what people hire lawyers for: to fix their problems, not create them."

"Maybe you should talk to Lulu."

"Talk to me about what?"

For the thousandth time I kicked myself for not remembering to lock my damned front door. One day it was going to get me in trouble. Bigger trouble than my best friend walking in on me talking about her. At least I hadn't been slagging on Richard Sinclair.

"You didn't buzz."

"Greg and Jason were heading out. I said hi and they held the door for me."

"Glad you could stop by," I said. Lulu didn't look so glad to be here.

"What did you have to tell me that was so important I'm skipping drinks with a senior partner."

"I didn't tell you to skip drinks. It's not like I have a day to live. We could have talked tomorrow." And right now tomorrow was looking like it would have kicked the can down the road a good bit. I wasn't relishing what I had to share with her.

"Well, you made it sound like you were on the verge of death."

It wasn't me on the verge of death, but her relationship with Professor Sinclair. I'd made a date to shatter her illusions.

"Do you want some wine?" Miles asked coming into my living room with a wine bottle, corkscrew, and three glasses between his fingers. I'd told him about Lulu and Sinclair and now Dr. Bloom. He'd been the one to advise the application of copious amounts of wine.

"I have to work in the morning," Lulu said. She waved away the glass.

"Take the wine." I grabbed the bottle from Miles as he set down three glasses on my steamer trunk. All of a sudden, I could see it then, that I was way too old to be living like I was a student. I promised myself a trip to the mall. There was nothing I could do about it now. Carefully I removed the foil and cork. I poured Lulu a generous amount, way more than any restaurant would serve.

She peeled off her age-appropriate belted gray wool coat, draping it over the back of my futon. I shook my head. That would have to go next. Adult furniture was best for a woman my age. Fiona Rose aside, this new Hudson relationship could prove to yield great money and further referrals.

This case alone would give me what I needed for a couch. Watching Lulu brush the cat hair from her skirt, I moved couch acquisition to the top of my list and pushed the car down a few more notches. The decade-old Honda wasn't pretty with its dings, dents, and scratches, but the engine still ran strong.

"Hey, Simba," I said when the cat slunk his way into the room.

"How old is he again?" she asked like always. Lulu wasn't an animal fan. Part of me suspected she asked the question while ticking off the years to his demise in her head.

"Eight." In my own head, pampered housecat that he was, he had another dozen, at least.

Perfunctorily, she rubbed her fingers through the cat's fur a couple of times before shooing him away.

"So?" Her eyebrows shot up over the tops of her round tortoise shells. The glasses were cute, stylish even, just not her.

"There's no easy way for me to say this."

Miles poured wine for both of us women. I took a healthy gulp before I laid into my story.

"I have this new adoption client." I was easing into what I didn't want to say.

"From Hudson?" Lulu nodded, smiling to herself. I knew she was proud to have added to my bottom line without having to write a check herself.

"Yeah. My first referral."

"Please don't tell me you're in trouble on this case already. That you've uncovered some crazy baby-brokering conspiracy. That would so be you."

I laughed uncomfortably, then took another large gulp. From the corner of my eye, I could see Miles' eyebrows shoot up and nearly meet his hairline. Until I got to the bottom of the noncitizen visa issue, I wasn't going to touch that comment with a ten-foot pole.

"Anyway, I bought a gift certificate from Babies 'R' Us to take to the happy mom."

Kidnapping, baby brokering, and conspiracies carefully pushed aside, Lulu visibly relaxed. I kind of felt like I was leading her on.

"Totally makes you smile, right. So much of what we all do is so cynical, but helping someone complete their family. How great is that?"

"So great," I agreed. Except for it being a work night, my best friend in a pencil skirt, and Miles standing at the ready with a full bottle of wine, it was going like any normal night together. At least that's what I told myself to assuage the guilt of what I was about to say. "Anyway, I'm standing in her living room giving her the card and getting her to sign some paperwork when one of her colleagues came over."

"That's nice. What did she get for your client?"

"Some great two-year-old toys. Not, old. I mean age appropriate."

"I knew what you meant, Casey." She smiled over the rim of her wineglass toward me like she was indulging someone for whom English was their second language.

"They were all super bright objects. Stuff I think the baby will appreciate in a few months."

"Not a newborn adoption?"

"Nope. My client was totally open to all races and ages."

"Cool."

"So my client's visitor introduces herself. Doctor Deborah Bloom."

A wrinkle furrowed my best friend's brow. "Why does that name sound familiar?"

"So this Doctor Bloom shakes my hand and mentions that her husband used to be a full-time law professor and was now adjunct at Cleveland Marshall. He gave up full time because he's doing death penalty work at Dalton Lacey as a partner in their pro bono practice."

I know Miles and Lulu were used to treating me as their dumb friend who they gave advice to and patted on the head. For once it wasn't me working through some startling revelation. Instead I watched all the emotions flit across Lulu's face as she put two and two together. It added up to five, or more like one and one and one was three. "Oh, God, you're not saying…"

"I am absolutely saying that her husband is none other than Richard Sinclair."

"Was she in a wheelchair?"

"No. She was absolutely one hundred percent ambulatory. As a matter of fact I asked her just that stupid question. I think my exact words were, 'are you okay, I'd heard you were sick, terminal?' After that I further embarrassed myself asking whether she'd been the recipient of some miracle medicine. Talk about undermining any credibility I may have had with my client."

"Are you sure she said Sinclair was her husband?"

"How many people do you think have husbands who taught Criminal Law and Procedure, work at Dalton Lacey, and have daughters at Vanderbilt?"

"You're just jumping to conclusions," she said. With logic like that, I wanted to point out, she'd have failed the law school admissions test. Which, she hadn't of course.

"A rational, reasonable conclusion. There are fewer than half a million people in this city, Lulu. We'd be hard-pressed to drum up another Richard Sinclair with exactly the same bio."

"You don't like Richard and are poking around for any evidence that he isn't right for me." My friend may as well have stuck her index fingers in her ears and said, "la, la, la, I can't hear you," like your average seven-year-old. I bet Deborah Bloom could pull out the perfect gift for that age of child as well. She seemed like that kind of woman.

"Poking? I'm not poking anyone or anything. She said she was his wife. Her only aches and pains come from her standing any number of hours and performing life-saving surgery on her patients. I mean she even sounded proud of him."

"Did you tell her about me?"

"I haven't lost my mind. I wanted to come to you first. Let you know that he's a lying, cheating ass. That he's a coward who hasn't changed one damned bit from the guy who stood on the sidelines while I got railroaded."

"Maybe I misunderstood her being sick."

"Yeah, it's every day someone confuses terminally ill and still married for insurance purposes with head of orthopedic surgery at Cleveland Clinic. That's an easy one to mistake." My voice was dripping with as much sarcasm as I could stuff in.

Lulu's gaze was riveted to the bottom of her wineglass which she got to after she drained the contents.

"Either way," I said, "he's married. You may be unconventional in a lot of ways, but I never thought you were the kind of person who'd break up a marriage."

"Of course not."

"Then you know what you have to do." I may flounder at my own moral quandaries, but I for sure knew that home wrecker wasn't something Lulu should ever do.

"I'll talk to him," she said with conviction. "I'm sure there's a rational, reasonable explanation for all that."

"Explanation?"

"Maybe he was embarrassed because she wanted the separation. There are a hundred reasons he may have wanted to hide the truth."

"Like say, getting into your pants, for one."

"Don't be crude." Lulu plunked her glass on the table, then rose. I was silent for only a moment while she gathered her coat.

"Are you leaving?"

"You delivered your message. It was received. I have work tomorrow."

"Don't you want to talk about it?"

"Do I want you to talk me out of the best relationship of my life. Nope. I'll get through work tomorrow, then I'll get to the bottom of this. No sooner." With Miles' help, she eased her arms into her coat. "Don't you dare talk to Richard about any of this."

"Except for that drink a few Sundays ago, I most certainly haven't talked to Richard and I'm not looking to. That is your monkey and your circus. I didn't think I'd be doing my job as your best friend if I didn't tell you about Bloom. That's all."

Lulu jammed a cloche hat on her head. It wasn't fire-engine red, but it was still a pretty cool mustard yellow.

That hat said not all of my best friend's personality had been stomped out.

Usually effusive, she let herself into the hall without so much as a hug, a kiss, or a backward glance.

Miles leaned forward in my papasan chair, the rattan creaking under his weight. "That went well."

"Do you have a better way I could have told her? 'Cause I can't figure out how that could have gone any worse. I've read the magazines. The women always think the man is going to leave. He's almost always lying. Eventually someone...or everyone gets hurt."

He lifted a single shoulder in a shrug that said to me, everyone was an adult here.

"Did you say where that baby was from?"

"No, I didn't say. It's in Africa. I'll have to have a close look at the documentation. I'll make a swing by Hudson for that next week."

"Africa?"

"Yes, as in that big continent south of Europe."

"Is it a transracial adoption?"

"Sure. The baby is black and the mom is white."

"How do you feel about that?"

"Why do I feel like this is a trick question?"

"It's not. I wanted your opinion."

"There was a baby who was probably abandoned in some orphanage. I hear that between AIDS and all the wars there, children are often the casualties. This woman, now mom, I guess wanted a baby. She was willing to open her home and heart to anyone, so it seems like a match made in heaven."

I kind of wanted to ask if I'd answered correctly, struck a balance between what was true and what was politically correct, but I didn't say a thing.

"Lulu was right. It's a work night. Let's turn in early," Miles said, his tone suggestive. I walked down the hall, not altogether sure if I'd passed the test.

16

"Are you tired?" the woman who'd introduced herself as Mrs. Barrera asked.

"Yes." It was a simple answer that didn't begin to touch upon my emotions. I was tired, yes. In the UK, it was well into the middle of the night. Whatever Dinha had gotten up to, she was most likely home, tucked into bed with Eligu. My own bed there was probably already taken by someone new. I'd never seen one vacant for more than a few days.

Despite all the mess and overcrowding, I missed Wolver-hampton. I'd even started getting used to the milky bitter tea and odd-tasting foods there. I'd have to do it all over again here.

"How was your flight?"

I looked out on the road. We were on the right side again. I wondered why some countries drove on one side, some on the other. I was glad that at least in this way America was a little bit like home.

I could feel the woman's eyes on me. She wanted a bit of a chat. These social workers were the same the world over. I tucked away my sigh and made to please her. "Long. But it was okay."

"The traffic isn't too bad for a Saturday night. We should be at the house in half an hour or so. I'm not sure how much information you got before the flight."

"Please tell me about the family." I didn't know anything more than the baby was African. I was coming into this situation completely blind. That didn't bother me exactly, I'd been moving from place to place for more than a year. It took a lot to shake me nowadays.

"It's not a family, so much as a single mom. She adopted a baby from Africa. You're from there, right? Was it Sudan?"

I didn't lie so much as nod.

"Right. Mozambique...no, that wasn't it. Something with a 'Z' Zimbabwe. That was it. The girl, the baby is a girl, is about a year old. She's a little bit delayed, having been in an orphanage for much of her life, but Fiona, that's the mom, is pretty sure Charlotte, that's the name she picked, isn't it beautiful? She's sure Charlotte will catch up quickly.

"And the mom has had the best advice. She's a doctor. Did I mention that? She's not a pediatrician or anything. She's a surgeon. But she works at the clinic and has access to the best doctors in the world. She took Charlotte to a pediatric developmental specialist who's pretty sure the girl will hit the right targets pretty soon."

"Targets?" It was the only thing I could think to question that wouldn't make me sound too dumb. I'd not understood much of what she'd said though it had been in English.

"Maybe you don't use those words where you're from. Milestones may be better. I'm sure you know that babies say their first word by a certain age, walk by another, can pick up small objects with their hands by yet another. She's mostly behind on walking, talking, and some other motor skill development."

I tried to not let myself worry that Yeni was falling behind in the same way. I could only pray that Umi didn't take out her hatred of me on Yeni. That my aunt was treating my little one like she was one of her own children. That Umi and the girls would cuddle her and hug her and read to her at night.

None of that mattered, though. Even if she was behind, I'd figure out how to teach her what she didn't know like my mom had done when my dad and brothers were away.

These same doctors that this mum had seen could see me too. That's how it was supposed to work in these countries. The rich and poor had access to the same services.

We swerved across a couple of lanes and exited the highway onto a wide street. Even though it was nearly seven in the evening, it was light outside. America looked big and empty. I looked out the window and there were a few buildings, but lots of unoccupied space. Nothing like England, its buildings jammed together cheek to jowl.

"This your first trip to the United States?"

"Yes. America seems big."

"Africa is bigger."

"Yes, but many different countries and many different cities."

"Cleveland is a city on the smaller side. It once had millions of people. But now, maybe, half million or so."

The road changed from something that looked like an abandoned industrial area to lots of houses very far apart, lots of grass and trees in between. There were so many electric lines everywhere. They must have had them in England. They must have been underground or something. Here everything was a wire. The lights swung gently on the wires they were attached to. And every light worked.

"Despite the size, I don't want you to think we aren't a world-class city. We have top-of-the-line medical care, museums, the Rock and Roll Hall of Fame, live music and plays. And you'll be able to attend college."

My heart sped up at the mention of school. Part of me had assumed that was only a pipe dream, something Emma and Rita had mentioned to get girls like me here, but that would be abandoned in the face of full-time child care.

"School?"

"I'm not sure if you're in time for summer session. We'll look into that and get back to you. If so, you can take one class during the summer, and maybe enroll in at least two in the fall. Usually one of them is English. You seem to get my English just fine, don't you, hon?"

"Yes, it's not my native language, but we learnt it in school from the beginning."

"Well then. That's great. You'll have no problem communicating with your mom."

The car slowed and pulled to a stop in front of a white house, it's wood boards straight across and its paint fresh. The grass was green and the shrubs trimmed. I couldn't believe I'd be living here. If I could send a picture to the girls in my village I would. They would think I'd become rich. Maybe the streets weren't paved with gold. I hadn't really believed that, but it was lovely nonetheless.

There was money everywhere. In the cars that were all new. In the grass that was all the same height. In the front doors that were locked tight. In this car that was so cold that gooseflesh raised on my arm. It wasn't even that warm outside that we needed air conditioning. On the ride here, I'd wanted nothing more than to open the window and take in the warm breeze. But the fact that not only were the windows closed tightly on this car, but every other, meant that open windows weren't something Americans did. So I didn't either.

A loud click sounded and I jumped. I'd heard there were guns everywhere in America. I didn't want to get shot before we could even get into the house. No one else was ducking or running so I pulled my shoulders down from around my ears.

"You okay? Oh, I forget things we're so used to here. Those were the door locks. Kind of loud, huh?"

I nodded and reached for the handle while the social worker got out of the car on her side. I fumbled a couple of times before I could figure out that I needed to pull the slick silver metal. I stepped out on the grass and took the deep breath I'd wanted to take for half an hour. Clean air tickled my nostrils and filled my belly. It smelled different. Drier than England, more antiseptic than home.

Before I could get my foot across the sidewalk to the path in front, a black woman came out from the house next door.

"Hello, I'm Mrs. Watson. Are you the nanny coming to live?"

I tried to swallow my shock. Yes, of course I knew there were black people in America, like there were black people in England. In the UK, though, they looked African. This woman could have been a mix of everything. The baby she was holding was kind of Asian and kind of black. Her accent like many in the UK was from the Caribbean, though. My brain couldn't quite take it all in.

Politely, I held out my hand to shake hers. "I'm Alile. Yes, I'm coming to work here."

"Alile. Nice name. You're from the mother country, huh? Welcome. Welcome. I can't wait to get a chance to talk to you about what it's like in Africa nowadays. We don't get much news here about anything that goes on over there— other than war and famine, I guess. It's the same where I'm from."

"There is that, yes. But there is so much more. Where are you from?"

"Trinidad. I live here with my son and his wife. She's from Korea. Melting pot, huh."

Even though she hadn't invited me, I reached out and smoothed my hand over the baby's curly hair. Different from Yeni's, reminded me a little of Eligu's.

"This is my grandbaby Dylan. He's sixteen months old."

Younger than my Yeni. If she were here, they could play together. She would have an American accent. Wear new clothes. I leaned down a bit looking into his big brown eyes.

"Hi, Dylan. I'm Alile. I'm going to be taking care of the little girl next door. Do you play together?"

"Oh, no." Mrs. Watson shook her head hard. "Doctor Fiona keeps to herself."

"Alile, let's get inside before it's too late," Mrs. Barrera called from the path.

"Sorry. It was nice to meet you. I hope to see you soon."

"I'm sure we'll see each other, baby. You're practically a baby yourself caring for another baby. Mm hm."

For the first moment since landing in this country, did I feel a bit of panic. Well, not the first time. The first was when a man and woman, guns strapped to their sides, pushed me to a line for what they called foreign nationals. My Sudanese passport hadn't been returned, so I used the one from Malawi I'd had to spend hard-earned kwacha on I hadn't had to spare.

After asking a lot of questions about my intentions, and I answered with believable statements about summer travel, I was able to go past one line and into baggage reclaim to go through a security again and onto my connecting flight to Cleveland. Rita had said that my immigration stuff would normally have been arranged, but there'd been no time before I took flight. So I was to tell them I was a visitor. For a country that probably had a lot of visitors, they'd acted like I'd come to raid the larder.

My heart was beating because I worried that I was cracking from too many lies. About my real reason for being in this country or even the UK or about my daughter or my true age. While I was in the UK, I learned that most white people couldn't tell my age or where I was from. I was just another black. I'd have to watch Mrs. Watson, though. There was something about her that made me think she could see right through me.

I nearly tripped over my feet as I tried to keep up with the social worker's brisk steps.

"You seem very nice." She patted my arm like nice meant feeble minded. "Africa is probably very different from the US with your tribes and villages that can help you raise your children and all that. Be careful of who you talk to, okay?"

"Yes, I understand." I nodded and pulled my pack a little closer to me. Mrs. Barrera rang the doorbell. It was a long couple of minutes before I heard footsteps approaching the door.

A thin woman, her mouth in a seriously straight line, answered the door. She was very pale and her stick-straight hair was very short. I wondered if she never got out in the sun, or if having a new baby had kept her inside and made her lose all her color.

Her "hello" sounded annoyed. "Oh, Merrill, it's you. I'm sorry to ask, but can you please ring me on my mobile or knock. The bell has a way of waking Charlotte up and it's a good hour and a half before I can get her back down."

"Oh, yes. I do tend to forget that." Mrs. Barrera looked back toward me. "This is Alile, your au pair."

"Right. I thought you were coming on Saturday." The woman's face was screwed up in dismay.

I didn't have a calendar, but I was pretty sure it was Saturday.

Mrs. Barrera corrected the woman. "It's Saturday night. Poor thing. Without sleep, you're losing your days."

"Without work, I'm losing my days. I love Charlotte, don't get me wrong, but one day of making food and diaper changes blends into the next."

As if on cue, the large plastic gadget the woman was holding in her hands lit up. With cries from a baby, the lights went from green to orange to red as the child's volume increased.

"There's no time like the present to meet her, I guess."

The woman disappeared up a set of stairs taking the wailing plastic speaker with her.

I lay my pack on the floor in a corner where it wouldn't interfere with walking. "What was that thing she was carrying. Is that a radio just for babies?"

Mrs. Barrera smiled. "It's a baby monitor. You will carry it around with you so that you can hear the baby crying."

"Can people here not hear their babies crying without it?"

"This house isn't huge, but some are. If a mom is cooking in the kitchen or watching TV, it can be the only indicator that the baby is awake, or hungry, or in distress. I suggest you take that from Fiona and keep it with you at all times you're on the clock. It'll be a big help for her."

I made a mental note that this big house was considered small and that I'd have to carry that plastic radio around with me.

A second later the baby monitor or where I would sleep were the furthest things from my mind. Fiona had the baby in her arms and was bringing her downstairs. The girl was in pajamas that covered her whole body. I think she was supposed to look like a little giraffe. Compelled by some force I couldn't name, I went to her. She smiled and stretched out her arms. I took her in mine.

Underneath the sweet chemical smell of soap and lotion and powder, she smelled like Yeni. She smelled like home. I knew then I'd lost my mind. I too was suffering the effects of little to no sleep.

"Yeni," I whispered into her hair. I walked her to the window where the remains of daylight streamed through. All the words I'd put away for so long tripped off my tongue in Yao. "My daughter, my darling, my love, how I've missed you. How I can't believe you've come here to America to be with me. How I've vowed to keep you safe from harm and give you a life of streets paved with gold."

"Alile? Alile!" My name on a foreign tongue got my attention.

"Yes. Sorry. Yes."

"Can you please make sure you speak with her in English," Mrs. Barrera said, her tone clipped. "French is usually permitted, but you've agreed to only use English."

I thought back to the papers I'd signed in a rush at Rita's shop. I hadn't read a single one, not that I could have done in so few minutes. My one focus had been leaving the country without being forced to trek back through Africa.

"Of course. I understand. They were just words I'd used with my nieces and nephews when they were young. I won't do it again."

The mom didn't say a word about that. Instead she took the baby from me and gave her to the social worker.

"Merrill, can you hold Charlotte for a moment. I should show Alile to her room. It's one in the morning in the UK. I imagine she'd like a nap."

Silently, I followed the woman up first one flight of stairs, then another narrower flight.

"When I bought the house, it came with this finished third floor. There's a bedroom up here. You'll have your own bathroom as well. Please make yourself comfortable. I can handle Charlotte tonight. She'll have another feeding, then be down for at least eight hours. Don't mind Merrill. I want my daughter to be a citizen of the world. She is already, so please feel free to use your tribal language around her. Okay."

"Okay."

The blue eyes that met mine were kind and warm if not tired. "Call me Fiona. Fiona Rose. She's Charlotte. It was my grandmum's name."

"Thank you...Fiona."

My heart skipped about, beating fast, then slowed when I realized that at least the mum here seemed kind.

I dropped my pack in the doorway of a big yellow room, the ceiling sloped on the sides and walked down the middle where I could stand and into my future.

17

"Casey Cort, nice to meet you in person." Paola Hudson shook my hand and turned. I took that as my cue to follow her through the door behind reception.

My low-heeled leather slides didn't make a peep on the floor. Plush carpet alternated with glossy wood floors, neither making a sound. I'd love it if my apartment looked like this. Kind of made me wish I could afford a decorator.

If I continued getting referrals from Hudson, I would be able to hire someone to make my living space nice. Probably I could even afford a new space once my loans were paid off. Maybe not a west side Victorian like this one, but something small in the CHALK area. I was starting to think I'd picked the right specialty this time around. Obviously money was no object for these clients.

"Lovely office," I said once we were in Hudson's space and she'd closed the door behind me.

"Take a seat, please."

Gingerly I placed my butt in the linen-covered oval-backed chair. I wasn't an auto mechanic or anything, but even with my office job, I worried about somehow getting a speck of dirt in the flawless space.

"It's good to meet your in person, Ms. Hudson," I started.

"Call me Paola. Ron said you were happy to handle our parents. Of course we'll be looking for a backup attorney should any of our families have a conflict with you. It's happened with divorce and custody being what it is these days."

"I understand." I used my best adult inside voice to try to match the surroundings which called for modulated tones and subtle movements. I wondered if a space could transform a person. Maybe I'd be more like Paola, well dressed, confident.

Pulling my mind back from the brink of distraction, I leaned forward, closer to the desk to exude what little poise I had. "I've been doing adoption for a while now. I'd hoped to meet you earlier to perhaps work with your families. Ron referring me was actually quite fortuitous." After that speech I leaned back a little and crossed my legs. I felt a little like an awkward Hillary Clinton in my silk gray pant-suit, water stains lurking around the ankles, but I kept my legs like they were nevertheless.

"Certainly is great timing, Ms. Cort." She paused for a moment assessing me. I didn't know if I made the grade, but she went on anyway. "Can I tell you a bit about Hudson?"

"Sure. I'd love to hear it." I scooted back finally feeling for the first time in a long time that I was in the right place. My job finally felt like a career and that I was no longer grasping at straws of what could have been.

"I founded the agency about twenty years ago," Hudson started. "These guys." She gestured to the poster-size color photos that graced the wall behind her whitewashed French desk, a companion to the chair I was in. "They're brother and sister. I adopted them from Guatemala. Unfortunately my husband and I weren't able to conceive on our own. We had waited for three years for a baby with nothing on the horizon when someone suggested international adoption."

"Do you specialize in that arena?" I asked. Domestic adoptions were like vanilla ice cream, a predictable mix of ingredients, parents, home study, babies. International, as I was learning from research in the Rose case, added a whole new dimension of complications. Each country did things a little differently. I wasn't afraid of the challenge of these cases, per se. It was more like I'd have to step up my game.

"Yes, and no. As I was saying I'm from Belize. I knew that there were plenty of children in Central America looking for homes, so I made some inquiries. This was all before the internet of course. In a few months, I was a mom of two toddlers from just over the border."

"They're lucky to have you."

"I'm lucky to have them. I really wanted to help people complete their families like they completed ours."

"Are they mostly couples with infertility issues?" I asked. International was one thing, but the personalities of the couples would be another entirely. I wanted to know where their heads would be when I came into the picture.

Although I kind of hoped that having a baby in their arms would replace the yearning and resentment with a new and overwhelming love—kind of how Fiona Rose was transformed the moment Charlotte was in her arms.

"Not always," Hudson said. Her answer surprised me. I shifted forward again keeping my eyes and ears open to the flood of information. "Some people believe they have a moral obligation to adopt rather than create more children in an overcrowded world. Then there are gay couples and moms like Fiona who are single."

"Yeah, right. I see."

"We complete about fifty adoptions per year. I anticipate that we'll be able to refer about forty of those to you. Ron mentioned that you're solo, will you be able to handle that caseload?"

I hoped there weren't dollar signs in my eyes as my head went through the rapid calculations. I could be loan-free in six months.

Six months.

Not another fifteen years. The house I'd envisioned buying when I walked into Hudson doubled in size.

"I can more than handle it," I promised. "I have an assistant, that's Leticia Vilagran. She handles all the administrative tasks so I can focus on the legal side of things." I didn't mention that Letty was part time. The moment I walked out of this office, I'd have to make her full time.

"Good help is worth its weight in gold."

"I was there when Fiona Rose picked up her baby. She was in my office for her consultation when your social worker called."

"Amazing to watch that, isn't it? She was willing to consider all races and ages up to three. With that wide-open field, she was at the top of the list when a baby became available."

"Right," I said. "Charlotte, that's her name now. Charlotte was from Zimbabwe the nurse said." In addition to handing over the baby, the nurse had given us a thumbnail sketch of Charlotte's background. She'd come from an orphanage in Malawi, but was from neighboring Zimbabwe.

The best estimate was that she was a year old. Her parents had perished, the dad to AIDS, the mom in an accident. The relatives had been overburdened with another mouth to feed, so had reluctantly turned her over months prior. The story itself had broken my heart. Made me want to promise my future children with Miles that nothing would ever happen to me.

"Yes the AIDS crisis has orphaned so many children in Africa."

"Do you bring children from China as well?" Seemed like every time I flipped past the news, there was some story about Chinese adoptions.

"Unfortunately, no. There's a certain demand for Chinese babies that's made it a bit…shall we say…unethical to deal with orphanages over there."

"I hadn't heard that," I said shocked—but not—by how money could quickly change the nature of the adoption equation.

"At first there were many, many babies available, all girls who were given up when the Chinese implemented the one-child policy. Unfortunately party officials have been accused of pulling babies from families and splitting the adoption fee with corrupt agency heads."

Even though I didn't have a baby of my own, the betrayal of that fundamental public trust hit me in the gut. "That's awful," I said trying not to think too hard about the Cuyahoga County public officials who did the same here in a different way.

"I couldn't sleep at night if anything like that were going on and our agency was involved. Our reputation for finding great parents and working aboveboard is what gives us access to available children in need of loving homes."

"You're doing a good thing then." I was more assured than I'd been in the days before I requested this meeting. Miles was right, I was looking to find fault where there was none. Maybe I needed a little of Lulu's faith that things were going my way, that everything would work out just fine for me.

"Absolutely. How's the Rose case going." She lifted her hands toward me palms face forward before I could speak. "I know you can't talk about the particulars. Will it be your first international adoption?"

"Yes, I've only tackled domestic so far. But I've done the research on the additional steps necessary to complete it. Not too difficult. Also, I had a chance to talk to Justin McPhee."

Her expression at the mention of Justin was inscrutable. "You know Mr. McPhee?"

"We met years ago at a juvenile court function. He said that Hudson would be a good fit for me."

"Yes, well. It was a shame to lose Justin. He didn't like the fast pace we move at around here."

"He was saying something about that," I acknowledged while leaving out the part about him crying in his second beer.

"We like to keep things moving forward. Give our families certainty. If you've been in Juvy, then you know how awful it can be for parents to wait and see how their case is going to turn out."

"It can be unpleasant, that wait."

"Don't I know it. I was explaining to Justin our philosophy, but I think he was too used to the pace of Twenty-second Street."

"He's a very traditional guy." Old-fashioned was more like it. I could see, though, with his upbringing how he could have such black-and-white thinking.

"That's honorable. Don't get me wrong. I admired his painstaking attention to detail. I need to keep up with how things are done now, though, if I want to remain the preeminent agency in Cleveland."

"I understand and agree. Completely."

Hudson stood signaling she was all done with chitchat. "It was great meeting you, but I do have families to meet with and birth mothers to call. Someone is always on the verge of labor. Do you have any questions for me?"

Her half step from the back to the side of her desk certainly didn't invite more back and forth. I took a deep breath and launched into my real reason for the meeting even though I'd couched it as a meet and greet.

I lifted my messenger bag and slipped the strap on my shoulder. "Just a quick one about the Rose case. I did some research and it seems noncitizens can't adopt internationally."

"Hmmm." Hudson's right hip leaned against the desk. "That's interesting. We've never had any issues before. Are you sure you have your facts correct?"

"There may be some exception...that I'm unaware..."

She snapped her fingers. The sound was muted by textured wallpaper and carpet. "Of course. That must be it. This is a country of immigrants. A country that's welcomed immigrants like me. I can't imagine that the government would make such a huge oversight..."

"Let me check again. I could have missed something." As sure of myself as I'd been going in, my mind started turning in cartwheels of contrition.

"Yes. Please do that. Does that mean that the paperwork hasn't been filed?"

"No. Yes. No, I haven't made the petition with the probate court yet. I'm waiting on the FBI check as well as the African birth and death certificates. I only have the final decree from Zimbabwe and I wanted to talk to you about those missing documents."

"It's your first case, so I'll...I understand your hesitation. One of the things we pride ourselves on here at Hudson is our expediency. Not only do we like to help our clients complete their families without excessive waits that other agencies impose, we like to finalize the adoptions quickly. Sure, the court gives us months to get the paperwork in, but you have to understand the parents' position."

"I can relate. The one thing about juvenile Court that drove the families nuts was the lack of resolution on the cases."

"So you do understand. I'm so glad. One of the parents' greatest fears is that they're going to lose their child. No matter what we tell them, they tend to lose sleep and fret until they have that final adoption order in their hands. From there it's a six-month countdown before the appeals time limit tolls. So in total, maybe we're looking at nine months, maybe a year. Let's do the parents a favor and keep that to a minimum if we can. Are you on board? Do you think you can do that. Fit these in with your other caseload?"

"Of course. I completely understand. First-case jitters and all that. Just wanted to dot my 'i's and cross my 't's."

"Attention to detail is a great asset, but remember not to let it hamstring you like it did for Mr. McPhee. So many professionals these days are more interested in fees than serving the clients. We're not like that here. As long as you understand our philosophy, you'll be a great asset to our team."

"Thank you for your time. I look forward to working with you going forward."

"Great. I'll have Merrill Barrera speak with you before you leave then about those papers you've requested. She'll let you know an ETA on those. Also I'll instruct her to give you a rundown of the adoptions that we have coming down the pike so you can be prepared. Maybe get any research done and questions answered before you meet with the client next time."

The rebuke was subtle, but I heard it nonetheless. Given the fees legal and otherwise the parents were paying, I would make sure not to mention any issues with the client present. I'd gotten into sloppy client management with my appointed clients who, because they weren't paying my fees directly, were okay with uncertainty. I'd have to step up my game. If I wanted to play with the big boys...

"Thank you again for the opportunity to work with your parents." I took my leave and found Merrill Barrera waiting for me in the hall ready to lead me to her office, my next cases, and a surefire way out of debt once and for all.

I had arrived.

I tried not to be too resentful that it was where I was supposed to have been all along.

18

"Fiona Matthews Rose. I love you!" A voice that sounded like Paul's warbled from some distant part of my mind. I turned over in the too-warm bed trying to banish the image of my missing ex-partner. Kicking off the duvet, I stuck a foot out and tried to shake off the dream. I'd had one similar off and on for the last couple of months.

While my logical waking brain knew Paul wasn't coming back—much less declaring his love while climbing the trellis like so many American movies—in the dead of night, in my not-so-logical lizard brain, I still had hope and dependency on a dream that was never going to be fulfilled. That hope scared me. I closed my eyes ready to drift off for a few more minutes at least. Have a bit of quiet time so I could banish Paul, so I could move on to what was my life now: Charlotte.

The sound of something rustling got my attention and woke me fully, banishing any dreamy thoughts. In the dusky light of dawn everything came to me. Paul's absence. Charlotte's presence. The fact that the new au pair, her dark eyes ever watchful, had moved in a week ago and I couldn't wallow in my pity and tears. For the first weeks that Charlotte was with me, I didn't have a moment to think of Paul. Exhaustion was the cure for grief. With Alile here, I was getting some of my time back. I wasn't sure I wanted it if that time only ended in tears and thoughts of my ex.

This time when the voice came, it was more insistent. "Fi! Let me in. I'm so sorry."

I shook my head again trying to shake off the "Paul comes back" dream. I'd gotten a lot of sleep since Alile had come. Auditory hallucinations should not be happening to me. Motherhood could not drive me to the madhouse.

"Dear God. It's five o'clock in the morning. Use your key. My grandbabies are sleeping. I'm sure yours is too." That was Dolores Watson speaking.

One voice was a hallucination, two was a conversation. I kicked off the duvet once and for all and went to my window. Paul, rucksack at his feet, was looking over toward the neighbor's house. Dolores Watson stood in her doorway, bathrobe clutched tightly at her neck, face creased deeply in a frown.

My annoyance at having my sleep disturbed was quickly replaced by elation. I banged on the wood until it loosened, little flakes of paint floating to the floor. Shoving up the sash, I leaned my head out into the soft warm air.

"Paul!" I shouted.

"Fi!" His head was tipped up. There he was. My Paul.

Barefoot I ran down the stairs and toward the door. It took me a good half minute to undo the locks and throw the doors open. Paul stood, looking a bit worse for wear.

Not caring a whit what Dolores Watson or any other nosy neighbors about at that hour thought, I ran down the walkway and threw myself into Paul's arms.

For a long minute I felt like the star of that American romantic comedy I'd despised a few moments before as he spun me in his arms. A second later the sprinklers went on drenching us in warm water. I wanted to peek to see if we were indeed being filmed. That scene from Dancing in the Rain quickly went out the door when the water turned from warm to icy cold.

"Gah!"

Paul pulled back, fire in his eyes.

"What?" I fiddled with my short hair plastered to my head. Following Paul's gaze I saw that it wasn't the only thing skimming my body. My white-and-gray-striped sleep shirt was clinging to me like a second skin. My nipples stiffened as I pulled back. Looking down I could see that nothing was left to the imagination.

"Looking good, Fiona," he said before he leaned in and kissed me again. I'd missed him so much. His familiar taste and smell were like a homecoming. It could have been England. It could have been ten years ago.

"Let's get inside," I urged. I cast a look toward my neighbor's house. Mrs. Watson was outside looking down her nose at the two of us as if we'd done the deed on the middle of the driveway that separated our two properties.

"We can do a proper welcome home then." Paul's smile was wolfish.

Clutching at each other's waists, we stepped toward the house in unison. My body was at once blisteringly cold and achingly hot. I counted the seconds until we could strip and run up to the bedroom.

After I pushed through the front door, the sight of Alile in her simple cotton dress, Charlotte on her hip, their brown skin a near perfect match, stopped me in my tracks.

"Am I at the right house?" Paul asked dropping his rucksack to the floor.

Looking back and forth from the toys and dolls on the floor, to the playpen in the corner, then back to Alile and Charlotte, I could see that I had a lot to explain. It was as if Paul had been gone two years instead of three months. My life had changed that much during that short time he'd been away. Alile's accusatory stare had me crossing my arms across my breasts.

"Paul. Meet my daughter, Charlotte Rose. This is my au pair Alile. She's been a godsend, Alile that is. Charlotte is a miracle." I stopped sounding foolishly sentimental to my own ears. Motherhood had, in a very short time, changed me.

"Daughter?" He looked between me and Alile and Charlotte. I could practically see his brain ticking away at all of the possibilities.

"Ali, do you have it? You okay for a few minutes?"

"Yes, we'll be fine."

"Paul, come upstairs. I need to talk to you." I wanted to have that talk in private without watchful eyes.

I'd never been that girl. The one who stood at a party rubbing her guy's shoulders in a semi hug, or the one to sit next to him and possessively pat his leg at the dinner table. Today, though, I wanted to be a different sort of girl for him this time 'round. So I grabbed his hand and held on for dear life as we climbed the stairs in unison.

I made sure the bedroom door was firmly closed before I sat on the unmade bed. Paul took a seat on a wingback chair I'd picked up from a secondhand shop in Shaker Square.

"You have a daughter? I don't understand." Confusion marred the features I'd known so well for so long. I wanted to reach out and smooth the wrinkles from his forehead. Instead I took a deep breath and spoke.

"I'm not fertile, Paul." I took a deep breath. "I can't have a baby, naturally."

His frown deepened. "We hadn't even been trying that long. You didn't have to rush to judgment. You're still young...maybe..."

"Paul. Listen to me. I hear what you're trying to say. I'm okay with it. I think you know that I wanted a baby. With or without you, I wanted the family we'd talked about so often. I was going to do it the natural way...with insemination, but..."

"Natural?" The creases of worry were so deep in Paul's face I wanted to warn him about it all freezing that way the way my mam would have done. I took it as a sign that he cared. It was a one-hundred-eighty-degree turn from the impassive face I'd had to look at across the table at the hotel where we'd had the bad tea before he'd left for good.

"As natural as I could get without a penis. I wanted to have my baby. Carry it to term. I wanted to have your baby, Paul. But before they shoot you up with hormones or even sperm, they needed to test me for fertility.

"I thought the tests were just a way to get cash or fulfill some insurance protocol. So much of America seems to be about testing, and testing, and billing. I'm getting off track, sorry." That happened to me when my brain wanted to avoid something hard. It veered. "So, I went in for insemination and they told me I probably couldn't ever have a baby naturally."

"Why not? We're young. We're not sixteen, but we're not sixty either."

I didn't want to blame him. I was past the blame. Having Charlotte come into my life had put me on a path to forgiveness that had swept up both my parents and Paul. They'd all loved me the best they could. The path I'd been on, the treadmill I'd hated had all led to Charlotte. That I would never regret.

I ran my fingers through my fringe, letting it cover my eyes a little. This was going to be the hardest bit.

"An infection gone wrong," I whispered.

For a moment his eyes roamed the walls as he worked out what could have gone wrong. The part of me who wanted to be that girl, took a back seat to the old me who'd been mad as hell. I waited while he filled in the blanks. In a sudden movement, his head jerked up.

"Bollocks. Bloody hell. Was it the clam?"

My nod was slight.

"I'm so sorry. Me mates were drinking. It was Johnny's stag do—"

"I'm as responsible as you were," I said, mentally bashing myself all over again for being so cavalier with my own health like the cobbler was with his own children. "I'm a doctor—"

He sat forward until we were inches apart. His large, roughened hands bracketed my face between them. His eyes met and held mine.

"Don't do that. Don't take on everything. I'm an adult, Fiona. I know that I haven't always acted like it, but I have to be responsible for all the decisions I've made."

"It's done. Whatever it is. It's done. Charlotte's here and she's perfect. You're here. You are here, right?" I'd been so busy making my own confession that I hadn't thought to ask whether his stay was permanent or if he were here for one last goodbye.

I took a breath to steel myself for whatever was coming. If I'd learnt anything in these past months, it was that none of this was going to kill me. Hurt yes. Kill me no. I had to live for Charlotte anyway.

Paul's eyebrows shot up to his hairline. "Hold on..."

He let me go and stepped back. In an abrupt about-face Paul turned and ran from the room. I could hear his leather boots pounding on the stairs. He shared some words with Ali. Then in a few minutes he came back into the room, giant rucksack in hand.

"Paul?"

"Your girl, Ali, did you call her. She said that she's going to take Charlotte to the park. I told her that was okay. She wanted, I think, for us to have some time together."

I could only nod and wait for what was to come.

"Anyway, this isn't perfect, Fiona. I wish I could do something for you worthy of something you'd see on one of those Sky shows on the telly, but here we go."

He knelt down and held out his hands. I took his. Gathering up all my mental strength, I finally looked Paul straight in the eye. His were shiny with unshed tears. I had to swallow about ten times to keep my own crying at bay.

"What..."

"Fiona. I love you. Always have. From the day you bumped into me at the fish and chip stand and called me all kinds of an idiot for spilling malt vinegar all over your clothes."

"I smelled like a chip shop for days."

"I love that you're smart and ambitious. That you support me in my artwork. I realized that you've been to every show that I ever had. Even that one in the lorry garage in Shoreditch. No matter what you were doing, if you had a big exam or even a surgery coming up, you put it on hold to be with me. I've been such an idiot, Fiona.

"I know now that I want to spend the rest of my life with you, if you'll have me. I'm going to do this right this time." He sat on his haunches and fiddled with some zippers. From a pocket in the army-green canvas, he extracted a box. It was navy, and square, and couldn't be mistaken for anything other than what it was, an engagement ring.

"Paul, you didn't have to—"

"But I did, Fiona. We did this all wrong before. Making it about citizenship and practicality. You deserve romance. We deserve it all." He held out his hands palms up. "Fiona Matthews Rose, will you marry me?"

I fell to my knees so that we were eye to eye.

"Of course, Paul. I missed you. Yes."

We were both sniffling as he fiddled the box open and slipped the ring on the third finger of my left hand. It wasn't big or flashy. The oval diamond, surrounded by a bunch of tiny diamonds in a simple gold band was something I'd be proud to wear every day. Even if I did have to hang it on a chain around my neck so it didn't interfere with surgery.

"It fits," he pronounced.

"You were always good with spacial relationships," I complimented.

He stood pulling me up with him. At six foot, Paul was comfortably taller than me. Despite my height and practical haircut, he had a way of making me feel feminine.

"Will you go away with me?" he asked.

"Where…"

"If we leave today, we can be in Niagara Falls by tea time. There's a little log cabin where we can get married. Just the two of us with pictures and bubbly. They can take us on Monday. Will you do it? Come away with me?"

"There are three of us, now."

"Right, of course. I can't wait to be a dad, be a family. But for right now, can this be just about us, Fi. We can be parents in two days, but let's be a couple for one last time."

I hesitated for only a single second. He was right. I needed to be with Paul, resolve the past before we could begin our future together.

"Yes, let's do what you've planned! Should I pack? What should I bring?"

Paul gestured to the rucksack that he planned to carry.

"For you? A toothbrush? Just you, Fi, is all I need. All I ever needed."

19

The white plastic monitor lit up like Lilongwe at Christmas. First green, then yellow, then red. I watched the little squares of light pulse for a full minute before I threw my legs over the side of the couch where I must have fallen asleep.

I had only a single thought. Yeni needed me. I wasn't dressed. But the baby wouldn't care.

Barefoot, I ran up the stairs to the second floor. For a full moment I stood outside Fiona's closed door trying to decide whether to knock or not. I had my hand ready to hit the wood, when I remembered two very important things. It wasn't Yeni waiting for me, it was Charlotte. And I was alone with the little girl for two more long days.

That man, who'd made Fiona cry night after night had marched back in after being gone who in the hell knows how long and she'd taken off with him, just like that, leaving me and her new child behind. They were going to be getting married in some place I'd never heard of. Some kind of falls.

Guilt that Fiona should have been feeling hung over me like a cloud. At once I hated her for running out on her own child without so much as a backward thought. I also hated myself for running out on my own daughter, for letting Umi intimidate me, for not fighting harder for my own flesh and blood, for leaving me with this child while I ached so much for the girl I'd left behind.

When I'd finally come back from the park, Fiona and Paul, he said his name was, were downstairs drinking tea. He shook my hand with two of his and smiled a crooked-toothed smile as he said words about family and being friends.

I put Charlotte into her high chair and got her some breakfast. Neither moved to help. Neither Fiona nor Paul moved from the stools they'd taken across from each other at the tall table. They couldn't stop smiling at each other.

I was invisible to them. I'd been planning that morning to ask Miss Fiona about going to school. I didn't have the phone number of the social worker who'd dropped me off. Without her help, I didn't have the least clue as to how I would find a school to attend or register or even get there. Or what papers I'd need to bring or how much the fees would be.

For this first week, I'd basically been catching up on my own sleep, caring for Charlotte, and visiting with that black woman neighbor in the afternoon. She was always cooking something good and it was less work for both of us when all three kids played together.

Yesterday, though, Fiona and her man didn't ask about my sleep or where I was taking Charlotte. They were out the door, having thrust a wad of green paper bills in my hand with promises of lots of time off before I could so much as work out what was happening.

I lifted Charlotte out of her crib, changed her diaper, and carried her downstairs with me.

It was lunchtime, but for a moment, I lay on the sofa with her plopped on my belly.

Like I'd done every day since I'd come here, I ran my eyes and hands over every inch of her skin. I wanted my own daughter so bad that I knew I'd been crazy to convince myself this one was mine, when she couldn't be. Even though she seemed to understand almost everything I said when I spoke Yao. I closed my eyes and opened them again trying to separate fantasy from reality. That just wasn't possible.

She certainly didn't smell like Yeni with all these perfumed soaps and lotions that Miss Fiona kept next to the bathtub and on Charlotte's dresser.

From the corner of my eye, though, she could have been my little girl. From her tiny toes that looked like tiny grapes the way Yeni's had, to the ear shaped like Uncle Onani's. Maybe Africans looked more alike than I'd always been told. Our tribe had one kind of genes. The neighboring tribes had something altogether different in looks, in language in customs. But Charlotte looked as if she could have come from my own family. While I was thinking like this though, I wasn't working on the biggest problem I needed to fix. My problem was still in Africa.

All the worry over what was going on thousands of kilometers away was going to make me crazier than my aunt thought I was. I lifted Charlotte and stood ready to get some kind of meal together in the kitchen.

"Alile?" The screen door rattled. "It's Dolores. Come on over. I have some macaroni pie. Made a little pan for you and Charlotte to take home with you."

With that announcement, it fell silent. Dolores did that a lot, knocked, announced, then walked back to her own house before I could so much as work the lock open and stick my head out to say yes or no. Maybe she did that so I would always say yes. It worked. I shrugged Charlotte up higher on my hip and made to leave.

With something hot and done next door, I abandoned the idea of heating up one of the dinners Miss Fiona had left. I slipped my feet in my sandals by the couch and was out the door in a few seconds.

"Where's the family?" I asked. It was more quiet than usual in her house. Normally her granddaughter, the half-Asian-looking one was running around like a chicken with its head off. The dad was grumbling about his daughter and hugging her at the same time. The momma didn't say much. I'm not sure she spoke English.

"Ain't no one but me tonight. Min-ji took the kids to see that man of hers while he's out of jail. My boy and his wife took themselves out to Charley's Crab."

Jail. That one surprised me every time it came out of Dolores' mouth. I don't think I'd ever known anyone in my village to go to jail. She'd made it seem like this boyfriend was in and out all the time. Maybe Americans shared more. Maybe we didn't talk about personal things back home because everyone already knew all your secrets. There wasn't much you could hide there.

"That's nice."

"Have you been to a restaurant?"

I shook my head. I hadn't had any extra money for that. Except for Dinha and others who did some kind of illegal work, none of the other women had eaten on the high street either. I may never be rich enough to eat out, but I hoped one day Yeni would be.

"Charley's serves seafood. Min-ji's mom, she grew up in the south part of Korea. Her dad was a fisherman. She really misses a fresh catch here in the middle of the country. So my son takes her out every so often to keep her happy."

"We were landlocked too," I offered in a rare candid moment. "There's a big lake though where people fish."

"What countries are around you?"

"Mozambique. Zimbabwe. Zambia. Tanzania," I answered. I may not have gone to school like the other girls in uniform, but my mother had tried to teach me all she knew before she had died. I remembered nearly everything she'd ever taught me.

"I wish to go there one day. Sounds like home a bit. A place where most people are black. I miss that here."

"So Trinidad is black?"

"You know about slavery, right?"

I nodded. But I didn't know much. Mama had told me that black Africans had been put in ships and sent to Europe and America to work. Then they got their freedom. Not a lot more than that. My ignorance was starting to embarrass me so I didn't add anything out loud.

"The islands were different from America," Mrs. Watson started. "The slaves had a much harder time there. Many died. But also we got our freedom earlier. After that many Chinese and Indians were brought over."

"So there are other kids who look like your grandson and granddaughter?" I asked. I'd wanted so much to ask about them with their folded eyelids but black coarse curly hair.

Even though Europeans had been in Africa for hundreds of years, there hadn't been much mixing. It had been mostly illegal everywhere. Also, I think we'd outnumbered them greatly.

"You know, now that you say it, there are a lot like them. No one would look twice. It was Dutch and French too. A lot of mixing. Also a lot of people keeping to themselves."

"Doesn't sound much different from anywhere."

I took the food and cut it up into small pieces. Yeni...Charlotte stuck some in her mouth on her own. From the six-tooth smile, I was guessing she liked it a lot. It would take her a long time to feed herself which was fine. I could have a moment to take a breath.

It was full on without any help. With me and Fiona it had been totally doable. But with Paul back and Fiona probably going back to her job as a doctor, it might be like this all the time. Except school and weekends, those were supposed to be mine.

I helped myself to a good chunk of the food and sat at the kitchen table. I pinched off a piece with my fingers and tasted it. Foreign but good. It was macaroni and cheese with some kind of stewed meat on the top. My mom would have loved this. When we had meat, she'd stew it and we'd have it on top of foufou or nsima. For a moment my heart squeezed with missing Mama.

That hurt must have showed on my face, because Charlotte's face turned down in a frown at the same time. Quickly I placed a smile on my lips. Seeing that all was okay in her world, she went back to pulling noodles and meat from her bowl and sticking about half of it in her mouth and the rest on her cheeks and in her hair. Bath time was going to be longer than usual. Cheese was a challenge I hadn't encountered in my life before now.

"What happened to you, Alile? You left us for a moment."

"Sorry. I was thinking about my mother."

"Where is she?"

"She died about three years ago."

"How old were you, poor thing, to have lost your mother so young."

"Thirteen," I said. Then I threw both hands across my mouth. I'd gotten too comfortable and said too much.

"Child. How old does that make you now?"

"Sixteen."

"Aren't you supposed to be at least eighteen to do the job you're doing?"

"Please don't tell Miss Fiona," I pleaded. "I'm sure it's not legal, what I've done. But I can't go home now. I'm so close to saving enough money to send for my daughter."

"Your daughter? You're just a child yourself."

"When my mother died, there was no one to protect me." I didn't need to say the rest. She seemed like the kind of woman who understood the way of the world.

"I'm so sorry, dear girl." She hung her head for a long minute of silence. "Where's your daughter now? What about the rest of your people. How did they let such a young girl go off alone?"

I looked at Charlotte, tried to keep it in, but I couldn't keep my thoughts to myself any longer.

"I think this is my daughter."

Dolores Watson who'd been kind, and inviting, and caring, looked at me like she was ready to call someone and have me shut up in a hospital for people who'd parted ways with their sane mind.

"I know. I know it's crazy. My Yeni can't be this Charlotte. But in my head I'm not so sure. She looks just like my girl—"

"How old was your daughter when you left?"

"Only a month old."

"They look so different from babies to toddlers. Are you sure you aren't filling in what you see with what you hope?"

"I know. I know. It's just she has my uncle's ear." I should know. I had watched that ear rather than the eyes that raked my body or the mouth that hung open like a horse's. "My mouth. I mean Fiona and that social worker don't seem too sure of where she came from. And I left Malawi because my aunt threatened to put her in an orphanage if I didn't pay her. I will finally have the money in a few weeks' time. But what if she turned Yeni over to the orphanage as soon as I left. And what if that orphanage offered Yeni for adoption. And what if she came to this place, this Cleveland. And what if I came to this same place."

It was the unlikely string of events I'd put together in my head during the week. It's what had made it okay for me to close my eyes and sleep. If Yeni was in the room below me, much of the fear and worry was gone. Or I'd traded a harder problem for an easier one.

"Dear, that's about a thousand coincidences that would have to happen all at the same time. It's so rare for even two things in life to match up."

"But it could be true. Watch." I spoke to Yeni then. Asking her to put down her food and lift up her arms.

"You spoke to her in your…tribal…language?"

"I did."

"It was like she understood you." Dolores shook her head in wonder. Do you think she could have learned all that in a week? Kids are very quick to pick up a second or third language."

"But she's been here a few weeks and she doesn't understand the same things in English." I demonstrated by asking her to repeat the actions, but this time in the English that we all used and understood and all I got for my troubles was a look of confusion on little Charlotte's face before she went back to smearing the food that was left all over the high chair tray.

Realizing she was done, I lifted her from the chair and pulled some paper from the hanger under the sink. I wet it and wiped at Yeni's…Charlotte's hands and face. I took aim at the tray next, wiping away any stray cheese sauce before it hardened.

Cheese was a new thing. But Dolores made a lot of foods with it. Kids ate it at the park. Fiona stuck it in the microwave. I thought it tasted okay, but getting hard, dried cheese off was terribly difficult. Having tasted it a few times, I wasn't thinking it was worth all the trouble.

"What if she's your daughter? What would you do?"

She asked the question in the same way the refugees in our house in England had asked what would happen if you won the lottery after we'd pooled our meager funds together and bought a strip of tickets.

"Take her…"

"Where? You're a child yourself. Legally, you can't do anything for yourself. Take it from me, at your age without a house or a job or any kind of education, the county would come take your kid and put them right in foster care. After the year we had with McKenna in and out of the system. Trust me that's no place to be."

I slumped in the chair. Deflated, I hauled myself up and lifted Charlotte from the floor where I'd put her. With a washcloth I carried with me in a big bag Fiona had, I wiped Charlotte's face and hands one more time making sure she was clean. Then I plopped her in a playpen where Dylan usually sat. Restless, I paced the room. Once I'd said it aloud, my belief that my daughter was a precious few feet away solidified.

"How could I find out if she was my daughter. Surely in America you have a way to do that."

Without saying a word, Dolores placed both hands on the table and pushed herself up. She walked out of the room and came back with a huge folder bursting with official-looking documents. She pushed a small plastic container with a lid toward me.

More food.

I tucked it in the baby bag in a little insulated pocket. I hadn't much liked cooking at aunt Umi's house. This I could rcheat and give to Charlotte later or even save it for me.

Next, Dolores upended the beige folder and the papers spilled across the table. Her brown hand starting its journey to claw, which for the first time I noticed was in the early stages of arthritis, shuffled through the papers. I could see in her raised eyebrows when she came upon what she was looking for. Plucking it from the stack, she slipped it toward me. While she gathered up the other documents, I looked at what she'd given me.

At the top in big black letters were the words "DNA Diagnostics." The rest was in English, but I didn't understand it. Min-ji's name was there as was that of her sometimes boyfriend. Then the words north American black population came next to a ninety-nine and a symbol. I shook my head feeling momentarily sorry for myself. I needed to go to school and study so I could read things like this.

"What does dunna mean?"

"Dunna? Oh, DNA. It stands for…it stands for the test that labs do from people's blood to tell if they're related or if they've done a crime. Like OJ."

"'O' what?"

"Skip all that. If you can get a sample from the girl and one from yourself and send it to this place, they'll tell you if she's your daughter."

"I'd have to take her blood?" I didn't want her to have to be poked with a needle or see her cry because I had a question that was at best a long shot of being true.

"No, it's a lot easier than that. They swab the cheeks with something that looks like a giant Q-tip."

"Can I go to this DNA place?"

"Of course. They're a cash business like every other one."

"So you have to pay?"

"Nothing is free. Not a single damn thing. Gimme a second." Dolores shuffled through the papers again and pulled out a second document. She pushed that toward me as well. "Here. It's six hundred dollars."

"That's a lot of money." I thought of the two hundred I'd gotten paid before Fiona had left. Inspired, I stood up so quickly the chair behind me nearly fell. Startled, Charlotte dropped the blocks she'd been putting in her mouth and trained her eyes on me. Retrieving the diaper bag from the floor where I'd placed it after dropping the food in, I searched for and found the envelope Fiona had slipped me before she'd run out the door. I took out the crisp green bills and counted them out. It was five hundred dollars. That meant I could go and have two hundred left to give back to her.

"Can I go there today?"

"They'll be closed. Only stores are open on the weekends. Offices are closed Saturday and Sunday."

"Tomorrow?"

"I guess. Are you this sure that you want to spend that much money based on a couple of coincidences in your mind?"

Resolved, I said, "I'm sure. If it's not her, at least I can stop my mind from being crazy. I can devote myself to getting the real Yeni from Malawi."

"I'll drive you, then." Dolores had her own car separate from the other three in the driveway.

"Will you?"

"If you take the bus, you won't be back before they get home from their one-night honeymoon. It's best you don't involve them in this. The test will be painless. Noninvasive."

"Thank you." I nearly fainted with relief that I could have an answer to the question that had plagued me every night for the last five. "Will they be able to tell me right there?"

"No. I don't know how long the results take, but it's not instant. Maybe a month, maybe more."

"I'm going to go take this baby for a nap. But tomorrow. What time should I be ready?"

"Eight should be early enough."

"Thank you. Thank you. Thank you."

"It's just a ride. I'm probably wasting your hard-earned money."

I shook my head fervently. "Yeni would want me to do this. She's worth more than all the money in the world." I lifted the baby I thought was mine and hefted her on my hip. There was nothing I wouldn't do for my baby. Not a single thing. I'd come this far. What was one little detour as long as it got me closer to the truth.

20

"Thank you, Ms. Cort. This is amazing. I can't believe Hailey will be ours."

Happy people in my office was a huge change for the better. I still had a box of tissues on my desk, but instead of mothers breaking down over the loss of family, new moms were crying happy tears over finally completing theirs. Mrs. Turner was no different. Through the tears falling down her checks a big smile beamed.

"Again you have my congratulations," I offered. "Letty will call you when your hearing date is set."

"Do we really have to bring the baby?" she asked. It was an oddity of the adoption process. In juvenile court, even though it was about the kids, they were never in the building. That was verboten. I'd asked about it during one of my first weeks there. From the response, you'd have thought I'd farted in the courtroom.

Somehow children's best interests were served with only a guardian ad Litem being their voice. With adoptions, the judge liked to eyeball the kids. My cynical side thought it was a bid to win votes in upcoming elections. My criminal defense clients, the few who voted, probably never cast a ballot for those judges who pronounced their guilt. I could see these parents happily punch a chad or two for those who left them with the warm fuzzies.

"Yep. It's required." I shrugged. "Don't worry. The younger the children, the faster your hearing gets called. They're used to kids down there. There aren't the long waits like with other courts."

The Turners, husband and wife, rose to leave, but each gripped my hands again like they had when they'd arrived. I was kind of afraid they wouldn't let me go. Fortunately Letty knocked and chose that moment to open my door.

"Your eleven o'clock is here."

I glanced at the clock on the credenza behind me. "Right. Thank you."

While Letty showed the Turners through reception to the door to the suite, I did some quick mental calculations. Paola Hudson had been right in her prediction that I'd have a boatload of cases. After the meeting, no less than six referrals had come through the door. I couldn't help but do the mental math. They'd gross me at least sixty thousand dollars. That plus Charlotte Rose's matter and I had nearly enough to pay off my loans. Or at least half of the money was mine. The rest belonged to the IRS. I knew I'd probably owe a crap ton of taxes on this cash. A good problem to have.

While I straightened my desk, filing the notes from the last meeting, and sharpening my pencil for the next, I called myself all kinds of a fool for not having pulled out of juvenile earlier. I'd slaved away there for eight long years barely making a living while my fellow graduates had been filling their bank accounts with money, buying cars and condos. Law was full of cash cows and I was milking one—finally.

Before I could get caught up in all the things I'd denied myself that I could all of a sudden buy now, Letty was showing in the next couple. I was surprised to see my neighbors from across the hall. People out of context were always startling.

"Jason? Greg? What are you doing downtown? I'd love to chat, but I have a consultation at eleven. Maybe we can go to lunch in an hour if you don't mind waiting around…"

Jason laughed. "I'll take you up on the lunch offer if you're buying, but we're your eleven o'clock."

I glanced down at the printed schedule Letty had left on my blotter first thing in the morning. Indeed the last names in the third hour-long slot were Corry and Salazar. How had I not noticed that?

"You want to adopt a child? When did you decide this?"

"It's been something we've been talking about off and on for a while now."

"You could have just knocked on my door. I'm only across the hall."

"You've never asked me for medical advice at dinner, right?" Jason asked. He cocked his head in such a way that Greg and I both found hard to resist.

My smile at him was automatic. "Of course not. Boundaries, as in I have them." I was not a fan of friends, relatives or church parishioners asking for advice. For Greg and

Jason, though, I would have bent my self-imposed rule. "I appreciate your consideration, though."

"So we thought we'd come see you in your office when we got the attorney referral. Merrill Barrera spoke highly of you."

"Oh my God, that's so weird, a third person telling you about me. Did you tell her that we share a hallway?"

"No. That seemed weirder." Greg's laughter made me laugh too. He continued, "I mentioned that we knew you, though. Told her that she was right about you being the greatest lawyer ever."

"I kind of love you for that. I just hope she doesn't think you have a checkered criminal background or some kind of child abuse record. So what's the story with the baby?"

"As you know, we've been together for seven years. Sure that we're past the itch, we're ready to commit, be parents." I remembered their seven-year-itch blowout celebrating the fact that they'd made it past the first couple of hurdles of being a couple. The four-year party had been pretty great as well. "Jason will continue to work full time and I'll work around the baby."

"Which one of you will adopt? I assume Paola or Merrill told you that Ohio doesn't...yet...recognize same-sex couple adoption," I said stumbling over the inequity. Made me wonder if Miles' parents had faced this kind of discrimination when they wanted to marry. I had to hope that gay rights would be the civil rights of the next generation. "Sorry."

"It's just one of a list of rights we don't have. You're not telling us something we don't know. Don't worry."

"So...one of you will be the parent, though they won't discriminate against you in the home study process at least."

"We both applied. I think it'll be Jason, though," Greg said. "Everyone loves a doctor. Freelance magazine writers, not as much."

"I love you both equally."

I leaned toward the drawer and pulled out my new folders. Gone were the generic red pocket folders replaced by slick white folders with my name emblazoned on the front. Seemed pretentious, but Leticia insisted that it was part of the stepping-up-my-game project that she'd voluntarily initiated.

"Are you hoping to adopt a baby?" I'd found the seemingly innocuous question turned out to be a loaded gun. It turned out to be common knowledge that non-white babies, older children, and those with special needs were the easiest to adopt while white babies were the most rare.

Turned out people thought of themselves as liberal until faced with a choice that challenged their beliefs. Because the court's requirements were different with each kind of adoption, I needed to know what I should expect and whether or not I'd need to get parental consent, or something from the county, or like Charlotte Rose's case where extensive international documentation was needed.

The question triggered people though. Half the time I spent at least ten minutes listening to justifications for why they weren't willing to take the most adoptable and vulnerable kids.

"I think we'd prefer a baby," Greg said.

"But we're open," Jason interjected. "Paola said it was better that way. Plus if I've learned nothing else as a doctor, it's that people's personalities are pretty fixed. The only difference is that a baby gives you a bit more leeway to figure it out."

"I'll leave that as an open question then. I hope you guys are ready. I'm learning that once home studies are done, Hudson can move pretty fast."

"That's why we went to her. She's known for working with people in the gay community and with people of color, the kinds of clients a lot of traditional agencies turn away."

"If you're ready and are okay working with a friend and neighbor, I am."

They both nodded, so I uncrossed my legs to keep the blood flowing and launched into my spiel.

For the next fifty-five minutes I walked them through the ins and outs of adoption. The explanations were almost longer than the hearing process itself.

"So that's it?"

"Yep. If you have questions, you can always come across the hall. My door is always open."

"Except when Miles is there," Greg added.

Another knock came. I swear I hadn't been so popular in my life.

"I thought it was probably okay that he come in if you're done," Letty said. I frowned at the total breach of protocol.

"Who—" Letty didn't get the opportunity to answer before my boyfriend poked his head in the door. Speak of the devil.

"Miles? What are you doing here?"

"Came to take you to lunch."

"Okay. Great. Jason, Greg, you want to join us?" I said like my neighbors had been here on a social call.

"Don't need to be a third and fourth wheel," Greg said. They stood. Jason stuck the folder in his ever-present black messenger bag. I'd once joked that it was like a modern doctor's bag.

"Are we a bicycle?" I joked.

"Go to lunch. We're going to go home and figure out where to put Greg's office."

"My office?" Greg looked affronted.

"What? a baby needs a room."

They both made their way across my office and bickered all the way out the suite door. I closed my office door again seeking a bit of privacy.

"It's weird seeing you here. It's not every day that you drop by my office." I was always the one going to Miles for advice, for comfort, for companionship. In a flash of insight our relationship looked decidedly one-sided. I tucked that one away for another day and smiled in a way I hope was endearing instead.

"Do I need an excuse to see my girl?" he asked. A half smile played around his own lips.

"No, of course not. What are you thinking for lunch?" Miles shifted and I heard the crinkle of bags. For the first time I noticed the delicious smell wafting from them. Sometimes when I was with him I forgot all about food. He was a diet all by himself.

Maybe I should rent him out, I thought, then thanked God and all that was holy that I hadn't said it out loud. Damn, I was offensive when I didn't mean to be. I decided right then that maybe I should forgive my parents since it was easy to see how what they said could have been meant in the kindest way.

The crinkle of bags and more good-food smell transported me back to the present. "I brought you something. Leticia said that you had back-to-back appointments. So, I have Thai."

"Thai as in Thailand? Where did you get Thai food in Cleveland?" I'd grown up with lots of local old-world restaurants—Italian, Polish, Hungarian, German. But Asian

restaurants beyond Chinese in Cleveland were a new phe-
nomenon that I hadn't really indulged in. Without lots of
disposable income I hadn't had time to be adventurous. The
future was looking so bright, I'd need shades.

"Have you had it before?" The way Miles asked the question told me he knew the answer.

"Not really. Maybe across the hall. Greg went through
an Asian food phase, but that covered a whole continent and
I don't remember all the specifics. What is it like?"

He hefted the bag on my desk. Quickly, I cleared everything off the blotter. The squeak of Styrofoam made my
mouth water. Or it was the smell of spices. Either way, I
couldn't wait.

Two plates came from another bag along with napkins
and real silverware. I hadn't thought his formality extended
beyond his house where paper plates, paper napkins, and
plastic cups were verboten.

"How did you do this?"

"I have magical powers." He set out the usual cardboard
Asian food containers, though these were red instead of
white. Wielding chopsticks like a pro, he heaped noodles
onto my plate. I tucked a napkin into my shirt. The last thing
I needed was a spot on the new suit I'd acquired courtesy of
Filene's Basement.

It was a pale periwinkle blue and reminded me of Paola
Hudson. In it I had her confidence. Not necessarily the pastel office or the beautiful desk not marred by something so
pedestrian as a computer or paper and pen, but when I put
it on this morning, I just knew I'd moved to the next level.
The checks deposited in my escrow account confirmed it.

"It's good," I said twirling noodles, shrimp and vegetable
on my fork.

"Pad Thai is always a crowd pleaser." He hadn't gotten whatever was on the exotic menu. No doubt it's what he'd order if alone. We'd had more than one discussion about my plebeian palate. I don't think I'd ever be ready to give up potatoes, though.

"Is it better in Thailand?" I jabbed my chopsticks in his general direction.

"Did I mention I'd been to Thailand?" A crease formed between his brows as he tried to remember what he'd sanitized for my benefit.

"You don't have to censor yourself for me, Miles. You grew up rich. People with money travel." He winced. I pretended I hadn't seen it. "You've been everywhere. It was an educated guess."

"I haven't been everywhere. There are something like a hundred ninety-five countries."

"So you haven't been to the Middle East or Tibet," I said naming the most obscure places I thought few Americans had visited.

Miles lowered his eyes, then dropped his head to focus on the food he was picking up with his chopsticks. "Those I've been to. Not Iraq or Iran, but UAE, Kuwait, and Israel. Oh, and Lebanon. Beirut is great. Nothing like it was when it was on the nightly news when we were kids."

Sometimes Miles made my point without me having to speak. "Like I said, everywhere."

Done with denial he launched into his next salvo.

"You can travel too. We could go to Thailand. Maybe next month when the rain stops."

Because of course he knew the weather patterns of foreign lands. I don't know why that intimidated me, but it did.

"I've never taken time off." Panic squeezed my heart. A vacation was a foreign concept in more ways than one. If I didn't work, I didn't eat. Not to mention the courts' unforgiving schedule. Without a bevy of associates at my disposal, I had to take the dates mailed to me from the courts via postcard. Postponement for clients worried about regaining custody of their kids or whether they would go to jail seemed both capricious and cruel. "You have colleagues who can work in your absence," I said by way of excuse.

"Seems like your current practice is completely different. I'm sure you could set hearings before and after you leave." Miles' was the reasonable tone of someone who knew where work stopped and leisure began.

"That's true." Although everything in my tone said it wasn't. "What's up with the spontaneous travel?" Except for his stint in Toledo, I hadn't known him to go anywhere not since he got to Cleveland at least. Although who knows what had happened in our months apart.

"Life is short. Watching my parents go through a divorce only proves that. Now that you have the money, we can finally enjoy some of the fun things in life together."

Even though I vowed not to stuff down my feelings with food, I took a big bite of noodles. Every last word Miles had said was true, but somehow it didn't feel good. I swallowed and spoke anyway.

"Are you saying you couldn't travel with me until I got money?"

"No. Casey, you are way too sensitive about this money thing. If you didn't have it now, I'd have been happy to pay." The, "I guess," that followed was so low that I was half convinced I'd made it up.

Now I was feeling unworthy of free vacations from rich boyfriends. I changed the subject.

"Do you think I should represent Greg and Jason?"

"Why wouldn't you?"

"Seems weird to represent my friends. Have you ever done that? Represent someone you know?"

"I've never been in private practice. My client is the United States of America."

He represented three hundred million people. How could I forget he had the country's biggest client. I was operating on a much smaller scale. "Right. It's just that if things went south somehow I wouldn't want them blaming me."

"You said yourself that adoption is one area of the law that's practically bulletproof and definitely appellate proof after only a couple of months. It honestly has to be the shortest statute of limitations ever. I think you should do it. Maybe give them some kind of friends and family discount or something. But what better way to be a part of your friends' big moment. You're such a worrywart. What could go wrong?"

21

"Do you trust her?" Paul had been lying on his back. He lifted the duvet, took a glance under it, then turned toward me. I tried to guess what was in his eyes. He was unreadable. "I'm not sure I do. There's something weird about her." He waved fingers like a fake hypnotist.

"Who? Alile?" She was the only other person in the house besides Charlotte. And the baby, despite her lousy sleep schedule, wasn't out to get us. Well, except in the usual way I was starting to think all kids were out to steal their parents' sleep.

"I feel like she's watching us," he whispered. With him lowering his voice, I flicked my eyes right and left. We were alone in the room. Alile was a full floor above. With the plaster walls and wood floors, I hardly ever heard her. I doubt she could hear us either. Or I liked to believe that.

I turned and rested my own head on my hand, my elbow on the pillow. For what felt like the twentieth time, I endeavored to explain the decisions I'd made after he left. I could kind of see how it looked like I'd gone crazy. I liked to think it was me finally resolving to do what was important for me.

"I know I'm not the posh 'nanny' type who leaves the raising of her children to someone else. You were to stay home, work in the studio whilst caring for the baby. That's all shot to hell, as they say here.

"Merrill warned me what it would be like having an older child. More separation anxiety, more of a need for adjustment. So she suggested Alile. I know I'm not one who trusts easily, but Hudson fulfilled my dream. They haven't pointed me down the wrong road. So I took their advice and hired the girl. I know she's a little awkward. But she's young. One thing for sure is that she loves Charlotte. She cares for my daughter like she's her own. I couldn't ask for anything better."

"How will that shake out when she leaves in a year for her or for Charlotte if Alile loves her so much?"

"I don't know, Paul. Maybe I'll extend her contract. Merrill said I could do that. Please cut her a little slack. Don't you remember what it's like to be eighteen? You thought you knew everything until something new stared you in the face."

For Paul, I think his moment had been years later when he realized that his raw talent wasn't enough to set the modern art world on fire. For me it was in medical school, coming upon the fact that being a doctor was a glorified service job with customer service requirements and a review component like I was a clerk on the high street and not a full-blown doctor.

Turns out the NHS had a lot of angry patients even though they were nearly the only game in town. Youth was both powerful and humbling. It was the reason I was willing to give Alile some space to find her footing, grow into herself a little.

"It's a new job in a new country. She's got a lot coming at her at once. Foreign travel. Looking into schools. Getting used to a new job. I can't imagine what it's like for her, living in like she does. First, she thought she was going to be living with a single mum, to now working for a newly married couple. Even I kind of feel like I pulled a bit of a rug out from under."

"I'm not going to let you do that, Fi. Feel bad about us or the way we came together. Everything was meant to happen exactly as it was supposed to." This new and improved Paul was so self-assured. I feel like someone had replaced my perpetual Peter Pan with this bloke. I wasn't one hundred percent sure I liked the switch.

"Was it? I worry. I foisted Charlotte on you." It wasn't that I regretted the decision to adopt exactly. If I'd known Paul were truly coming back, I may have waited. We could have faced Dr. Ivanova and the whole infertility thing together. I couldn't help to wonder if we'd have done it a different way...as a couple. I closed my eyes blocking him out. I refused to let my mind go down that road.

"Not at all," Paul said breaking into my thoughts. "I've come back and I accept the situation as it is. Do I wish I were part of the decision-making process—yes, of course I do, but I understand that you'd thought I'd gone—for good. Plus I know you wouldn't be—"

"Can you accept Charlotte?" I got straight to the point. There was no need in beating around the bush. If I had to choose between the two, my choice was easy. Realizing how us versus him I sounded, I almost backtracked…almost.

"I know it's been a rough go," Paul offered. "She's a prickly one. Only seems to want to take a bottle or sippy cup from you and food from Alile. Plus it's like Alile has her under some kind of spell or something. She whispers to her in that weird tribal language and it's like she's the dog whisperer for babies. The little girl is obedient to a fault."

"Give it time, Paul. It all needs a little time to shake out. You've only been back for three weeks. Let's get your visa fixed, get her adoption final and then we'll have the time and brain capacity to move things forward—as a family." With time, I knew, he'd love her as much as I and even Alile did. Charlotte could have melted Margaret Thatcher's heart.

"Are you still going back to work next week?" he asked. I listened closely for the telltale whine that went with discussions of me and work. Either I couldn't hear every dagger sent my way, or it wasn't there any longer.

I sat up, letting the duvet fall away from my breasts. Paul gave me a lingering glance, but that was all. Relief fought with guilt. We'd finally exhausted ourselves last night.

"It's only six weeks at partial pay." I explained America's backward rules concerning maternity leave—the fact that there were none. I'd heard my hospital was generous. I don't think I agreed, but it was the job I'd vied for and accepted. "I can take more time, but it's with no pay. The fees for this adoption and this house hoovered up my savings. And now I've added a mouth to feed and another salary and expenses to pay. I really have to work. I'm not even through my full probation period not to mention the visa issue. I think we're all better all around if I get back to work."

"I could care for Charlotte. We can send the au pair back to wherever it is she's from. I mean the situation has truly changed. We shouldn't have to be on the hook for decisions that were made before things settled."

"Shhh. She's coming down to get Charlotte up. I don't want her to hear us talking about her like this."

I nearly jumped from my skin when I heard a hesitant knock at the door.

"Yes?"

"It's me. Alile. Can I talk to you, Fiona?"

Paul looked at me as if her intrusion was evidence of his earlier assertion about her weirdness. I patted his arm, my silent reassurance that Alile was on our side—that there were no sides.

"Hold on a second. Let us get presentable." I picked my shirt up from the floor and fiddled around until I could find fresh knickers. Paul did the same. Smoothing the duvet, I sat on the bed, cross-legged. There really was no position of authority for a boss in their own home that I could figure out on short notice. "Come in."

"I wanted to talk to you before Charlotte woke up," she said. No greeting. No preamble.

"She's sleeping better since you came. I was just telling Paul that you loved her like your own and that I couldn't be happier that you came here to help us out." I hoped the words were a start—a way to smooth a path of understanding between Alile and Paul.

"A matter of routine, I think. She'd always slept well as a baby."

The dead calm of that last sentence sent a shiver down my spine for a reason I couldn't put my finger on. I reached over and grabbed Paul's wrist. My fingers tightened around him like birds' talons in search of purchase.

"What? Did Merrill...Mrs. Barrera tell you that?"

"No. I haven't spoken with her. I remember. I was the only one who cared for her even though my aunt surely told the people at the orphanage that Yeni was abandoned."

At this point, I was starting to think that University Heights was some kind of alternate universe. Either that or I'd entered some kind of horror movie where the au pair went crazy. Either way I wanted out.

I must have been silent for some moments, because the next voice I heard, as if from a thousand miles away, was Paul's.

"Alile. I'm not exactly sure what you're talking about, but the little girl sleeping in the next room is Charlotte Rose. She's our baby. We're adopting her."

"But, Mr. Cooke, she's not your baby." A paper I'd only noticed in the periphery of my vision was being waved in front of me.

Paul took it. For a long moment there was not a single sound except for my heart beating a rapid pulse between my ears.

"I took a test at a center somewhere not too far from here. These are the results that came in the mail. They told me because I paid the extra four hundred dollars that I could use these in court."

"What does it say?" I turned to Paul who could only shake his head. He flicked the paper and thrust it at me. Far more familiar with test results than Paul, I gave it a quick read. In black and white it was there. It was a ninety-nine percent chance that Alile was Charlotte's mother. This wasn't a dream or a movie, this was a living, breathing nightmare.

"When did you have this done?"

"Mrs. Watson took me while you were away in the Niagara Falls." She pronounced it as if the indigenous name were four syllables instead of three.

"Why did you do this?" Why would some crazy girl come to my house and claim a link to my daughter. None of this made sense. There was no statistical way this made any sense. The probabilities were against this. Six and a half billion people in the world and mother and daughter both in my house from Africa. It couldn't happen, shouldn't happen, but it was happening right here in Ohio.

"Because she is my daughter. Because I left her at my aunt's house. She threatened to turn her over to the orphanage if I didn't pay. When I couldn't, she sold Yeni. I don't know how much you paid, but it's not enough. I want my daughter back."

22

As of this morning I was done stewing in my apartment. I'd searched my mind for clues that would somehow explain how at every turn I made the wrong choice. I'd sworn that this adoption thing would be my way out of chaos. There was no way this should have gone as wrong as it had.

Embarrassed, I hadn't said anything to Miles. Not that he'd noticed any change in me. He'd been caught up in a big political corruption case this summer—taking down a family that had been associated with the Brodys—to their detriment. I think he was gunning hard for them because he'd been hamstrung with Eamon.

My fault, natch.

As was his lack of success with the container case. Between work and his worrying himself to death over his parents' breakup, he didn't have the bandwidth for my problems, nor should he. I was happy to keep it all to myself. The label of "screw-up" girlfriend wasn't one I was eager to pile on top of all the others.

Resolved to get to the truth, I shook off thoughts of my domestic life, straightened my fitted black and white gabardine dress and strode past reception on the seventh floor of seventy-five Public Square. In seconds, after reading the variety of name plates engraved upon the doors, I came across Justin McPhee, Esquire. He'd paid extra for those four additional letters of the alphabet. Without knocking I twisted the handle and pushed the door open.

I'd called the receptionist ten minutes ago and knew he was in his office. He looked surprised to see me which is how I wanted it.

"What are you doing here? You don't have an appointment." Justin stood, his chair rolling back toward the window. I never knew why people didn't want to be able to see outside, though if my view was of the Justice Center, maybe I'd have my back to it as well.

"You need to level with me," I demanded walking right up to the desk and laying my hands on the wood.

"Casey. What time is it? I have to be in court at eleven."

The clock behind him said it was ten fifteen.

"Justin, I don't care about that. Well, I do, but I kind of don't. You're beating around the bush."

Justin looked at me like I had few marbles left.

"I'm beating around the bush?" His question was a near shout.

"You rush in my office when we haven't seen each other for weeks, and before that, who knows how many months. Now you're demanding an explanation."

I must have looked apoplectic because Justin finally stood from his chair, came from behind his own desk and took my arm. Like a dog, I followed him. Mostly because we were attached. When we got to the other side of the room, I sunk into his denim couch. It smelled like musky cologne and Justin. It was a strangely comforting smell.

I lifted my bag and extracted a white security envelope. Inside it was a single blue striped business check for one hundred dollars. Since I was stumbling over my words far too much to be effective, I merely handed the envelope over to Justin and waited.

He flipped it back and forth like it was a foreign object. "What's this?"

My shrug was resigned. "Open it."

Justin tore the paper. Read it. Looked at me like my few remaining marbles were all over the floor. He stated the obvious, "A check written to me."

"Retainer."

He dropped the little bit of commercial paper and steepled his fingers. "Well, this just got interesting. Casey Cort needs a lawyer."

After years of serving my clientele, I'd never wanted to need a lawyer. It seemed painful from the other end. "I don't quite think of my life as interesting so much as a walking disaster."

"As long as it's not a capital crime, I'll accept this. What do you need?"

"Advice. Information. A place to confess. I don't know." I didn't really know why I was here. He'd got out of his representation of Hudson and he looked unscathed. I wanted him to turn back the clock, but in place of that, I'd take an answer on how to fix the Charlotte Rose problem without court-ordered sanctions.

He got right to the point. "Hudson."

"How did you know?"

His headshake was slow and pronounced. "I tried to warn you, Casey."

"What are you talking about?" I'd been going over everything everyone had said in my head for the last few days. Except for my father's dire warnings, no one else had said a thing.

His eyes bored into mine. Something about his frank gaze made me shiver.

"Drinks," he said. "Amazing and sad drinks."

"We talked about growing up first generation and stealth nuns." I'd thought about that conversation quite a bit. Both because Justin was amazingly funny and because he sort of made me long for a relationship that was easier; where my boyfriend was a lot more like me.

"What happened? How many cases have you closed so far?" he peppered me.

"Seven. I have a final hearing on an eighth tomorrow." Up until a few days ago I'd been proud of my growing practice. Now everything about Hudson was making me think twice.

"Sounds like you're in the black." He reclined a bit in his chair like he was some wise man from whom I'd come to seek counsel. Because I was desperate, I played along.

"In the black. Very much. I'm about three cases from paying off my loans."

"But..."

"You have to know that I normally don't break confidences. I'm not one of those lawyers who'll spill all their clients' secrets for a drink."

"I know what a retainer is for."

"Fine. Sorry. This all makes me really uncomfortable. That's all. I'm used to handling all my problems, question, I don't know, issues myself."

"Maybe you should ask for help more often." The cryptic way Justin said that unsettled me the tiniest bit, but I pressed on anyway. Because I really did need to get to the bottom of things and I didn't want Miles to know how much I'd potentially fucked this up.

I took a deep breath and launched in. "There's something highly wrong with the Rose adoption."

Justin's equanimity was not what I was hoping for.

I continued, "The mom or well, soon-to-be adoptive mom, called me a few weeks ago. First, it was that she was getting married and wanted to amend her petition. That kind of thing I didn't really expect in an adoption case, but," I shrugged, "I'm used to it. You know how it goes in Juvenile—families are fluid. Anyway, it was the second call that freaked me out. The mom, Fiona, calls me, frantic. She's saying now that the au pair she hired has some paper that proves she's the genetic mother of the girl."

Justin sat forward in his chair, equanimity gone, instantly attentive. "Run that by me again."

"The au pair is the biological mother of the girl my client wants to adopt."

"What in the hell?"

I raised my hands in an "you're telling me" gesture.

"Merrill has some papers verifying the baby girl's background, but they don't match up with the au pair's story." The adoption would have been long done had those papers arrived with the girl. It had taken longer than Merrill had predicted to get the final adoption papers from Zimbabwe.

None of what she was saying in this case had matched up with the research that I'd done on how international adoptions were conducted. But I'd tamped down my suspicions assuming like everything else in life, money eased the way. That what Hudson offered was a certain baby concierge service as it were, for those well-heeled enough to afford it.

"And the au pair?" Justin asked.

I hung my head for a moment, then lifted and shook it simultaneously. "Another suspicious one. According to her, Alile is her name, she was in the UK illegally and got some lead from an NGO that she could apply for this job without papers."

"And now you're worried that if you go forward with this case, that you're on shaky ethical ground. Maybe shaky legal ground."

I nodded.

"I know how this played out," he said. "Let's see. You went to Hudson about the irregularities in the case, because the client was in a baby haze and was no help. Hudson wasn't your client, but you figure after all their years in the business, they could give you some explanation for the hinky paperwork."

"It's like you read my mind."

"When you get there it's all cappuccinos and herbal tea in their somehow soundproof Victorian mansion. After you spend ten minutes touring the place, sinking your feet into the deep pile, they gave you the snow job and a bunch more referrals. So maybe you forget about the paperwork because you're so busy with the new cases. Before you know it, you've raked in a ton of cash, more than you've ever earned in such a short time, don't want the gravy train to stop, but don't know what to do about this one case. Is that about right."

"Exactly right." It was eerie how right he was. "How did you know?"

"It's why I left Hudson."

"Why didn't you tell me any of this that night? If you had said, Casey, run like your hair is on fire. I wouldn't have signed on."

Justin's eyebrows slowly rose toward his hairline, which was kind of far.

"Well, okay, maybe I wouldn't have taken your word for it immediately, but I'd have done some more digging and if what you'd told me turned out to be true, I'd have politely declined. I'd have walked the other way. I'd have used any one of those euphemisms."

For a long moment we were both silent. Justin and I sat with that. I felt like I was vibrating with uncertainty.

Finally, he lifted his arms and thrust them outward. "Look around."

I followed the arrows his arms created. For the first time since I'd walked into his office, I had a closer look at everything. It was a big office. Like "successful lawyer" big with paneled walls and actual hardback case reporters lining the bookshelves. His desk was wood and about six feet wide. The chairs were newly upholstered in blue and gold. He had a couch. I was sitting on it. It was nice. His three-piece suit fit like it was made for him, not like he'd bought it off the rack from Men's Warehouse, a look Common Pleas lawyers favored.

"I thought maybe you'd inherited money when you sent those change of address cards." I remember the cream-colored notice on impossibly thick card stock. Since he'd never, to my knowledge, left Juvy, I assumed he'd inherited a pile from somewhere.

"First generation. Polish mom who escaped Communism and Irish dad from a family that had more mouths than they could feed. There's no money there."

I could see how I'd done it. Made him into something else so that I could justify his success in the face of my own failure.

Into the silence, he spoke again. "It was about forty cases before I got one or two hinky ones. A girl from China who was two. The mother had studied Mandarin and swore the girl was having nightmares about being stolen from her family. Another from Bulgaria with a lot of paper problems. The adoption certificate from the country said one thing. The birth certificate, another. Bulgaria wasn't China, so I did a little research and according to my contact there, the papers were likely forged.

"Poor country, a little money goes a long way. Probably only took a couple thousand to get the papers and grease the necessary wheels. The baby was probably from Romania or Ukraine would be my guess, but those adoptions, especially the Romanian ones are more well-known here. So they picked a random third country, got some papers, and had the baby brought over."

"Are any of the adoptions at Hudson legit?" The thought of opening all those files, going to probate court hat in hand wasn't something I relished.

"Probably eighty-five to ninety percent."

I tried not to sigh my relief out loud. "And the rest?"

"Sneak in. It's like taxes. Use a whole bunch of legitimate deductions to cover over the one you're trying to slip past the IRS. Probably works ninety-nine percent of the time in that case."

"You still haven't answered my question."

"What's that?"

"Why didn't you tell me any of this ahead of time?" I gave him a half smile. "Remember I have a hundred euphemisms for turning Hudson down."

"Because I didn't think you really wanted to turn Hudson down. You came to me looking for a way to take those cases. Everything I've read about you in the years since I met you says to me that you walk a fine line."

"What are you talking about?" I asked. His implication got my back up. "Are you saying that you think I'm bent or crooked?"

"The first case I heard about with you involves Judge Grant. She flees the jurisdiction and you claimed in the paper that you didn't know anything about it."

"I didn't." My teeth were clenched when I'd bit off that last bit.

He lifted his fingers like he was ticking off enhancements to a criminal sentence.

"Then you're mixed up with the Brodys. If you look up the word corruption in the dictionary, Liam's picture would be there."

Despite my promise to myself that I wouldn't do it, I found myself explaining away my relationship.

"Tom Brody was my boyfriend a bajillion years back. I got out when it was clear that there was a cover-up of Eamon's activities on the bench."

"Lastly, the news on the street was that you were somehow representing the guy behind the biggest sex trafficking ring to ever be busted in the Midwest. And that guy was never found or put on trial."

I didn't say anything about that. What could I say?

"It's not how it looks."

"I figured maybe Hudson was right up your alley."

"Did you report either of those two cases you mentioned to anyone? Whomever licenses adoption agencies. The probate court. Ohio BCI or even the FBI?"

"On a hunch from one mom who studied Chinese a few weekends before adopting a baby. From a friend who thought the Bulgarian papers weren't legit? I'd have been laughed out of court. I decided after talking with Paola that it was better if we mutually agreed to go our separate ways."

I wanted to ask, but didn't, if he had closed those cases— holding his nose the entire time or if there was yet another attorney involved in the deception.

"What are you doing for money now?" I asked instead.

"I paid off my loans. But, I didn't move to a nicer apartment. I didn't get a newer car. I still share a secretary with five other guys. I'm diving into some plaintiff's work right now. Bigger payoff even with some upfront investment of the rest of the money. It's going there for my future."

When I got a cramp in my right hand I looked down to see it was balled in a fist. As my fingers unfurled my anger came alive as well.

"I can't believe you thought I was the kind of person to play fast and loose with ethics. I'm the total opposite of that person. It's me being a rule follower that put me here right now." I was indignant. "I'll tell you that story over drinks some other day. I need to figure out what I'm going to do now."

"You have to get out of the Rose case at least. Whether you continue with Hudson is up to you." I guess he didn't believe me about the nature of my ethics. I let the slight roll off.

"Do I have an obligation to tell Ronaldo Pinheiro?"

"My classmate? What's he got to do with this?" he asked as if everyone but me were on the moral high ground.

"He's the associate working on the Hudson matter. I think he's even one of the client contacts. My best friend works at Dalton Lacey. Lulu Mueller."

"I hear she's well on the wrong side of right and wrong as well." Justin sat back again like a judge on the bench who'd heard all that he needed to here to condemn the accused.

I bowed my head. It didn't take rocket science to figure out what he was talking about. At least that's what I hoped he was talking about. Moral failings somehow seemed better than legal or ethical ones. That was somehow my exclusive domain.

"What have you heard?" It was kind of a pleasure to take the heat off me for a second.

"Pinhiero says she's seeing a married partner."

I shrugged. "Not my business. I got my own shit to deal with—apparently."

"Do you seriously need more advice?"

"I know what I have to do. It's not necessarily what I want to do."

"Why not?"

I spoke the absolute truth because it was something a person like Justin would understand, even if Miles wouldn't.

"Having money looked like it was going to be amazing. Don't you think I had visions of a house. My boyfriend was planning a vacation for the first time ever."

"Why can't you go on vacation any other time?"

"He's rich and I'm not and before I got these cases, he never mentioned it."

"That sounds like a boyfriend problem not a money problem." Bull's-eye. His comments hit like a dagger, but I stuffed it down somewhere deep where I'd deal with it later—much later.

"No more Hudson," I said grudgingly. "I'll call Paola. And as for Charlotte Rose...what?"

"Do what you'd do in any other case where there were no nefarious doings."

"Did you just use the word nefarious?" I had to smile at that. I wish I'd talked to him anytime in the last six years. He'd have been fun to hang out with. In this context, it was just amazing and sad.

"I did."

"So I'm going to have to play let's make a deal?" I'd done it before even if I hated the Solomonesque nature of the brokering.

Justin nodded Monty Hall style. "Have the two mothers pick a door."

23

I couldn't believe how much at peace I was after finding out Yeni was mine. No more worry about Umi or Onani. The way I saw it, I'd never have to go back to Malawi. I was free of everything bad that had ever happened to me. No one here would ever believe I was trash or was here to be their servant.

"I want to be clear, Alile; I can't represent you."

That voice with its strong accent brought me back to the room. This morning, I'd been told to drop Yeni off with Mrs. Watson, who'd been so kind as to take her even though I couldn't say when I'd return.

Then Fiona had stayed home from work and driven the three of us to this lawyer's office in the downtown of Cleveland. Fiona and Paul hadn't said exactly where we were going. If I'd known, I had have worn my best dress rather than the thin cotton one I had on right now.

"Represent me?" I asked. The woman, Casey Cort was her name. She looked kind. Her eyes had that look that told me she wasn't cruel or out to exploit me or out for herself. She held herself like a woman who was fair even when it wasn't to her benefit. So I sat forward, expectantly awaiting her explanation.

Paul hovered behind us, Fiona having taken the only other seat that was on this side of the lawyer's desk.

"Mr. Cooke? Paul. Let me have Letty bring you a chair from reception."

"I'm fine," he said pushing aside her offer then shifting from foot to foot, noisy even on this rug.

She ignored him and pressed a button on her phone. In a few seconds, the door opened and a green chair appeared in front of a woman with dark hair and eyes in complete contrast to the lawyer and Fiona. America surprised me so much with all sorts of different-looking people living and working together. Africa had whites, of course, and Indians and Chinese, but mostly everyone kept to themselves.

I could breathe a little easier when Paul took the chair to the other side of Fiona closest to the window.

"Anyway, Alile, as I was saying, I can't represent you if you choose to pursue custody or seek to declare parental rights to your daughter. Please understand you are well within your rights to do that. She's your daughter. Obviously obtained under some kind of false pretenses. Under Ohio law, there's no reason she couldn't live with you, and Fiona and Paul here would have no rights to see her again."

I kept my face a mask, like I had when my uncle came to visit me in the night. But underneath that mask was stark disappointment. I may not have been as old as Paul and

Fiona or even as old as the lawyer, but I knew what she said was only the beginning. Everything that came after it would be bad for me.

"I understand."

"That's the good news for you, I guess. The bad news is that you're under eighteen years old."

I nodded wishing that I'd never shared my true age with anyone. That I'd kept that secret as close to my heart as I'd kept all the others about what I'd had to do to get from my village all the way to London. But when the DNA place had asked for ID, I'd handed over my Malawian passport without a second thought. They'd carefully copied my real age onto a new form asking for a test. Fiona and Paul had confronted me about it later when there was nothing to be done about sending me back.

"What does that mean for me?"

"That if you file something in court asking for you and your daughter to live alone, that while the court may be sympathetic, they'd probably place you both in foster care."

"Foster care?" Those were the same words Mrs. Watson had used. Her mouth had pulled together in a tight line though. Somehow I knew by Casey's tone as well that it would not be good for me or Yeni.

"It's where children under eighteen live with families other than their parents or relatives because they are dependent—unable to care for themselves."

"And where would Yeni go?"

"To another foster family. Or possibly to live with Paul and Fiona as they've already had a home study. I could see a judge moving you out so you can go to school and live a 'normal' teenage life while your daughter would be cared for by someone else."

"I do not want that," I said. I swallowed back my tears. It could not be that I had done all this—sold my body, traveled nearly all the way around the world and then actually found my daughter—only to be separated from her once again.

"I couldn't imagine you would. I've worked with kids and parents with kids in foster care for the last eight years and I assure you it's not pretty. The system is rife with abuse and neglect of children in the county's care."

"Why can't we just adopt?" Paul asked, his voice tight with frustration.

"Paul, I've gone over this with Fiona. You don't have valid papers. While the documents you received from Africa look authentic, a challenge from Alile would show their falsehood. And even if the judge thought Allie had given the child up legally, or at least voluntarily, the DNA test calls all of that into question. And it's not a question I can see any judge in Cuyahoga County eager to work out."

"What do you think a judge would do?" Fiona asked.

I hadn't imagined her to be any kind of woman who chewed pencils or bit her nails, but she turned out to be a hair fiddler. In the last couple of weeks, I'd seen her twist and untwist the same forelock about a thousand times.

"It's a complete tossup. It isn't like there's a ton of precedent—cases like yours—for them to go on. Their legal remedies would be to put mother and child in foster care together if there's a family that would take both. Put them in foster care apart. Or even possibly refer both of them to Homeland Security for immediate detention and deportation."

"If you still represent me," Fiona pressed, her voice sharp, "then why are all three of us here?"

"You're all here because courts can agree with one thing. Cases resolved by the parties are their preference. Keeps the judge from having to make a decision. Despite their title, they don't much like making decisions. Also if the three of you agree on something you'll have certainty. You won't leave your fate, or more importantly Kantayeni slash Charlotte's fate, up to one person who may not have had a good night's sleep or breakfast."

For the first time, I felt some hope. In a way, I was equal to Fiona and Paul. We all wanted Yeni and we all stood to lose her unless we could come to some kind of agreement.

I glanced at Paul who looked more upset by the second, then at Fiona who was as teary-eyed as she'd been since I'd taken my papers to their bedroom. Then I looked at the lawyer who didn't look happy, but looked like she was ready to do what she could to fix this.

"You have an answer, miss?" I asked.

"Yes and no." She lifted her hands in a bit of a shrug.

"Why are we here?" Fiona moaned. Because you can't keep my baby, I wanted to say, but I did not.

"I have a number of ideas, which I'll outline for you in a second. But no matter what I come up with, I don't have to live with it. So I'm going to give you a few weeks to consider if one of these ideas is something the three of you could live with. Then I'll take it to the court and get it memorialized."

The lawyer looked at us and we all nodded.

"Good. One thought is that you all go to the United Kingdom. I talked to a solicitor there and she says Fiona and Paul, you could get a Certificate of Sponsorship for Alile. You'd employ her as you are now and she could live in or out, but she'd be able to work for you and see her daughter as often as you could all agree on."

My heart slowed as the lawyer talked. She was saying things that wouldn't be perfect, but wouldn't cut me out of my daughter's life completely. She didn't have me back in Malawi under my uncle's thumb. Almost anything had to be better than that.

I looked at Paul and Fiona, sad that there was no magic solution to be had. We were not much better off than we'd been when we'd come in the door. I had Yeni and I didn't have her, all at the same time.

24

Even though I knew it was coming, I jumped at the knock on the door. I uncurled my legs from the couch and walked to the door. The Rose adoption still plaguing me, I'd taken a long bath with salts and bubbles and probably enough chemicals and carcinogens to cause cancer. But I smelled good and the two glasses of wine had gone a long way to calm me down.

It had been one week since I'd seen Alile, Fiona, and Paul in my office. I was thrilled that I didn't have to be in a house with them. Seemed like a hellish landscape to navigate for all of them. I just wanted it done and off my caseload. The guilt of the whole mess was weighing me down.

Before I pulled open the door, I hesitated a long moment. I was expecting Miles, but quickly realized it could have been Greg and Jason instead. Especially as Miles would have to have been buzzed in if he hadn't walked in behind someone.

I wasn't nearly ready to see my neighbors. Every day they made a point of telling me about what plans they'd made for a kid as well as giving me hugs and pats on the back for the part I was playing in making their family complete.

I knew that I had to share my suspicions about Hudson with them. There was a huge likelihood that everything would be okay. They'd get a baby that was available to adopt and everyone would have a happy ending. For that slim chance something could go wrong, I didn't want to be responsible even if by omission. I took a deep breath heavily fortified by cheap wine and reminded myself to pester the super for a peephole.

I puffed out my breath when Miles was inside the door. He had at least three bags with him.

"Did you just come from the airport?"

"I didn't want to waste any more of my Labor Day weekend going to Coventry then coming back. Okay if I stay over and change for work here?"

Ushering him in, I took one of the bags and swiftly pushed the door closed behind him. I still wasn't interested in seeing my neighbors just yet.

Doing the silent dance I imagine any wife did when her husband came home, I took his duffle and walked it to the bedroom. While he undressed, I turned on the shower, filling my little bathroom with steam. While he was in I threw vodka, Kailua, Bailey's, cream, and ice into my new blender. I'd sent a bunch of money to Sallie Mae, but I'd splurged on a couple of items. One was a blender. I'd made quite a few margaritas and mudslides like the one I was about to make.

The other was a sofa from Arhaus. I'd always loved walking through the expensive furniture store. A month ago for the first time, I'd actually gone in there with the express intention of making a purchase. A couple thousand dollars of my hard-earned money went to them and last week a truck with two burly drivers had carried my new curved-back sofa and matching table because of course I realized while a near-antique steamer trunk was cute for a student, it didn't fit how I'd felt when I'd bought it—like a successful lawyer on her way up.

I finished moving the drinks to tall glasses and in honor of my slimmer hips, skipped the whipped cream. I took them to the metal-topped table in the living room, and sat and sipped.

"New furniture. Wow! It came. I thought you'd have a futon and trunk in here forever."

"Girl's gotta grow up some time," I said airily, though I was feeling anything but. I hadn't quite told Miles about the disaster I'd made of Hudson. I wasn't quite ready for him to go down the "sympathy for walking-disaster-Casey road."

"Speaking of growing up, I wanted to talk to you about something."

"Oh, gosh. How was it with your parents?"

"That's not—"

"What did they say about your impromptu visit?"

Miles sighed. "My mother's hired a lawyer. Served my dad with papers last week. She's found a rental in the building she wants to buy in. I...I helped her move in a bit."

"That must have been hard."

"It's just that she moved so fast. One minute she was talking about it, the next she was moving out."

"I read somewhere—probably in a magazine at the dentist or something—that by the time a woman files for divorce, she's been thinking about it for at least a year." I pushed the mudslide toward him. Sugar and alcohol could probably make almost everyone feel better.

He took a sip. "You went heavy on the vodka."

"Thought you might need it."

Miles took another sip and pushed it away. "I don't want to talk about my parents."

"I'm sorry. I didn't mean to stick my nose where it didn't belong."

"It's not that it doesn't belong...It's that...this is more awkward than I thought. Give me a minute."

Miles stood and disappeared from the room. I sipped at the drink while wiping condensation from the glass. I didn't worry about the table as I mentally patted myself on the back for going with the hammered zinc. I needed something indestructible and metal fit the bill.

Of course the minute I had that thought, Simba wandered in and did a big stretch on the floor. In a moment, he was glancing at me, and when I pretended to look away, his front claws sunk into the couch. Carefully, I extracted them, then planned a trip to the library or at least on the internet. I had to figure out how to keep the sofa from looking like a cat post. Or maybe I'd drag Miles to the pet store with me to buy a cat post, once we'd both sobered up, of course.

Simba scooted once Miles came back in. For the first time today, I took my boyfriend in. He'd changed from his weekend Ivy League sweats combo into well-worn black jeans and a maroon top. He was the only man who I know who could carry off sandals. Today's were soft-looking leather flats.

I was almost jealous at his effortless style. I didn't know if it was something about me or my body or maybe too many years in Catholic school, but getting dressed was an everyday struggle that never got much easier.

I lifted my legs ready to surrender at least part of the new couch, but Miles sat close and draped my thighs and calves back over his.

"What's up?"

"Remember how we talked about traveling together?"

"Sure. Thailand was on the table last I checked."

"How about either Bangkok or Gibraltar?"

"As in the rock of? Where is that? Europe or North Africa?"

"Off the coast of Spain. These two locations have something in common, though."

I looked at the melting drinks, out the window through the trees, watching them sway as a bus rolled down North Moreland. This was a quiz I was unprepared to take. "I give up."

Miles pulled it out then, a little velvet box and the world narrowed to a very thin shaft of light and reality. It was happening again. I'd wanted the first proposal, but it had come seven years too late. I wanted this one too, I'd thought until just this moment when nerves overtook me.

"Casey," he started as he turned toward me. My feet plunked noisily to the floor. "I've been a fool these past couple of years. I love you and want to spend the rest of my days getting to know every single thing about you. Will you elope with me?"

"Elope?" I asked as the velvet box hinge creaked and he extracted a beautiful ring with diamonds in between multicolored stones.

Miles held the ring up between us. "The platinum is a symbol of true love, purity, rarity, and strength. The pink is rose quartz and is for trust, amethyst is for protection, and aquamarine for communication. And of course diamonds are forever. Will you wear this ring. Will you marry me?"

I wanted to say yes. I wanted to want to say yes. "I gave up proposals for Lent," is what I said instead.

Miles tilted his head as if he didn't get the joke. Even I wasn't sure I got the joke.

"I...uh...if you'd proposed before Easter. That's what I was going to say."

"So I proposed on the wrong holiday?"

"Yes...no...I knew what I was going to say if you proposed at Easter dinner with my parents. I had that all worked out in my head. Now, I don't have any idea what to say..."

"The appropriate answer is yes if you want us to have a future together."

As well as I could from the side, I threw my arms around his neck and kissed him on the cheek. Fruity cologne greeted me. For a flash I thought about Justin McPhee's musky scent and how much I'd liked that. I untangled myself from Miles, and hit the side of my head V-8 style.

"Then yes, of course, I'll marry you. But what were you talking about with Gibraltar or Thailand?"

I watched as Miles slipped the ring on the third finger of my left hand. The heaviness Hudson and the Rose case had laid on me lifted. Buoyancy filled my chest. I leaned forward and this time kissed him square on the mouth.

That kiss was like coming home. It reminded me of all that Miles and I had together. Before we got carried away, I pulled back. One time more I admired the ring and wondered what my mother would think or even what Lulu would think.

"The situation with my parents is a mess. The same goes for Lulu. That's all temporary, but I thought maybe we'd elope and take that trip we've been talking about. We can do a reception later with friends and family. But this. This could be just about us."

Lulu would dump Professor Sinclair sooner or later. My parents would come around. His parents would reach some kind of equilibrium. Did I want to wait to start my life until all that happened? The resounding answer was no.

"I love that idea. When would we do it?" I started mentally flipping through the strong box in my bedroom closet. The one with my birth certificate.

"The middle of October? We don't have anything going on in the office that Rachel or Chas can't handle."

"I don't have a passport." Miles' head snapped up as I threw a wrench into his plans.

"Really?"

"I didn't take the bar trip I'd planned." God knows I didn't want to go down the Brody road with him again. How I'd planned to go to Ireland and Germany on our bar trip before we moved in together. But Tom had dumped me before I'd ever gotten down to the post office.

"I'll get the tickets. Then we'll pop on over to one of those overnight passport services."

"Overnight? That's amazing."

"There's always a service for those who wait."

"So which? Gibraltar or Thailand?"

"I vote for Gibraltar with a honeymoon in Spain. You'll love Spain. The seafood is amazing. We can dine on wine and tapas. They eat late and keep it amazing. I can't wait to show you around."

Spain with Justin McPhee would have been both amazing and sad. I was glad that with Miles it would just be amazing. "I think we should celebrate," I announced.

"On a Monday?"

"I wasn't talking about going out…" Letting that lie right there, I sashayed as best I could given my non-hip-swinging European background. I was going to be Mrs. Miles Siegel. Everything else would have to work itself out.

25

The voice mails from Casey made it feel like there was a dragon breathing down my neck. I had fantasies of never calling her back. I'd been dodging calls from Hudson too. I just knew that their solution would be to take Charlotte back. Substitute in some other baby like a high street shop when you made a return. I wasn't sure how much Paola or Merrill knew about Alile and Charlotte. I was mad as hell at them, but couldn't see the benefit of confrontation.

I'd even dreamt of calling the local news. But all I could see is all three of us sitting on a couch, crying on Oprah or the like, while state and federal officials suited up with guns, pulled Charlotte from my arms and repatriated her to Malawi.

I'd seen those Elian Gonzalez pictures. I didn't want that to happen to us. I opened my eyes and turned. Paul was awake. Returned my stare. His eyes were as grim as I imagined mine were.

"We could take her, you know," I whispered. "Just fly to England and disappear somewhere in the midlands or even the Scottish highlands. We'd have our little family and be done with all of this."

"Fiona, Charlotte doesn't even have a passport. I'm not sure how Hudson got her into the country, but you have no way of getting her out. What are you going to do, run downtown and find some kind of shady document forgers who are going to give you a passport? You don't even have a birth certificate from the United States or even England for that matter."

"I know. Paul. I know. It was magical thinking on my part. I just want things to go back the way they were when I knew that Charlotte was mine. That she was going to be mine forever."

"I want to go back to the day before I got the clap and passed it on to you. If we'd had our own daughter, our own biological girl, then none of this would have happened. Responsibility for this rests squarely on my shoulders. I don't know what I can ever do to make it up to you. Ever, Fiona."

"Let's not do this. No 'What if?' No 'What could have been?' Or the blame game. The question is what do we do now?"

"What do you think the girl wants?"

"The same thing I want, Paul. My baby."

"Do you think the best thing would be to give up Charlotte—"

"Paul, she's my daughter—"

"Hear me out, Fiona. I know you love Charlotte. I know that you bonded with her the instant that nurse or midwife or whatever placed her in your arms. But it's been only a few months. We can go back to England. Maybe even Scotland. I've done some research. There are tons of children and even babies up for adoption all throughout England. And if we do it through the state, at least we know it's on the up-and-up. We can begin again. I'm here now for you one hundred percent. You won't have to go it alone this time."

"I'm not ready to make that decision. I need more time."

"There is no more time, Fiona. Our time ran out weeks ago. You heard what the lawyer said. You know that this situation can't go on as it is. We can't take her anywhere. Register her in school. Even the health insurance company is sending notices demanding a social security number. We have none of these things that normal parents have."

"You don't love Charlotte."

"I do love her, Fi."

"Then how can you suggest giving her up?"

"I love her, Fi. Not like you. I'll admit that. I walked into a situation that wasn't right from the beginning. Where I would be bonding with her, I've been accosted by her biological mum and a noose slowly tightening around our necks. Don't tell me you don't feel the stress too. You've come back from work looking like you've been in Her Majesty's coal mines instead of in the surgical theater. You haven't even had your period since you've gotten back."

"I haven't had my period?" The minute I asked the question, I knew something was different. Everything about me was different. I'd thought it was stress. But there was another equally valid possibility.

"Not once. Fiona."

In a flash I ran from the bedroom and into our bathroom down the hall. I threw open the medicine chest and tossed out everything until I could find what I was looking for.

There in the back were two or three of the tests I'd pilfered from the hospital's supply.

"What are you doing, Fi?" Paul had come down the hall and was standing at the jamb. "Are you going to be sick?"

"Close the door," I hissed.

He looked down the hall and hustled into the room, firmly shutting the wood door behind him.

"What is that thing? Are you doing some kind of pH test of the water?"

I almost laughed at the craziness of that. Is that how he saw modern mums these days, running around testing water safety from the bathroom tap? Suddenly deflated, I wanted to be that mum. The one for whom bio versus conventional or peeled fruit versus whole were the biggest decisions of my day.

"It's a pregnancy test."

"I thought you couldn't. I thought I'd ruined…"

"I don't know anything," I insisted, though in my heart the truth was already there. "Can you back up so I can do this."

Paul threw up his hands, then promptly shoved them in his robe's pockets, pacing back and forth over the small space on the tile floor. I squatted awkwardly and placed the stick in my urine stream. I put it on the side of the sink, flushed, then waited.

First the control line came up bright blue. Then, slowly faintly the other line darkened, turning as blue and bright as the first. I wanted to faint, but I'd learned better from gross anatomy that hitting a hard floor from nearly six feet wasn't a good idea. Instead, I closed the toilet lid and used it as a brace as I slid to the floor.

"I'm in the pudding club."

"Pregnant? How can that be?"

"You know how it works. We haven't used any birth control in years."

"Why now? You told me that you couldn't and that's why Charlotte."

"There are lots of anecdotes about women getting pregnant after they adopt." It was supposed to be something about their bodies relaxing, I'd read somewhere. Probably utter nonscientific crap, but maybe true this time. "Maybe having a baby made my body realize it wasn't hostile to new life." It was the kind of hippy explanation that should make him happy.

Paul squinted at me. "Are you going to keep the baby?"

"How can you even ask that?"

"Are you going to tell—"

Either we hadn't heard the knock or Alile had abandoned all rules of decorum. With Charlotte on her hip, she pushed open the door and looked between the two of us. We probably looked as guilty as sin.

"Yeni—"

As if drawn by world's strongest magnet, her eyes snapped to the thin stick lying on the sink. I had no idea Alile's experience, but any woman my age, at least, knew exactly what that tiny strip represented.

Our eyes met and we shared a moment of deep understanding. We had a single thing in common that forged a bond where no other would flourish. We were mothers. Soon I'd join her in the group of women who'd carried babies and pushed them out of their own bodies.

"You said you couldn't have a baby. That's why you needed my Yeni. Now, you'll have a baby of your own coming. We each get one baby. That seems fair."

She murmured something to the baby in their own language and disappeared from the bathroom.

I watched the girl, too young really for a baby, walk away and I knew then that I'd waited too long. Casey Cort was right. We needed to come to a decision. The time was now.

"Go," I said to Paul. "Get dressed. Make some kind of breakfast. I'll be down in a bit."

I took the longest shower I'd ever taken. Working through everything in my head. Fifteen minutes later dressed in jeans and a simple navy flowered wrap top and Jerusalem Sandals, clothes that I thought made me much more approachable than scrubs, I came downstairs.

We ate Paul's muesli and yogurt in silence. Even Charlotte who liked to make nonsense sounds and flap her arms was relatively quiet for once.

I put down my spoon and looked directly at the girl who'd brought me both my greatest joy and greatest sadness.

"What are we going to do about this, Alile?"

She put down her own spoon. She hadn't eaten much of Paul's breakfast. She seemed to like Mrs. Watson's food much better. She turned her intelligent brown eyes on me. They held sadness over a short life filled with tragedy. Despite that, I soldiered on.

"What we're doing can't work long term. I need...we all need some kind of certainty. I need to know what's going to happen going forward for me, for Paul, and even for the baby to come."

"When I was thirteen years old, I lost my own mother. If I could change anything about my life, it would be that I could save her. I didn't know that she'd protected me from the world until she wasn't there anymore to do it."

"I'm sorry about your mum. I never really got along with mine."

"Maybe you want my Yeni to fix your problems. I want her because she's the only link I have to my family and my homeland."

"What happened to your father. Did he leave?"

"Leave? He gave my mother HIV, then blamed her for it. So when she died, he married a new woman. Moved to Lilongwe. But his new wife, she didn't want me to come with them. They took my brothers, but not me. So my father offered me to my aunt and uncle. I was to cook for them, clean for them, and take care of their little ones."

"What about school?"

"No one thought I was smart enough for school. No matter. At least I had a roof over my head."

"And Charlotte?"

"My mother used to forbid me from going to my uncle's house alone. And when he married aunt Umi, she still forbade it. We could all visit as a family, but I was never to go by myself. I thought she didn't like Daddy's brother because he was loud or sometimes drank too much or spent his money foolishly. That wasn't it. Not long after I moved in, I became pregnant."

I'd heard these stories before. Who hadn't? Every other documentary talked about babies being raped as a way to cure men from AIDS in remote African villages. The whole thing was a huge tragedy that I could do little about except save Charlotte from the same fate.

"You were so young."

"Not too young for my uncle. If my mother had lived, this never would have happened. My father shunned me. His wife called me a...bad word for women who sell their bodies for money. My aunt spread the story that I was a prostitute. Everyone believed her. Just as the orphanage probably believed her when she turned over my baby."

"I'm so sorry all this happened to you."

"I know that you people in England don't think much of how we live, our customs, that we're all barbaric."

"I don't think that, Alile. I've never thought that. I didn't adopt Charlotte to save her. I wanted to adopt a baby because I had so much love to give. I love you like that as well." And I did. Pity and anger had given way to grudging respect, then a kind of love for this girl. My heart hurt with what she'd gone through. If I could make it all better I would.

"I will not be able to rest if I can't protect Yeni from the things I should have been protected from. I thought I could go to your country, live there, go to school, and raise my daughter to be a proper girl with education. But no one in England believed I deserved to be there. Either way, my daughter deserves better."

"I can give her that life. I'm a doctor. Paul is an artist. He can stay home during the day. Take her to museums. Teach her about the arts. She can go to the best schools, go to college. Get that education that you want for her."

"Will you want her once you have a daughter of your blood. One with white skin like you. Who you know from birth?"

My experience with my own mum caused me to doubt myself for a long second. She had loved her kids from her second husband more than she'd ever loved me. I wouldn't do that to Charlotte. There had to be enough love for both her and the new one to come.

Thank goodness Paul jumped into the silence that was spreading through the room like a fast-growing cancer. "We'll love him or her just the same as Charlotte. Alile, I can guarantee you that. I'm from a big family and there's always more than enough love to go around," he said.

"They can be raised together," I echoed Paul. "They can be sisters. Or even sister and brother. Kids do better when they have someone to play with. A sibling they can share secrets with. I promise you, we will treat your daughter like our own. Please don't oppose the adoption. That's all I'm asking."

"You're asking me to give you my daughter."

"It's the best thing you could do for her."

"What about what's best for me?"

That question kicked me in the gut. Alile was right. I was asking her to make the ultimate sacrifice because I couldn't.

26

I sat in my apartment, gazing at my engagement ring—alone.

I wanted to call Lulu, but we'd hardly spoken in the last few weeks. The final straw had come when she'd gone away with Sinclair for the weekend.

She'd said she was going on the weekend trip to Montreal to make him choose once and for all. But they'd had French Canadian food. Stayed in a boutique hotel, and walked hand in hand along the water and still he hadn't chosen her.

Instead he'd smeared a lot of bullshit about needing time. And my best friend had lapped it up like she'd lost every brain cell she'd ever had. I'd always thought she was smarter than me. Not more intelligent, but smart as in good schools, good parents, good head on her shoulders. It seemed, though, all I'd ever thought had been wrong somehow.

I wanted her take on Miles and our future marriage. Her advice regarding Tom a few years back had been priceless. Now, though, the price of her counsel was too high. I couldn't condone her relationship with our former professor. Not because he'd hurt me, or maybe had never really cared about me. But because he didn't care for her.

And she didn't care enough about herself to not be with a man who could give to her fully, not divide his time and attention between a fully healthy and functional wife, a daughter in college, then my friend as a third or maybe even fourth after his dog or cat or something.

As if sticking up for cat kind, Simba meowed woefully and I picked her up. Snuggling my head into her fur was a kind of balm that soothed the soul. She didn't care if I were fat or thin, single or married, ethical or not. The cat was happy to be fed, be pet and sink an occasional claw into the new furniture.

Moving her off me, I picked up the phone wedged in the new couch cushions and started pressing in my first phone number, the seven digits so familiar to me. When I got to the last "5" I hit end instead of send. Mothers were a tricky bit of business. A phone call would never do. I tossed the phone back to where it had been and mentally reverted to my earlier plans.

It was best if I waited to talk to my mother and father until I could see them in person. Bring Miles around with me. Maybe spend the day with them helping them learn how much they would love him without his own mother hovering about looking for any opportunity to jump on any comment that could be misconstrued.

With Miles working weekends lately, I'd kicked the can down the road. I almost stood and gripped the knob, ready to talk to Greg and Jason. It was another conversation I'd put off. But before I could make that mistake, I stepped back.

I nearly fell to the carpet in fright when a loud knock came at the door as if I'd manifested a visitor straight from my thoughts.

Before I could think better of it, I turned the knob and pulled at the door. I'd never been a chain girl, and goodness knows I often didn't remember to lock.

There was Jason smelling of yeast and sugar.

"Yes," left my mouth before an invitation had been issued.

Jason threw his head back in laughter. "Greg had decided that he's going to tame yeast before the baby...or little kid comes. Cinnamon buns, vanilla glaze, and cappuccino await."

Pulling my door closed behind me I followed my nose directly across the hall in to my neighbors' warm and cozy space. As it always did, the beautifully stained oak, excellent decor, and smell of great food beckoned.

And as I always did I promised myself to talk to my landlord about pulling up the horrible industrial carpet I struggled to keep free of cat hair, and ditch the so-called art posters that screamed college dorm. Those changes wouldn't cost nearly as much as the Arhaus furniture I'd already bought. I could do that even if...no when...when I gave up the Hudson cases.

I wandered into the mirror image of my own apartment through the dining room to the kitchen where Greg was making magic happen.

He thrust a small glass bowl toward me. "Taste."

I obliged and was not disappointed. Creamy vanilla sweetness coated my tongue.

"What's in this? It's like a thousand times better than what you get at the mall.

"Shut your mouth," Greg said. "What they sell at the mall isn't food. That's diabetes in a cardboard box. This is the real deal."

Greg always said that when I reacted to his Asian food, or Mexican fare. And now it was baking. Sometimes I imagined, would never say out loud ever, but imagined, that if he and my mother teamed up, we'd all fall into a food coma. He had a way of adding just a little bit of zing or something extra special to whatever cuisine he attempted.

"Why is it you don't work at a restaurant, again?"

"I actually considered it. Culinary school, that is. I'd seriously thought of turning my passion into a career. One summer, though, in college, I got a job in a kitchen."

"Is this true?" I looked to Jason for confirmation and he nodded then went back to fiddling with drinks. Probably a mimosa with a thousand yummy fresh fruit ingredients. I wasn't disappointed when Jason handed me exactly that.

"I don't tell this to everyone. That summer was filled with a lot of stupidity otherwise. I'd just come out to my parents. Instead of facing them head on. I ran and took my newly out gay self to P-town...Provincetown, Massachusetts for the summer."

"Sounds good so far." Sounded ideal actually. I'd never thought of running away from my reality, even for a moment.

"Got a job in the kitchen of a place called the Clam Shack. Fried clam strips. Fried oysters. French fries. I think the lobster roll and coleslaw were the only two things that didn't go into a deep fryer."

"I thought you wanted to cook."

Greg lifted his eyebrows and looked at Jason over my head. "This one's a genius. Figured out in five seconds what I didn't." He looked down, brushed something, butter maybe on a second set of buns. "So I had this grand idea of coming in to this fry shack. Getting knives from some magical place where real chefs got knives. Then prepping my way to chef. I was going to be so brilliant at chopping cabbage that I'd be chef, or at least cooking alongside him in a matter of weeks after he was awed by my brilliance. I'd have a fabulous menu and people would be lining up on the sidewalk waiting for a table."

"Did you cut cabbage?"

"Came preshredded in a bag with carrots already added. I poured it in a bowl. Got a five-gallon-sized jug of coleslaw sauce, and applied a humongous metal spoon."

"Sounds killer. If you'd added lemon zest, called it Salazar Slaw, probably could have upped the price a dollar or two."

Both men burst out laughing.

"Come sit in the dining room," Jason offered pinching my flute from my fingers and settling it on the table next to a plate he must have set for me.

Greg was in with a flourish moments later, a platter in his hands brimming with a fabulous-looking frittata, bacon, and sausage. I'd known these two for years, and they'd fed me many times. More times than I could count, but most meals were impromptu. Something about this was different.

When we'd all sat, Jason's hand hovered above the platter.

"Casey. I know we went a bit overboard without formally inviting you. But this is just our way of saying thank you. Thank you for guiding us through the process of creating our little nuclear family."

As if he'd used the spoon and punched me in the gut with it, my appetite was gone. I put down the drink. No boozy brunch for me. I needed to fess up before this thing went any further. I'd buried my head in the sand. Wanting to pretend that I could push forward with the adoptions already assigned to me.

The chances, I'd convinced myself, that they'd have a problem like the Rose family were one in ten, one in a thousand, one in a million. No matter how I did the math, I couldn't play the odds and still be their lawyer, or their friend, or their neighbor or even a guest at their table.

"Oh, my, God," Greg yelled. I nearly jumped out of my chair convinced he could read my thoughts. Jason looked at him cockeyed, but started dishing out food anyway.

"What?" I asked.

"You have a ring on the third finger of your left hand. Did you forget to tell us something. Jason, I think we're going to need more champagne."

"It's not official yet," I demurred. "Miles gave it to me last weekend. We haven't told anyone because we're going to elope."

"Wow. Congratulations! Elope? What does your mom have to say about that? There's a woman built for a wedding if there ever was one."

Jason saved me from having to answer. He said, "The definition of elope is secret wedding. No one brings their mother to Vegas. Are you doing that?"

"I think we're going to Gibraltar."

"The Spanish Mediterranean? Fun. No offense, but I didn't think you'd be the kind of person to run off. You have friends and family here," Jason added.

"Miles' parents are separated. His mom filed for divorce about a month ago," I explained, my sigh heavy.

"Jesus. Well, that changes the complexion of things," Greg said.

"You could wait six months to a year. By then his parents should have their shit together enough to show up to an event," Jason added.

The stone of truth that filled my gut was too much to bear.

"I…uh…need to talk to you about something else. About Hudson," I blurted out.

"Hudson?"

"I'm sorry, I know this is completely out of the blue. But I can't handle your adoption. I'm withdrawing from my remaining cases there. I won't be taking on any new ones. I was going to have you into the office to tell you, but I might as well tell you now."

"I'm confused." Greg shot a look at Jason who shook his head. "Why not?"

I chose my language carefully. Picked among all the English words I knew. I said, "It has come to my attention that there may be some irregularities surrounding some of the adoptions Hudson has facilitated."

"In plain English. We're your friends. Can you give it to us straight?" Greg asked.

"You sound like me," Jason interjected, "when I don't want to give someone bad news. The worse the prognosis the more syllables I start using. Tell us plainly."

"I can't break confidences, but one of the families I'm working with, the baby isn't clear for adoption."

Relief stole over Greg's face. "Oh, gosh, Paola warned us about this. Sometimes the paperwork can get hinky. Especially if the child is older. Mostly absentee-father issues. I know that can delay things, but it always gets worked out she said."

"It's more than that. A lawyer friend who worked with them for a few years...thinks that maybe all the babies or children aren't willingly given up by their parents."

"Bureaucracy at its worst, huh?" That was Jason speaking to Greg. I looked between them. They weren't getting it. I needed to break into their little echo chamber.

"You guys aren't hearing me." I raised my voice above the smooth jazz coming from some invisible speaker. "A baby was stolen. The mom has confirmed it." I pushed my chair from the table and stood. "I'm really sorry, but not only can I not do this, I think you know you can't do this either."

"Where does that leave us? When we called around there were no other agencies in the state that worked with gay couples."

Greg's plaintive tone struck me to the core. I wanted to get married, maybe, and have babies, definitely. There was no one, but me, standing in the way of that goal.

My friends. My dear, sweet friends had the church, and the state blocking their path every step of the way.

"Maybe foster care? There are families who take foster-to-adopt kids."

"How is that not a path to heartbreak?"

"I can't believe I'm suggesting this. But maybe you guys would be perfect. The one thing I hated most about foster care was the sort of low common denominator of the foster parents. I'm not saying they were all bad or bad intentioned. I was never in the position, really, to ask people why in the hell they'd signed up for it. But ninety percent of the people who did it were low income, low education single women. I'll spare you stories of the bad ones. But the good ones were no more than a layover. A place in between where the kid came from and where the kid was ultimately going to end up. But being in a way station is no way for a child to live. For them it was like being at the airport forever because the next flight never comes."

"Geez. That's awful."

"Foster care can be awful. The kids aren't," I said. "Kids end up there because their parents are in jail. Because their parents do drugs. Because their parents are poor and can't get a leg up so end up with no heat or food or home. There are some problem kids...but you'd get to pick and choose. You could only choose to take kids that are adoptable."

"Would there be a bunch of social workers in our house every day?"

"After the initial approval, honestly, not really. They're supposed to visit at least monthly. But the better off the home environment, the less likely they are to visit. It's a job about putting out fires. If you're not burning, they're not here to bother you."

Jason and Greg looked at each other for a long time. A completely silent conversation was taking place.

"Look. I'm not here to pressure you. I just dropped a bombshell about Hudson. For that I'm truly sorry. But you know that my honesty will be the death of me and my career. I couldn't, in good conscience, string you along. Maybe there's a silver lining here both for you and a kid that needs you."

"Come finish breakfast," Greg said urging me back into my seat. I hadn't realized I'd been standing. "Tell us all about eloping in a foreign land."

I sat, pleased that they weren't angry with me. That my entanglement with yet another dishonest person hadn't ruled out continuing my friendship.

For the rest of the morning, I plastered on a smile and pretended to be excited about marrying Miles. I needed to keep that smile plastered on. At least until I figured out why I wasn't as excited as I should have been.

27

I had all the power and none of the power. It was the very definition of being African, I thought.

With a single phone call, I could destroy the life that Fiona and Paul were trying to build. But I would destroy myself in the process. We would all lose. It was like the impossible problems my mother and I used to try to work out.

"Alile! Alile, come quick. You have to see what's happening."

That was Paul. Since Fiona had gone back to working ten- to twelve-hour days, he had fallen into the role of dad so quickly it scared me a little. He was always picking her up and chatting to her. He offered to get her out of the crib after naps, take her for walks in the park, even feed her. Even though I was relieved that I didn't have to work so many hours, I missed the time with my baby. It was almost as if they didn't need me anymore. It was so clear how life would look without me that it hurt to imagine their future as a mom-and-dad-and-two-babies family.

I ran from the kitchen where I'd been cutting up fruit for Yeni's lunch to the living room.

Paul had Yeni's little hands in his while he crouched behind her. She looked up at me with a silly six-toothed smile and bent her knee. In an awkward dance she placed one foot forward. Then like she was swinging a heavy sack, she lifted the other foot in a high kick and put it forward.

"She's walking. My baby girl is walking!" It took all I had to resist the urge to run forward and scoop her up in a joyous hug. Instead, I focused on the determined look upon her face and watched her take a few more steps. Paul had let her go on the third and when she looked behind her and realized that she wasn't being held up any longer, she crashed onto the floor. Tears and wails flooded the living room. This time I gave into instinct and picked her up.

Fortunately, she was easily soothed. I think her feelings hurt a lot more than her hands or legs. Gathering her on my hip, I went back into the kitchen. Before I could get her into her high chair, she was reaching for the bananas on the counter and started stuffing them into her face. Until I'd landed in the UK, I hadn't had more than a handful of bananas in my life. They'd been expensive after most had been wiped out due to banana bunchy top disease.

Here, like the UK, they were cheap and plentiful. I'd seen both Fiona and Mrs. Watson let them rot on the counter before throwing them out. It still startled me, that waste of food.

"Can I show you something?" It was Paul again. I'd forgotten he was walking about and his words startled the hell out of me. I jumped about a mile in the air. "I'm sorry. I didn't mean to scare you." His tone said his apology was real.

I used to sleep like a brick. My mum and dad and brother could walk through our house without me so much as noticing. After living with Umi and Onani, I couldn't settle. I'd never known when Onani was tiptoeing around to try to get to me. Or when Aunt Umi was going to come behind me and pull the broom from my hands and hit me with it for not sweeping fast enough or not cleaning well enough or not doing something...anything...enough.

"I've got to finish this," I said. I popped Yeni into the high chair and finished stirring the pot on the stove. I found the bowl Fiona had bought. It had sand in the bottom or something that made it hard for Yeni to push it from her tray. I poured the chicken stew in I'd made the day before. I stuck my little finger in making sure it wasn't too hot.

It must have been perfect because Yeni took her spoon and got more than half the food in her mouth.

"What do you want to show me?" I knew my tone wasn't friendly. But I couldn't remember a time when a man had offered to show me something that wasn't about their private parts. I'd not thought him that kind of man. But I shook my head. Of course, all men were that kind of man.

"It's nothing bad. Give me a minute. I'll be right back."

I put the food in front of Yeni and mashed in a hard-boiled egg. Excited to see food that she liked, she took the spoon from me before I could offer it to her. Whatever Mrs. Barrera had said about my Yeni being behind in development no longer seemed to be true. She was feeding herself more days than not and she'd just walked. My heart squeezed so tight I couldn't breathe for a moment.

"What do you think? Does it look like her?"

Yeni and I turned when Paul came into the kitchen. He was carrying a sketch pad in his hand. When Fiona had gone to work, he'd disappeared into his studio for a few hours each day. I had no idea what he did in the room, but I followed Fiona's rule to never disturb him back there.

"What?" I said lifting my eyes to Paul's.

He thrust the pad at me. I took it and looked down at what was on it. I nearly dropped it when I saw.

"That's Yeni." I rubbed my fingers against a corner, smudging it a little. "I'm sorry. It's just that it looked like a picture."

"It's pencil," he said.

I took the pad and looked at it again. It wasn't finished by any means, but I could see that the picture emerging was going to be my Yeni. The top of her head and a single eye had been finished. I could see every little hair that stood upon her head and the tiny scar above her eyebrow.

"How did you do this?"

He flipped down one sheet and showed me a black-and-white photo I hadn't seen before. But he and Fiona took a thousand of what they'd called digital photos. Our pictures were stored on a tiny electronic disk in the camera. Since they didn't cost anything to store like film, they took thousands. Some had been made and were hanging about on the walls.

"I drew it."

"But it looks so real."

"It's called hyper realistic drawing. I saw some artists at the National Portrait Gallery in London and decided to try my hand at it."

"This is your first try?"

"It is. I haven't even shown Fiona yet. I wanted to see if I could do it first."

"And you picked a picture of Yeni to do?"

"I love her, Alile. I'm sorry that we're in the situation that we're in, but I want you to know that I love Charlotte...Kantayeni...is that how you pronounce it?"

"Kantayeni, yes, that's it. It means go and throw her away."

It was kind of funny the name I'd picked. I'd chosen it at first because there had once been a school girl in my village with that name. When my aunt had laughed and told me what it meant, I'd thought she was surely wrong. Now I think it may have been God's way of preparing her for this journey.

Paul didn't say anything about her name. Instead he closed the pad and laid it on the counter. "We can't go on like this." That was Paul talking.

"This whole thing is holding all of us hostage," Paul said. His hands were shoved into the pockets of his jeans. He was wearing a sweater because the hot weather had already gone away. It looked like winter here was going to be as bleak as it had been in England where even with the rain and cold is where I'd wanted to be with my daughter. Instead I was here, with her, though I couldn't take her anywhere.

"So I should just give up my daughter because Fiona wants her? Because you're enjoying playing at being a 'dad'?" I wanted to believe he loved her, but I wasn't quite sure. Not sure enough to walk away from my little girl a second time.

"Because we can give her a better life. You know that. Good schools. Food, shelter, all that she needs and most of what she wants. I'm here. I can teach her to paint, ride a bike, ride a horse, I don't know. All the stuff little girls like to do."

"And you want what, for me to disappear? I am like a breed mare? It's like all of you treat Africa. You want our resources, but not the people who own the land."

"This is not political, Alile. This is about Fiona loving Charlotte. It's about doing what's best for her."

"And what about me. I've been to the library and adoptions in the Unites States are different. The birth parents stay involved. They can send cards or letters. Some even have visits for holidays and birthdays."

"I hear you." He shook his head. Stepped backward toward the door. "I'm going to step out for a bit. I'll be back later. Can you handle things here?"

"My daughter and I will be okay."

And we were. I put her down for a nap, then sat in my room with one of the books I got from the library on how to finish high school. I tried not to cry as I realized there was so much in the world I didn't know. Math and English and all the states in the United States, not to mention all the countries in Europe or Asia or South America even.

How long would it take for me to learn all this. If I left Yeni with Fiona and Paul, she'd never have any of these problems. Maybe it was time for me to let go, to walk away. There had to be some kind of services for a girl like me. A place for me to stay. A school that could teach me all I needed to know. In a way Fiona and Paul were right, I needed to figure out what was best for my daughter. I did and would always come second.

I stood and lifted the handset of the telephone in my room. Twelve buttons lit. Fishing a card from my dresser, I carefully pressed in the seven-digit number.

"Can I speak to social worker Barrera," I said to the woman who answered with a perky, "Hudson Agency."

"She's with a client at the moment. Can she return your call?"

"My name is Alile Rubidari and it's an emergency," I said unwilling to wait a moment longer.

I was seeking answers and this woman was sure to have them. If they wanted this adoption to go through, I'm sure that they'd figure out a way. The money these parents paid for babies was enough to help me.

After only a moment's hesitation, the receptionist spoke. "I'll put you through immediately."

When I heard the social worker's voice come on the line, I sucked in my breath. "I'm sorry. It was a mistake my calling. I'm not ready."

For a second, a short moment, I thought leaving my daughter's life would be the best idea. But the thought of it if only for the moment it took for Mrs. Barrera to say hello nearly took the breath from my body.

I couldn't do it.

28

"Miss Cort, you've brought us an unusual one today," the white-haired judge said. He took off his reading glasses and perched them on the bench. Then finally able to see, he brought the stack of papers closer to his nose. He was quiet for a long moment as he scanned first one page, placed it on the highly polished wood, then did it again until he was all the way through the stack.

His slow perusal of the documents made the pulse jump in my neck. Casey had seemed relatively calm when coming in, but I was sure something was going to go wrong. That he'd ask one question too may about how Charlotte had come to our house and he'd have some social worker grab her out of our arms before we could flee the building. It wasn't without irony that I realized we were back in the same building where Paul had deserted me so many months ago. I'd tried to make a family once here and it hadn't worked out. I was afraid to try it a second time. I looked up when the judge cleared his throat.

"All my papers are in order," Casey said standing behind the thick wood table with four chairs behind it, mine, Paul's Alile's, and the lawyer's. After she spoke, she chanced a glance behind us. Another attorney whom she'd introduced to us a few days back, Justin McPhee, was in the nearly empty gallery. Due to my unusual request, she said it would be best to involve another lawyer. Like I'd done a dozen other times over the last months, I wrote a check and didn't ask too many questions.

"Ms. Cort, Mr. Cooke, Dr. Rose, and Miss Rubidari. Did I pronounce your name correctly?" His sharp blue eyes fell on Alile.

"Yes. I'm Alile Rubidari."

I looked at Alile and wondered how I'd ever thought she was eighteen. In her white long-sleeved dress, roses the size of a one-pound coin patterned across it, she looked no more than twelve. I caught her eye and gave her a slight smile. I wanted to slide my hand across the polished wood and grab hers. I wanted to promise her that she wouldn't have to again make an adult decision—not until she was ready.

"To be clear, Ms. Cort, Mr. Cooke and Dr. Rose wish to adopt Alile and her daughter, Kantayeni Rubidari."

"That's correct, Your Honor."

"It's unusual for the birth mother to be adopted as well. As a matter of fact, I'd say that I've never seen this and I've seen a lot of things come across my bench in all my years in probate."

"As you know, Your Honor, open adoptions have become the norm in the last decade. Like many birth mothers, Ms. Rubidari was without resources. Dr. Rose and Mr. Cooke have decided to provide her with the same love and education that they've promised to provide for the little girl. Not only have they kept this little family together, they've expanded their family to make space for those who need them."

"Miss Rubidari, I see here from the papers that your mother has passed away. Is that true?"

"Yes."

"I'm sorry to hear it. I'm also reading that your father had already abandoned you to your aunt and uncle and is willing to consent to the adoption. I have his declaration duly notarized by the US embassy in Lilongwe, Malawi."

"Yes, my father is in favor of this arrangement."

"You aren't being coerced in any fashion."

"No, Your Honor. I want to go to and finish school. Also I want to help care for my daughter while providing her with all the opportunities that Mister Cooke and Fiona…Doctor Rose can provide."

"Doctor Rose, I very much admire the decision you've made here to adopt this little family. It's a wonderful thing that you're doing."

I looked around not knowing if I could speak. Without the wigs and robes I was used to seeing on the telly, it all looked so informal. I didn't want to talk out of turn, however, so I looked to the solicitor for guidance. Casey nodded in my direction, so I did as she had done and rose from my seat

"Thank you, My Lord."

"No need to be so formal."

"Right, Judge…Your Honor. Sorry. I want to thank you for hearing us out today. While my new family may be unconventional, my actions come from a place of love. I want the best for Charlotte…Yeni…and keeping the family as in tact as possible. I think the future of the two girls is very bright."

"Hudson is a top agency in this city. They make beautiful families with some difficult placements. You couldn't be in better hands. I hereby grant the adoption of Alile Rubidari and Kantayeni Rubidari who shall hereinafter be known as Alile Rubadiri Rose and Kantayeni Charlotte Rose. It is so ordered. Counselor, you can come on through for the judgment entry if you want to walk it through."

"Thank you, Your Honor." Casey took a deep breath as if she were stilling her nerves. Maybe she had been as worried as I'd been. She threw a look over her shoulder at Mr. McPhee and he gave her a slight nod of acknowledgment.

"That's it?" I asked so relieved that this little ordeal was finally over. Beyond happy that Paul had been the one to find a brilliant solution that spared anyone heartache.

Casey Cort lifted and dropped her shoulders in the suggestion of a shrug. "That's it. I'll get your papers and everything will be formalized this afternoon. Birth certificates will come via mail in a few weeks."

I lowered my voice. "And that thing you mentioned about me being a noncitizen. The court isn't going to come back to void the whole thing are they? I want to know this door is closed tight, shut, locked."

"I followed Hudson's lead. The assignment clerk called me and let me know that my original judge had been replaced by Judge Curtis Floyd. His bailiff called to let me know that the filing was considered complete when the hearing was scheduled. I'm going to say that you can be assured that your ruling won't be disturbed. There's really no one to object. And without objections or appeals, no one is going to scrutinize the papers after the fact. They'll go in a thick leather-bound file in the dusty basement of this building to be forgotten like so many other cases down there."

"That's it then."

"Congratulations on your pregnancy. I'll get your documents to you by messenger tomorrow. Please call Hudson should you have any questions."

"Thank you for bending the rules. It was important to me."

A slight wince creased the solicitor's eyes, but in a flash it was gone, replaced by a tentative smile. She shook my hand and went to speak with McPhee. The two went to the room behind the judge's bench and disappeared.

29

"Mom, Dad, there's something I want to talk to you about," I said. Miles was holding my left hand. His large brown fingers undoubtedly engulfed the ring that I'd show them in a few minutes. I was gesturing with my right trying to get them to sit on their couch for once. Sometimes trying to have a serious discussion with them was like trying to hit a moving target.

"Should I get some coffee. Maybe kaffee plätzchen. I could have it together in a bit," Mom offered. While I loved the quarter-sized chocolate bites, and given my nerves would gladly eat a dozen, I deferred.

"Mom. Stop. We don't need sweets. We're going to eat in a few minutes anyway, right?" I was there for lunch. That I'd organized a few days back. I could smell something delicious wafting through the house. "I want to talk to you first about me and Miles. About a trip we're going to take in a few weeks."

"A trip?" My mother clasped her hands at her waist. I couldn't help but notice she hadn't removed her apron. "That's exciting, lieb, you never travel. Where are you going?"

Before I could blurt out the part about Gibraltar, the doorbell rang. I held in my sigh. No doubt my mother had offered one of the empty seats at the table to one of St. Ignatius' parishioners with a sob story.

I was about to pull away from Miles and open the door when my father uncharacteristically popped up from the couch he'd been reluctantly sitting on and went to the door.

"If it isn't my favorite surrogate family," I heard my best friend shout out.

Miles looked at me. Raised his eyebrows in question.

"I didn't invite her," I whispered. This was going to be hard enough as it is. I certainly hadn't sprinkled in crazy best friend for laughs. I was not in search of life as a sitcom though I was teetering on the edge of absurdity with the way things were going lately.

"I heard that," Lulu said as she bustled in and gave me a generous one-armed hug. "Your parents invited me. Said you hadn't mentioned me in a while. They were worried that we'd had a falling out or something."

I grabbed my friend's arm—covered in a Sinclair-inspired silk blouse natch—and pulled her out of the back door onto the deck my parents used even less than the formal living room. I was proud of myself for not commenting on the complementary wraparound skirt. She could have been straight out of a J.Crew catalog. Her married boyfriend's effect on her was so weird.

I pointed to her skirt. "Is that really plaid?" The question had practically fallen out of my mouth despite my best efforts. "Does Sinclair have Catholic schoolgirl fantasies? You should tell him that we were never allowed to wear heels." I gestured to her two-inch navy pumps. "Scratch that. I don't even want to know." I mimed rubbing my eyes like I was scrubbing an unpleasant image from my mind.

"Can we declare Richard Sinclair off-limits?" she asked glaring at me.

"Sure. Whatever. Why are you here?" My question was uncharitable, but what I was planning to tell my parents was going to be hard enough without adding a third ring to the circus.

It wasn't that Lulu hadn't been to my house before. She'd been there a handful of times. Mostly when we did the parent thing, though, we went to her house. It's not that I felt poor exactly. I'd grown up distinctly middle class—on the lower end. But I always held myself in comparison to her. And I had always fallen short.

She'd grown up in a modest—her words not mine—six bedroom in Cleveland Heights' North Park Boulevard. One of those streets that just screamed old money as the acre lots backed upon Shaker Lakes.

Her father was a doctor, her mother the president of the largest Jewish nonprofit in the city. They did things like go on vacations and go to charity balls. I'd gone down to Edgewater Beach and helped my mom dish up chicken for parish fundraisers. For a hot minute I wondered why Lulu hadn't gone after Miles herself. They had a lot more in common with each other than either of them had in common with me.

Everything would be so much easier if I were at their engagement party instead of the announcement of my own.

"I wanted to talk to you. You've been avoiding me like the plague. Ron even said that you'd given up Hudson cases. Are you seriously that angry with me?"

"I had a conflict." It was the big lie I was going to tell anyone who asked.

"What's going on with you? I'm finally able to help you and you toss it."

"So that's what I am to you? A charity case?"

"No, it's just none of this makes any sense. I mean I knew you'd be a little put off initially by my relationship with Richard. But to be so pissed that you fuck up your career is nuts."

"Jesus, Lulu, Hudson had nothing to do with you and Richard. I have a life, you know, that doesn't revolve around begging for crumbs from Dalton Lacey."

"I'm sorry what I said a minute ago. You're not a charity case. You're my friend and when I was finally able to help you, I did.

"I'm sorry that there's this wedge between us. It's never been this way." Her eyes strayed to the reflection my ring had made against the side of the house. For a moment it reminded me of the refracting light Shaker Lakes sometimes made on the back of hers. My sparkle was manmade.

"Is that a ring?" she asked, everything else forgotten as she zeroed in on the semiprecious stones.

"Miles and I are engaged."

"Engaged? Today? Is that why your parents are having this brunch?"

"Shh. They don't know yet. I wanted to tell them with Miles here. I want them to know that we're a unit."

"Was it last night? Did you call? I had my phone off."

"No...not last night. A few weeks back actually."

Lulu's face crumpled. "Seriously. This is where we're at. You don't tell me about the most important stuff in your life anymore."

"It's...that's not quite it."

"Then what is it? I love you, Case. I don't want this Sinclair thing to drive a wedge between us. No man should."

"I...Miles proposed, but with a caveat," I admitted reluctantly.

"Did he actually say, I'll marry you, but..."

"No, of course not. It's that his own parents are getting a divorce. He told me about them the night we were in the Gateway District before you and Richard showed up. He's pretty torn up about it. But his mom just moved out. Papers have been served. It's not a good time for a wedding. He wants to elope."

"Is that what you want? I mean I've always seen you as a get-married-at-church, have-a-reception-at-a-country-club person. At least that's what you talked about when you were engaged to Tom." I threw her a look. "Okay, at least the club part."

"I don't know what I want," I blurted, violating the one promise I'd made every day for the last month that I'd keep my doubts to myself.

Lulu hooked an arm around my elbow and moved us to the farthest corner of the porch away from anyone's view. Her head came close to mine. Her voice was a whisper when she spoke.

"Do you want to marry Miles?"

"I don't not want to marry him," I equivocated.

"Jesus, Mary, and Joseph." The epithet was unnatural for her.

"You're not a Catholic."

"It's what you'd say if I showed up half engaged."

"Half engaged?" my father said. Neither of us had heard the door slide open. I turned to see my father, confusion marring his face.

"Dad. Hi. Um. Miles proposed." I held out my hand and showed him the ring.

My father's "Did you want a diamond?" question was not the congratulations I expected.

"The stones don't matter. Miles mentioned that these each stood for different things like love and loyalty and trust." I tried to sound upbeat when I said that. Somehow I was failing to keep up the façade.

"You're going to marry him?"

"Dad. What are you asking? Do you have a problem with Miles? You didn't raise me this way. You always told me that everyone was equal. There were no good or bad people. Race didn't matter. Now, you and Mama are acting weird."

My father had always been my rock. Something was going on. He was crumbling before my eyes. Dad wiped his hands on his khaki pants, once, then again. Finally he lifted his head up and looked me in the eyes. "There's something I need to tell you."

"What?" I couldn't imagine him having any secrets I didn't already know. They weren't like the Brodys or the Siegels. Everything had always been an open book with my parents. I waited a beat for him to speak.

"I'm adopted."

"What do you mean? You knew who your parents were. They're from Dębniki."

"That's not exactly true. I...think...they are from else-where. Some things have made me unsure as to why I didn't grow up with them. I...was a Lebensborn child," he said. His tone was somber like he was announcing that he was dying. I tried to sort through what he was saying. Not a single thing made sense, so I latched on to the least familiar word, the German one.

"Lebensborn?"

Lulu's face was a mask of shock and horror. "You don't know, Casey?"

"What am I supposed to know?"

"The Nazis, they took children mainly from Poland, from Yugoslavia and a few other countries. The children if they looked Aryan enough, were put into orphanages, German-ized and adopted out."

What Lulu was saying didn't compute in one part of my brain and in another it made a horrible kind of sense. Scenes from Rabbit Proof Fence rolled through my mind first. Then wisps of discussion about the Indian Adoption Project in the US came next. Of course if it had happened here, it had probably happened before. My stomach roiled at the idea that my father, my very loving and solid father, had a child-hood where he was separated from his parents.

"Daddy, did that happen to you? Is that why you were in Germany when you met Mama?"

My father, whom I thought I knew better than anyone in the world, proved then that he wasn't who I thought either. It seemed these days that no one was.

The bend of his head was so slight that if I hadn't been looking for it, I might have missed it. "Yes, that's true."

"Oh, God. That's why you weren't a fan of the adoption. Because you know of many children who were stolen from their families and given to other, better, families?"

"Yes. Although maybe it wasn't fair to put that on you. You're not doing anything of the sort."

But of course, I was doing that exact thing. That exact thing that he'd warned me about. Cautioned me against. That exact thing that I brushed off as impossible. There was nothing I could do about Hudson except to keep it in my past. I turned to my dad who seemed to be hurting in the present.

"Why are you telling me this now?"

"You weren't the only one who had an announcement for brunch. I wanted to tell you that I'm planning to go to Poland and maybe also Germany at the end of this month, maybe in October if I can't get a ticket now. I got a call from the German Red Cross. The government has finally opened the records from the war years. I want to go and find out what happened to my parents. Find out why I was taken. Why I was deemed white enough where my sister wasn't."

"You have a sister? I thought you were an only child."

"There's much I have to tell you, dear girl. I was hoping you'd come to Poland with me."

"I was…" The word Gibraltar didn't leave my lips. I couldn't tell him this way.

"Casey and Miles were planning to elope," Lulu announced.

I looked at my friend wild-eyed. "That was not the way I wanted to tell him that."

"You wouldn't have said anything. Your dad has the right to know."

"I was going to tell him. With my mom and Miles after the food and dessert and maybe a couple of drinks."

"You should go to Poland," Lulu said as if it were the most brilliant idea in the world. "If you're at all on the fence about marrying Miles. You should go with your dad. Have a minute to think about what you're doing."

"You're not sure?" My dad looked pained for himself, for me...

"Dad. I don't know. I love him. I do. I want to get married and have kids. I want what you and Mama have. It's just a little sudden. It feels like Miles and I just got back together and now he's ready to make it permanent. I mean is there a reason to hesitate when I can have everything I want?"

"You not being one hundred percent on board is a reason."

Suddenly Europe with my dad seemed like a brilliant idea. If Greg could run to Provincetown, I could run to Europe. Everything could hold while I helped my dad navigate the waters of his past.

"I'll go with you, Dad," I said. "I can help you do the research. Talk to officials. Lulu, you have to come too."

Looking like she stepped from a catalogue, my best friend turned to look me square in the face. "Me. What are you saying?"

"You've always said you wanted to visit your grandparents' birthplace. See the concentration camps. And if I need time to think about Miles, I think you need the same amount of time to think about Sinclair. He's married, Lulu. He hasn't left his wife. I think you need to give him an ultimatum if this is the guy you really think you want to be with."

For the first time in months, my best friend's gaze was clear. It was like the spell of Sinclair had been broken. It may have only been a crack, but I wanted to put a crowbar through it, open it wide.

"I'll do it if you do," she dared.

"Dad, would it be okay to bring Lulu?"

He nodded sagely. "I think all of us need to go. To think about the past and the future. Take the time, honey. I don't believe in divorce. Ending a marriage is much harder than beginning one."

He was right. There was no rush. And if Miles would only marry me if it were in the next few days or weeks, then I needed to find that out now.

I pushed open the sliding door ready to find out more about my father's past while I postponed my own future. Miles would just have to understand.

ABOUT THE AUTHOR

Aime Austin is the author of the Casey Cort Legal Thriller Series. Casey is almost always in trouble. Aime's full time job? Rescuing her. Good thing Aime's got experience. She practiced family and criminal law in Cleveland, Ohio for several years—so she has the skills for the job. When Aime isn't rescuing Casey from herself, she's hosting her podcast *A Time to Thrill*, raising her son, or traveling between Budapest and Los Angeles.